ALSO BY ISAIAH CAMPBELL

The Troubles of Johnny Cannon

THE STRUGGLES OF JOHNNY CANNON

ISAIAH CAMPBELL

Simon & Schuster Books for Young Readers
New York London Toronto Sydney New Delhi

SIMON & SCHUSTER BOOKS FOR YOUNG READERS
An imprint of Simon & Schuster Children's Publishing Division
1230 Avenue of the Americas, New York, New York 10020
SIMON & SCHUSTER BOOKS FOR YOUNG READERS is a trademark of Simon & Schuster, Inc.
For information about special discounts for bulk purchases, please contact Simon & Schuster
Special Sales at 1-866-506-1949 or business@simonandschuster.com.
The Simon & Schuster Speakers Bureau can bring authors to your live event.
For more information or to book an event, contact the Simon & Schuster Speakers Bureau
at 1-866-248-3049 or visit our website at www.simonspeakers.com.
Book design by Lucy Ruth Cummins
The text for this book is set in Adobe Garamond.
Manufactured in the United States of America
0915 FFG
2 4 6 8 10 9 7 5 3 1
Library of Congress Cataloging-in-Publication Data
Campbell, Isaiah.
The struggles of Johnny Cannon / Isaiah Campbell. — 1st edition.
pages cm
Sequel to: The troubles of Johnny Cannon.
Summary: In Alabama in the summer of 1961, twelve-year-old Johnny Cannon gets
mixed up in a Mafia blood feud as he searches for his happy ending with Martha Macker.
ISBN 978-1-4814-2631-2 (hardcover) — ISBN 978-1-4814-2633-6 (eBook)
[1. Adventure and adventurers—Fiction. 2. Organized crime—Fiction. 3. Family life—
Alabama—Fiction. 4. Fathers and sons—Fiction. 5. Alabama—History—
20th century—Fiction.] I. Title.
PZ7.C15417Str 2015
[Fic]—dc23
2014025239

FIRST
EDITION

TO THE REAL-LIFE MR. THOMASSEN,

WHO NEVER OWNED A CLUB IN CUBA,

BUT I EVENTUALLY GOT OVER IT.

I MISS YOU, ROGER.

THE
STRUGGLES
OF

JOHNNY
CANNON

Acknowledgments

I'm so very grateful for every person who believed enough in Johnny that this second tall tale came to exist. First of all, for my wife, the real reason I write anything. Also for Nicole and Erin. For my magnificent agent, Marietta, my incredible editor, David Gale, and his assistant, Liz. For the students in my ninth-grade English class, for the kids in my drama class, and for every person who read, loved, and shared Johnny Cannon's troubles. It all started with one boy's dream, and you have all made it come true.

CHAPTER ONE
THE BOY WONDER

My grandma always said there ain't much learning in the second kick of a mule. Reason being, if you didn't shoot him after he kicked you the first time, then he might be a mule, but you're a jackass.

Same thing goes when a dog bites you, she'd always say, or if a horse bucks you off, or if any other bad thing happens to you 'cause of an animal that ain't listening. That's why the Good Lord made bullets.

Of course, that was an old-fashioned way of thinking, back from the turn of the century when folks hadn't never seen *Bambi* and didn't know nothing about happy endings.

In other words, it was back when folks was smarter.

See, there ain't never been a lie in the history of man as big or as terrible as the lie about happy endings. Everybody these days believes in them, everybody waits for them, and when you get to the end of a story, as long as everybody's smiling, folks think all is right with the world.

But it ain't true. There ain't no such things as happy endings. Some things get to be happy. Other things get to end. But trying to mix them things together is like trying to shake up oil and water to make a new kind of medicine. Once you've swallowed it, it does a number on your stomach and you realize you're the biggest fool in the whole wide world.

Which is why, if you look up the word "fool" in the encyclopedia that came out in '61, you'll see my picture staring back at you. 'Cause in spite of everything inside of me that knew better, I was still hunting my hardest for my happy ending.

It was the middle of August, the weekend right before school was set to start and seventh grade was primed to hit me like a ton of bricks. It was hotter than a two-dollar pistol, even out there on the water of Smith Lake. We was in my brother Tommy's rusted old paddleboat, and by "we," I mean me and the girl I was hunting that happy ending with, Martha Macker. And if there's a better way to get tangled up with the girl of your dreams than hunting catfish in the heart of Alabama, I'd like to know what it is. No, really, 'cause this wasn't turning out the way I'd hoped.

I was wearing my coveralls, which had been passed down from my grandpa after he'd had a heart attack reeling in a sixty-pound catfish. Hadn't been washed since then either, 'cause it don't matter that he died in them, if they was lucky enough to land

ISAIAH CAMPBELL

a sixty-pounder, that's the sort of luck you don't wash off. My Cincinnati Reds baseball cap was perching on top of my head. It didn't fit so good 'cause it had been a birthday present from Tommy back in '58 and was about five sizes too small, but it was a fishing tradition. And them are sacred.

Meanwhile, Martha was wearing a wide-brimmed hat and Foster Grant sunglasses, which hid her blue eyes but made her red hair look even more pretty, and she was also wearing an Auburn University sweatshirt her pa had sent her up from Montgomery, where he was off doing business. I didn't have the heart to tell her she wasn't dressed sensible for fishing. I reckoned she'd figure it out on her own after we got some catfish blood on her white leather oxfords.

I'd put the worm on her hook for her 'cause I reckoned she felt a bit squeamish, even though she claimed she didn't, but I knew better 'cause she was a girl and all. Then I helped her cast her line 'cause she didn't want to hook her skirt. I reckoned she'd start enjoying herself directly, even though her face looked like she was as miserable as could be.

"When do they start biting?" she asked.

"They'll start biting here eventually," I said. "Or they won't. It don't much matter. Fishing ain't really about getting bites—"

She smacked a mosquito that was trying to sting her arm. It was squished to her palm and she looked around her seat on the boat to find something to wipe it on. She finally wiped it on my sleeve. I didn't mind, it meant she was touching my arm.

"I knew I should have used some bug spray," she said.

"It scares off the fish," I said. "Besides, you can make a game of it." I smacked one that was chewing on my ankle. "See, that's twelve for me."

She sighed and didn't say nothing else for a little bit. We bobbed up and down as the water moved us farther along and we listened to the sounds of birds singing love songs to each other. Bugs hummed along with them off on the shore. Martha kept time by swatting more mosquitoes.

"Am I doing something wrong?" she asked. "I feel like I'm doing something wrong. The fish aren't biting."

"They ain't bit mine yet either," I said. "You're doing all right."

Just then the tip of my fishing pole started jerking down to the water. I sat up and got to reeling in whatever was gobbling on my worm. I fought with it for a bit, 'cause it wanted to have a little fun with me. Finally, I got the big ol' catfish up out of the water. It was twenty pounds, easy.

"Grab the net and get him," I said.

"Eww," she said, "it's still alive."

"Well, yeah," I said. "They don't bite nearly as good when they're dead. Get the net, he's about to fall off my hook."

She dug around the boat for a bit to find the net. Once she got it, she tried to hand it to me.

"No, stick it out there and get him."

"But it's flinging water everywhere."

It sure was, twitching and fighting against the hook and sending a shower of water in our direction. It felt real good, but she didn't seem to appreciate it. I tried to hold the pole with one hand and grab the net with the other. I put the net out there, but just before I got it under the fat catfish, he gave a big shake and went sailing off my hook. He landed right back into the river and took off to warn all his catfish buddies that there was a couple of walleyed yahoos out there fishing.

I couldn't hold back my groan.

"Maybe I should reel in the next one," Martha said. "I don't think the net job is for me."

I was just fixing to tell her that it was okay, after all, she was a girl and it wasn't important that she be able to net a fish as long as she could cook it. But then the air got split wide open with what sounded like a buzz saw cutting through a plague of locusts, and then there was a fuzzy voice.

"*Superman. Superman, come in. This is Batman.*"

Birds flew off like they was escaping an alien attack and I'm pretty sure the fish even ducked for cover. I dug through the tuna salad sandwiches we'd brought with us and pulled out a fancy walkie-talkie. I stretched out the metal antenna and clicked the big button on the side.

"Dadgummit, Willie, you pick the worst times."

"*I thought we agreed on code names. I'm Batman and you're Superman. Remember?*"

Him and his code names. He'd been in supersecret-government-agent mode for the past couple of months, ever since he met Short-Guy, a fella from the CIA that almost took my pa to prison 'cause he thought he'd sabotaged the Bay of Pigs invasion. But that got all cleared up and we was sort of friends with him now. Except I couldn't never remember his name, which is why I always just called him Short-Guy.

Anyway, he'd given Willie the darn fool idea of working for the CIA someday. I tolerated it at first, even bought him those walkie-talkies since we was blood brothers and all, but he was starting to get annoying about it. Still, since he was a crippled black kid and there wasn't much else he could look forward to in life, I reckoned I'd let him hold on to his dream.

"Sorry, Batman, go ahead."

Martha giggled. She always thought me and Willie was a hoot when we was together.

"How goes Operation Happy Ending?"

My face turned as red as my hat.

"It ain't going," I said, and hoped Martha hadn't been listening.

"What's Operation Happy Ending?" she asked.

Dadgummit.

"It ain't nothing," I said. "I mean, it's just us boys doing stupid things. Like farting and scratching ourselves. Like how we always—"

She grabbed the walkie-talkie from my hand.

ISAIAH CAMPBELL

"Batman, this is Wonder Woman, do you copy?"

There wasn't no answer for a bit and I could imagine Willie was sweating from his forehead.

"Copy that, Wonder Woman, go ahead."

"What is Operation Happy Ending?" She had a possum grin on her face when she said that, and then she bit her lip while she waited for him to respond.

And she had to wait for a spell, too. Dang, Willie must have been sweating enough to fill up a bathtub. Which would really defeat the purpose of taking a bath. Unless you used the right soap, I reckon. Maybe Dove or something.

"It's . . . uh . . . it's . . ."

I started praying that the Good Lord would make something happen to get me out of that mess. Or kill me right there on the spot. But then I wouldn't never get to see the Reds win a World Series. So he had to come up with another plan.

Right then, Martha's fishing pole got yanked out of her lap. I dove across the boat to grab it.

"Holy cow!" I hollered. "You caught something."

She jumped up and just about lost her mind.

"No! I'm reeling them in, remember?" she said. She tried to grab her pole, but when she did, she knocked the walkie-talkie into the water.

I didn't even give no second thoughts about it, I dove in after it.

The walkie-talkie sank pretty fast and I had to fight with a dead tree branch for it, but I finally got it and swam back up to the boat. Martha wasn't going to be no help getting me back in 'cause she was too busy fighting a losing battle with whatever creature was yanking on the end of her fishing line.

I pulled myself into the boat and went to help her. We fought and fought with that fish, and my arms was getting sort of sore. It surprised me that she hadn't given up yet, but maybe I was doing more of the work than I thought. Didn't look like it, but looks can be deceiving.

Finally she got it up to the surface.

"Oh, look at that," I said. "You caught a gar."

She peeked at what I was looking at, the long fish with the even longer nose and teeth peeking out from its jawline.

"An alligator? You didn't say anything about alligators!" She let go of the fishing pole. The gar took off swimming and took her pole with it.

I had to laugh. It was the only natural reaction besides cussing.

"Not an alligator, a gar," I said. "It's all right. Girls is skittish, I understand."

She glanced behind me.

"Hey, Mountain Man, isn't that your pole?"

I spun around just in time to see my pole go flying off in the other direction, another victim of a hungry gar.

Martha was laughing something fierce at my face, and it brought back memories of when me and Tommy used to go fishing

ISAIAH CAMPBELL

together. So I reckoned I'd do what he always did when I thought I'd gotten him good.

I pushed her into the water.

In retrospect, that probably wasn't the best plan. Definitely didn't help Operation Happy Ending any.

She was splashing and flopping in the water like a chicken getting a bath and she was hollering about as bad too. Her hat was soaked and hanging all down on her face, her sunglasses had dropped into the river so them lake mermaids could wear them, and she had gotten some lake weed stuck on her ear. It was real funny and I finally understood why Tommy did it so much.

I reached out my hand to help her into the boat. She grabbed it and pulled me back into the river instead. She held my head under the water and I was pretty sure she was aiming to drown me, but then she let me up so I could gasp at the air. She climbed back into the boat and didn't offer me any help getting in myself.

After I got in and looked her once over, I couldn't contain myself. I started laughing again. She just looked so darn funny, like a waterlogged redheaded bunny rabbit.

She hauled off and slapped me across the face.

"You're a jerk!" she said. "You're lucky you're my brother, or else I'd never speak to you again."

Yeah, real lucky. See, that's one of the biggest reasons my happy ending was getting further away every single day. 'Cause, the night that Short-Guy almost arrested my pa, she and I got to hug each other for the first time ever. I reckon it had something to do with the fact that my real dad, a fella named Captain Morris that was the biggest polecat there's ever been, almost shot her and me both in the head. And it was nice, hugging her like that. But then I slipped and told her I loved her. And, of course, she freaked out, so I scrambled and said I meant like a sister. Which fixed that situation, but killed any chance I had of kissing her. 'Cause, I don't care what you've heard about Alabama, we don't kiss our sisters down here.

She pointed back up the lake.

"Home, Jeeves," she said. "And you'll be rowing all by yourself this time. That will be your punishment." She dug into her purse and pulled out a little mirror, and then she got to work fixing her face back to normal while I paddled. Once she finally had everything situated, she grinned at me right before she unwrapped a sandwich and ate it. Didn't offer me a bite. Girls was as evil as rattlesnakes. But cuter. A lot cuter. Which is why I reckon folks don't generally marry rattlesnakes. Except maybe in Arkansas.

We finally got to the spot on the shore where I'd parked me and Pa's new truck and I steered us up close to the dry ground. Yeah, I was just barely thirteen, but in Cullman County it was absolutely normal for a kid to drive himself to go fishing. Hunting, too. About the only place you wasn't allowed to drive yourself was to your own funeral. Unless you timed it right.

As soon as I got the boat up onto the shore, she hopped out and went to get into the truck. Left me to tie it up onto the truck bed and everything. Dadgum lazy girls.

After I got it all tied up, I went and got into the driver's seat. I started the engine and opened my mouth to say something. She reached up and shoved a big mud ball right under my nose.

"There," she said while I spit out the window, "now we're even."

She turned on the radio to listen to some music and we drove down the road for a bit. Dee Clark was singing "Raindrops," and it made me think of the wet butt prints we was leaving on the shiny new seats. I'd wrecked our old truck in a tornado. We bought the new one with money Pa was earning from working for Mr. Thomassen, the local barber who used to own a casino in Cuba. I'd helped Mr. Thomassen get his money back, so he helped us make some of our own. I wasn't real sure what exactly Pa did for him, but he claimed it was for God and country, so I left it alone.

After a few more songs, Martha turned off the radio.

"So, Mr. History-Man, what's today's thing?" she asked.

I had a book of daily history facts that I was prone to spout off. I was under the belief that history had lessons we could learn every day that would keep us from screwing up the way they did back in them olden days. 'Cause there ain't many stories that end well in history. Studying it had worked out pretty good for me so far. Except when I tried to adopt the once-a-week bath system. And even that wasn't so much bad for me as it was for everybody else.

"Well, today's August 26, so it's the day the Nineteenth

Amendment was passed for the Constitution back in 1920, which gave women the right to vote. See, back in them days, the womenfolk was thinking that the menfolk wasn't doing the best job at deciding—"

She stopped me.

"Not that I don't enjoy hearing about what the 'menfolk' decided," Martha said, "but today's actually the twenty-seventh."

"I sure hope not, 'cause we'd be missing church if it was Sunday the twenty-seventh. And I don't reckon Willie would be missing church, what with him being the pastor's son and all."

"Well, I go to mass on Saturdays, and Willie faked a stomach-ache to stay home," she said. "Seriously, it's the twenty-seventh."

I slammed on the brakes and pulled off to the side of the road. The boat yanked against the ropes I'd tied it up with. I didn't care.

"Dadgummit, in the summer it's hard to keep track." I opened the door and hopped out. I had to find some flowers.

"What are you doing?" Martha said.

"It's the twenty-seventh," I said. I kept looking, but the best I could find was a mess of dandelions and some purple wildflowers that was probably weeds.

"And?"

"And I need to go by the cemetery real fast."

I bundled them flowers up and got back in, then I did a U-turn and headed over to Mount Vernon Cemetery.

ISAIAH CAMPBELL

Martha watched me as I drove and didn't say nothing for a bit. Finally she put her hand on my shoulder.

"Is it a birthday?"

I shook my head.

"August 27, 1954. That's the day the doctors in Havana unplugged all my ma's machines that was breathing for her and feeding her. The last day she ever had breath in her lungs." I rubbed the scar on my cheek, without really thinking about it. "Today's the day she officially died."

She didn't say nothing else, but she left her hand on my shoulder, which I was fine with.

We parked outside the cemetery and I got out.

"You going to come?" I asked.

She smiled. "Maybe another time. This seems . . . private."

"She'd probably like to meet you."

"Another time."

I nodded and headed through the gate. Mount Vernon Cemetery was one of the oldest cemeteries in Cullman County, and it wasn't all that popular with living folks 'cause they said it was awful run-down, but it was just the sort of graveyard you'd hope to be in if you was dead. It was surrounded by real tall trees that cast good ghost-hiding shadows no matter what time of day it was. There was also plenty of spiders and beetles in every nook and cranny to keep lonely spirits company, along with a few small animals like rabbits and squirrels and such that they'd enjoy haunting and scaring half to death. And there was a few rocks and downed tree trunks that was perfectly situated to make even the smallest breeze sound like a howl from the depths of hell. So, you know, it was nice.

I made my way through the gravestones, trying my best not to think of all them ghosts that was just itching to haunt my soul for eternity, and I got to the corner that was set up for the Cannon family. Grandma was out there, along with most all of the Cannons that had ever been in Cullman. Tommy's stone was there too, though his body was still in Castro's basement in Cuba, thanks to him crash-landing during the Bay of Pigs invasion. Something about that made his stone seem even lonelier.

Ma's grave was over in the corner of our section that I'd visited the least, which is just another illustration of how messed up the whole idea of happy endings is. 'Cause for most of my life, thanks to me being in the accident that killed Ma, my brain couldn't remember a darn thing from when she was alive. People'd tell me stories, but they was just that. Stories. Like when we studied Hannibal crossing the Alps with his pet elephants. And visiting her grave didn't hurt one bit. It didn't mean anything at all, really. So I never did it.

But then I got my memories back and folks claimed it was a happy ending to the story. These was the same folks who had already grieved for my ma and done mourned her death. But now I was just getting started. And I was having to do it all on my own.

Anyway, I got over to Ma's grave and I put them weeds on her gravestone. I sure hoped she thought they was flowers. I didn't know how good you could see from six feet under, so I tried to position them to where she might not tell. Then I knelt down in front of her stone and tried to think of what to say. Actually, that ain't exactly true. I had plenty to say. Plenty more to cry about, if I wanted to. But I didn't want to. So I had to find something to talk about that wouldn't get me to blubbering. And that was hard to do.

"How's it going, Ma?" I asked, then I cussed. You ain't supposed to ask a dead person how it's going, 'cause if they haven't noticed that they're dead and decomposing under the dirt, it ain't polite to draw their attention to it. They might just think all them worms and such is pets. Or that they're aiming to go fishing. But once they realize they're dead, then they'll figure out what them worms is really there for. And that just ain't right.

"What I mean is, how's the weather been?" Nope, that was stupid too. She didn't have no idea of rain or wind or nothing from where she was lying. Dang, this was a hard conversation. It always was.

"I reckon you know what today is. Well, I actually hope you don't. I sort of hope you don't remember none just like how I didn't." I thought about that for a second. "Except that might mean you don't remember me none. And that wouldn't be no good."

I got a lump in my throat, which meant if things didn't change,

I'd be sobbing like the time I broke my model car back when I was eight. I said a quick prayer that something would distract me.

I heard what sounded like another car pull up down at the gate to the cemetery. It shook the lump out of my throat for a bit.

"Anyway, if you do or don't remember, it don't much matter. This here's the day you and me got taken from each other. That's why I wanted to make sure I dropped by. So you wouldn't be alone." That darn lump came back.

Martha started talking to somebody a ways off. Finally, a decent distraction.

"Do you hear that? Maybe you can't from down there, but that's Martha, the girl I told you about. She sort of reminds me of you. I think."

I heard footsteps coming through the cemetery and I reckoned maybe Martha'd changed her mind about meeting Ma.

"I think she's coming, actually. She's a mite bit soaked and muddy, but I swear it's my fault. Don't go judging her none."

I stood up and turned to call Martha over, but it wasn't her. Well, it was her, but she wasn't alone.

There was a Chinese girl with her. And, by the looks of it, she had a baby Chinaman in her belly.

Martha pointed her over to where Tommy's gravestone was and then came by me.

"Hi," she said.

"What's she doing here?" I asked.

ISAIAH CAMPBELL

The girl was looking at them gravestones one by one, all around where Tommy's was.

"She said she was looking for your brother," she said.

"Did she say why?" I asked. Martha shook her head.

The Chinese girl found Tommy's gravestone, and she fell down onto the grass in front of it and started crying.

"What in tarnation—" I said. Martha shrugged.

I wouldn't normally get involved with foreigners, but since she was at Tommy's stone, I figured the only polite thing to do was to at least check on her. Plus I wouldn't want her going into labor or something. That'd make for a real bad place to birth a baby. I went over and knelt down next to her.

"Hey, listen, I don't speak no Chinese or nothing," I started.

"I'm Korean," she said with snot coming out her nose. She was covering her face and sobbing like there wasn't no tomorrow, so I didn't reckon I'd point out to her that it didn't much matter which one she was, since she apparently spoke English. Martha came over and joined us.

"Is everything okay?" Martha asked.

"Not sure," I said. "Is it?"

"It's just . . . ," the Korean girl said. "I was hoping it wasn't true. Hoping . . ." She started sobbing again. "Hoping he was still alive."

"Tommy?" I asked. "You're this ate up over Tommy?"

She nodded, then she wiped her nose and I finally got a good look at her face. She was pretty, for a Korean. Her hair was as black as a crow's back, her eyes sparkled even though they didn't have no color, and her face was shaped the way them models in magazines' faces are shaped, only she wasn't white, so it didn't look quite the same. If I'd had to guess, I'd have said she was the same age as Tommy. Maybe.

"I'm sorry, I'm being so rude." She held her hand out to shake mine. "My name is Sora Sa."

I went ahead and shook her hand and tried to not puke at how slick and snotty it was. I wouldn't want to be rude.

"Well, my name's Johnny," I said. "And this here's—"

"You're his brother? You're Johnny?" she asked, then she grabbed me and hugged on my neck. "He said you'd be here! Oh, it's so good to finally meet my baby's uncle."

I was at an awkward angle in the hug, 'cause she'd pulled me over her belly like a chicken on the chopping block. Then her belly punched me in the throat. I jerked away.

"Wait, what do you mean by that?"

"Are you saying . . . ," Martha said, and her eyes got real big. "Are you saying that your baby is Tommy's?"

Sora nodded and Martha gasped like she'd done seen a Martian come waltzing across the yard or something. And it was a surprise for me, too. But I reckon it wasn't too big of one. Half my life had been spent watching Tommy come home sauced with some girl he'd met at a bar. As soon as I found out storks didn't bring babies, I was waiting for one of his girls to announce that she was.

Still, she wasn't exactly like one of them girls he used to mess around with. Besides the fact that she wasn't white, she also seemed higher class than them. Probably couldn't dance on a table or cuss me out over her cigarettes and waffles if she tried.

I liked her already.

It had been five seconds since anybody had said anything, and Martha's eyes was practically floating in midair as she stared at Sora, so Sora cleared her throat.

"And you are?" she asked. Martha blinked a few times and stuck out her hand.

"Martha Macker."

"Oh, I've heard about you!" Sora said, and she smiled at me. "So you two finally—"

"Finally became friends, yup," I said. "Tommy told you about that?"

Sora glanced at Martha and then nodded.

"He told me all about you, and about Cullman, and everything else."

"Wish I could say the same," I said. Martha kicked me. "I mean, Tommy didn't say a darn thing about you." Another kick. "I mean, it's nice to meet you, too."

Sora laughed.

"Tommy always said you were funny."

He always told me I was a moron. Maybe that's along the same lines as funny.

"Um, where are you staying?" Martha asked.

Sora brushed her finger down Tommy's gravestone and traced along the dates that was under his name. She sighed.

"Nowhere," she said. "Not yet. I just got here from Mobile. My luggage is still in the car."

I looked over at the gate, expecting to see a yellow taxicab or something. Instead it was a gold Buick LeSabre. And a fella was leaning on the hood, wearing a slick blue suit and a white fedora, smoking a cigarette.

"I'm sure Mr. Cannon would want you to stay with him and Johnny," Martha said. I almost kicked her back, but I reckoned that would be detrimental to Operation Happy Ending. It wasn't that I was being inhospitable or anything. It was just that me and Pa was private folk. Partially 'cause we was both a little shy. And also partially 'cause of the work Pa did for Mr. Thomassen. But I couldn't go and tell about all that, so I just nodded instead.

Sora grabbed me and hugged on me again. Just about threw my back out contorting like that. Then that baby in her belly socked me in the gut. Dang, it was definitely Tommy's baby. It punched just like him.

Martha went to help Sora up.

"So, the car, is that a friend, or—"

"No," Sora said, real quick. "No, he's just someone that offered me a ride."

"Well, you can send him away now," Martha said. "We'll

backyard where Pa had rebuilt his radio shack. That was where he did his work for Mr. Thomassen.

"As you can see," Martha said, "there are no women living in this house." Sora nodded in agreement.

I looked at the place again and couldn't see what they was talking about. I mean, sure, we didn't have no flowers or nothing, or curtains on our windows, or a porch that looked pretty. And sure, there was tools in the driveway that had been there for a week and the grass had gotten to growing longer than it should have. And, sure, we had some squirrels and rabbits hanging on the front porch 'cause I still had to skin them. But really, what about all that made it unfit for a woman?

There was several cars parked in our yard, which didn't cause me no stir 'cause they was just Mr. Thomassen's white Cadillac and Carlos Martí's blue Chevy pickup. Carlos had been Mr. Thomassen's bandleader back in Havana, and he and I had escaped from Castro's clutches together. That's another long story. Now Carlos worked for Mr. Thomassen same as Pa, only Carlos did a lot of running around while Pa stayed put.

I parked next to the Cadillac and hurried to get inside before the girls. I was kind of hoping to prepare Pa for meeting his grandchild. He wasn't the healthiest fella in the world, mainly 'cause he only had half a lung and a quarter of his intestines thanks to the war. He also told me quite often that he had half a mind, but that was usually in context of him yelling at me, so I didn't think he was serious about that.

When I stepped in the door, I forgot what I was aiming to do, 'cause there was somebody there that I wasn't expecting. Sitting there with Pa, Mr. Thomassen, and Carlos in our living room was a fella that still scared the bejeezus out of me.

It was Short-Guy, the CIA agent.

They was all deep in a conversation, but Carlos elbowed Pa when he saw that I'd come in. Pa looked over at me.

"Oh, hey, son. How'd the fishing go? Did you catch anything?"

Right then the screen door behind me slammed open and Martha and Sora came in.

"Yeah, I reckon I caught a big one," I said. "This here's—"

"Sora Sa," Sora said.

All four of them men stood to their feet, 'cause that's what you do in Alabama when a lady has done entered the room. Pa cleared his throat and wiped his hands off on his shirt.

"Pete Cannon, Johnny's pa. It's nice to meet you, miss," Pa said. "What brings you—"

That's when Sora stepped out from behind me to show off that beach ball of a belly she had.

"Well," Pa said. "Congratulations on the baby."

Sora smiled and bowed her head.

"Thank you," she said, then she glanced at me. "It's your son's."

All of them fellas' eyes practically popped out of their sockets and looked at me, though I couldn't figure out what for. Pa's face turned as red as a fire engine and he started breathing the way he did when he forgot he couldn't breathe so good. Then they all started hollering at once.

"What in the name of all that is good and holy—?"

"You aren't even old enough yet!"

"¡No tienes dos dedos de frente! What were you thinking?"

"Hold the dadgum telephone!" I yelled. "It ain't mine, for crying out loud, it's Tommy's."

Talk about throwing a bucket of water on a bonfire. Pa went from being as mad as the devil to as giddy as a naked angel baby. He hurried and got up next to Sora and walked her over to the couch, the whole time grinning like a possum with an ice cream cone and babbling sounds that didn't none of them make sense strung together.

He fluffed up a pillow for her to sit on, then sat down right next to her.

"Ain't that just like Tommy," he said. "Going off and getting married without telling nobody."

Come to think of it, no, it wasn't like him at all.

"Well, we didn't ever actually—" she started, a little embarrassed. "What I mean is, we planned to take care of that when he came back."

Yeah, that sounded more like him.

Pa's face showed his shock again, but I reckon the happiness from finding out he was a grandpa took over and he just started smiling again.

"Oh well, water under the bridge," he said, then he patted her on the leg. "And this just proves that the Good Book is true. *'Whatsoever a man soweth, that shall he also reap.'* Here I am, doing the work I'm doing, and in return the Lord brings a happy addition to my own family."

Sora smiled and nodded.

"When are you due?" Mr. Thomassen said.

Martha plopped down next to Sora and put her arm around her.

"In October," she said, "and she doesn't have a place to stay."

"Not true," Pa said. "She can stay here."

"Pa!" I said. "What about the hotel or something?"

"What?" he said. "No, nonsense. This place could use a woman's touch. Sora can stay in Tommy's room. It's only right."

She hugged his neck and I reckon the baby took a jab at him too. He didn't seem to mind it. He put his hand on her belly to feel it contort and he laughed when it did.

I announced that I was going to get her luggage and Carlos offered to help me, but then Short-Guy said he'd do it 'cause he needed to talk to me about something. Which made my stomach get back into the bag of knots it had been when I first saw him. I hurried outside and he hurried to follow me.

I started grabbing bags real quick and he stopped me.

"How much do you know about what your father is doing with Mr. Thomassen?" he asked.

"Why?" I asked, and I felt all them knots tighten up in my stomach. "Is he getting into trouble again?"

"No," he said. "Not—just tell me, how much do you know?"

"Only that they call themselves the Three Caballeros, like that old Disney cartoon. And that Carlos goes away for two or three days to do jobs that Pa finds for him. And that not a one of them talks about it none."

He listened real intent to that.

"And that's all?"

"Yup." I pulled out another of Sora's bags from the truck. "Why? What's up?"

"Have you mentioned their name to anyone? The Three Caballeros, have you told anyone about that?"

"No," I said. "Well, Willie, but he's my blood brother, so I tell him everything."

He nodded.

"Now, listen to me. I need you to answer this question completely, and don't even think of lying to me." He grabbed me by the shoulders, which was a little weird since he was an inch smaller than me. "Who have you told about Captain Morris? That he is your real father?"

"Only the folks that was in the room when I recorded my testimony," I said. "So, the Parkinses, the Mackers—well, Martha and her ma, at least—and Mr. Thomassen and Carlos. Oh, and Pa, of course."

He sighed.

"That's more than I'd like, but it'll have to do. It can't go further than that circle. Do you understand me?"

"Sure, I guess," I said. "Why, what's going on?"

"Nothing you need to worry about. As long as you do as I say, nothing at all."

Oh good. 'Cause there wasn't nothing about what he said that made me worried or nothing. I was as cool as a cucumber now. A cucumber that was worried he might get shot in the head while he slept. That'd be a real pickle.

See, I wasn't nervous. I was almost peeing my pants, but still, I had jokes to spare.

We headed back inside and went to carry Sora's things up to Tommy's room. She stopped me and told me to leave the duffel bag down there. When we came back down, she had a gift-wrapped box and a manila envelope sitting on the coffee table.

"What's this?" I asked.

Sora smiled.

"Tommy made me promise I would come here to give you your birthday present. He wanted to make sure it was hand delivered."

The whole room got quiet, the kind of quiet that makes the air start itching at you. Adding the itchy air to the nervous stomach I had from Short-Guy's conversation, and I almost puked.

"What?" she asked. I looked over at Short-Guy, and he threatened my life with his eyes, so I had to come up with something else that was wrong.

"My birthday is in July," I said. "You're late."

"Johnny!" Pa yelled.

"Really?" she said, real confused. "Then why did he say it was—" She shook her head. "Oh well. Tommy wasn't exactly in the clearest state of mind when he and I were together in Mobile. He was so nervous about shipping off."

"To Nicaragua," Pa said.

That was a sputter in the conversation, and Sora seemed to get a little nervous over it. Or morning sick, there ain't no real way to be sure with pregnant women. She shot Pa a glance, one of them "do you know what you're talking about?" glances (or maybe one of them "I'm about to puke on your face" glances. Like I said, pregnant women).

"Did he tell you he was going to Nicar—"

"No, no, not Nicaragua," Pa said, real nervous like, I reckoned 'cause he was worried she didn't know what we knew. "My brain plays tricks."

"Where did he tell you he was going?" she asked.

Pa shot me a look.

"Korea," I said.

"Right, Korea," Pa said.

"Korea," she said, and she looked a little more sure of herself. "He told you Korea?"

"Sure did," I said. "'Cause that's where he went. Not to Nicaragua, or Narnia, or any of them other places."

"Exactly. Korea," she said.

"Yup, Korea," I said.

She peered into my eyes, then over at Pa's, and then she let out a satisfied sigh.

"Anyway." She handed me the manila envelope. "Here, I don't know what's inside of this and I've been dying to see."

Short-Guy cleared his throat and I knew why. He was naturally suspicious anyway, and that whole talk between me and her and Pa was enough to get him calling for backup. 'Cause Tommy hadn't gone to Korea. That was just his cover story. He went to Nicaragua to train the Cuban exiles for the Bay of Pigs invasion. So it probably didn't sound right to Short-Guy that Tommy'd have told the woman he was going to marry a lie like that. But that was 'cause Short-Guy didn't know Tommy. Tommy was inclined to lie to women.

I opened the envelope and slid out three comic books. All of them Superman comics, of course. 'Cause nobody knew me better than Tommy.

"Read the letter," she said. "Out loud, please." She seemed real excited about it. Everybody else, too. So I cleared my throat and did a quick scan so I wouldn't stumble over no words.

T. Cannon
Springfield, Fla.

April 7, ~~1861~~ 1961

Dear Johnny,

Wow, my FIRST LETTER! Can't believe I haven't ever written a first letter to you before. But I figured, if there was ever a time to write a first letter, it would be on your birthday. Wish I could remember when it is. It's in the summer, but I don't think it's a J month, so August? Yup, that's when you'll get this first letter.

But what I really need to say is

Knowing every elected politician yesterday only undoes right belief. Looking over our deeds satisfies as failure elevates failure, rusting our men. Hear Antonia + Rose's message.

Anyway, I love you, little brother. I also love the lady that brought you this first letter. Treat her right.

Tommy Cannon

I tried to read it out loud, but I couldn't even get past the date. It was so dadgum weird, it made my brain hurt to think about speaking it. I folded it up and mumbled a thank-you to her.

"Too emotional," Carlos said. "I understand, *compadre*."

Everybody else seemed to think that was a good explanation, so I let it be.

Sora slid the gift across the table.

"Open it," she said. "I think you'll like it. Tommy was always saying how much you like superheroes."

I unwrapped the present and opened the box, and for the first time I felt a tinge of that same disbelief that Short-Guy had been showing on his face. 'Cause either Tommy had been running on a few bottles of Jim Beam, or that present hadn't come to me from Tommy. Not a chance.

It was a statue of Robin, the Boy Wonder's head. And Tommy knew, more than anybody else, how much I hated Robin. When I was ten, I'd even gone through all his Batman comics and cut out all the Robins just so I could burn them on our grill. Robin was a dadgum nincompoop who ran around in women's underpants. Worst superhero ever.

I looked around the room, a tad bit worried that they was all going to start accusing her at once. It might not be good for the baby to have so many fingers pointed, and especially if they threw her out on her backside, well, it might give the kid a flat head or something. I got ready to start making excuses, just like I usually did for one of Tommy's girls.

Pa stood up and picked up the Robin statue. Good Lord, was he about to smash it over her head? I jumped up to stop him.

"This—" he started, and I poised myself to jump in between them. "This is wonderful. Let's put it over here on the mantel so we can all think of Tommy every day."

Wait, what?

I looked at Mr. Thomassen. He didn't never let nothing get past him. He'd probably cut right to the heart with whatever he said. I needed to figure out a good joke or something.

He was patting his eyes with his hanky. Okay, no joke needed. Which was good, 'cause the only one I thought of on such a short notice was the one about the car crank and the fella's butt.

"Makes me think of my own brother," Mr. Thomassen said. "I haven't thought of him in a while."

Whew. She was probably safe. I mean, sure, it was a little weird about the statue and all, but still. She was going to have a baby. That covers just about everything, doesn't it?

I looked over at Short-Guy. Nope, apparently not. He was scowling like a judge at a hanging, and I don't reckon he cared much about the baby or nothing else. There wasn't going to be no making him happy about Sora.

And that made me as nervous as a cat in a room full of rocking chairs. Add that to what he'd done told me, and all of a sudden I needed to get some fresh air.

"I'll be back in a bit," I said. I grabbed the letter and headed out the door, and then I hurried to go find the only fella I could tell everything to.

I hurried over to Willie's house.

Willie's porch was a little cluttered when I got there. They had one of them porches that was designed to have family reunions on, and it looked like they'd had a church get-together just before I came over. His pa was the pastor of the church in Colony, which was the place in Cullman County where the black folk lived.

I knocked on the door and Mrs. Parkins answered it.

"Willie's sick," she said. "But you're welcome to come in. We have lots of leftovers from lunch."

"I heard he was sick," I said. "That's why I brung him something." I looked around real quick and saw a tuna can that somebody'd put potato salad in. I picked it up. "It's an old family remedy for a tummy ache."

She gave me her usual suspicious look, which I'd grown to learn was what a mother does to a boy when she cares something about him, so I felt good. She took me down the hall to Willie's room. As usual, I could hear him talking.

"*Traversing the snowy mountains of the ice planet, Mercury is starving. He hasn't eaten in days. His only rations he split between Smokey, his faithful canine companion, and the green, two-trunked elephant, the only creature that can safely navigate the treacherous terrain. Now, sitting in his camp, he watches both creatures sleep. Our hero must make the impossible decision. Which warm-blooded friend will be his dinner?"*

Mrs. Parkins knocked on the door. Willie said an almost cuss-word that wasn't and then we heard a ruckus that sounded like somebody with only one good leg diving across the room into his bed.

"Johnny's here," she said, and opened his door.

He was wrapped up in his blanket and blinking his eyes like he just woke up.

"I sure hope he don't catch my chicken pox," he said, then he coughed a few times. His ma shot him that same suspicious look.

"I thought you said you had the measles."

"That too," he said. "Dadgum, I might have to stay home from church for the next month, huh?"

She covered her mouth and I reckoned maybe she was protecting herself from his germs. Course, it almost looked like she was smiling, but there wasn't no way that was true, so it had to be the germs thing. She left me and Willie alone, and as soon as she was out of earshot, he hopped out of bed.

"So," he said, "did it work? Did you finally get your Happy Ending?"

I shook my head.

"Not even close. Pretty sure I'm further from kissing Martha now than I was yesterday."

He sighed and went over to his bookshelf, where he had a whole row of red notebooks lined up. He pulled one off, which had a white label on the cover with the words "Operation Happy Ending" written in permanent marker. He opened to a page that had "Fishing Trip" written on top and he wrote, in big letters, *FAILED* straight across all the other writing. He turned to the next page.

"We won't give up yet," he said. "We got plenty more good ideas, and I got the equipment to make them all work." He pointed at the top of the new page. "Next up is 'Drowning.' See, you're going to fake like you drown and she's going to give you mouth-to-mouth."

"Does that count as kissing?"

"Maybe not when she first starts," he said, "but when you're done, it will."

I shrugged. "Whatever, you're the junior agent, not me."

He nodded. "By the way, did you bring me back that walkie-talkie?"

"Dadgummit, no," I said. "I left it at the cemetery."

"The cemetery?" He flipped back to the fishing page in his notebook. "That wasn't part of the plan."

"A whole mess of stuff happened that wasn't part of the plan," I said, and then I told him all about visiting Ma and Sora showing up, and the baby that was Tommy's. He was real interested in that and even fished a notebook off his shelf that said *Tommy Cannon Case File* and wrote some stuff in it.

"Why do you got a case file on Tommy?" I asked. "Dead folk don't usually do much that needs investigating. Their ghosts might cause some mischief, but you ain't supposed to look into that."

"I have a case file on everyone," he said. "It's what Short-Guy said agents do."

Now, he knew Short-Guy's name, but since I couldn't never remember, we both just called him Short-Guy behind his back.

"He was up there too," I said. "Him and the Three Caballeros was having a meeting."

"He's up at your house?" he asked. "Dang it, and here I'm claiming to be sick. I wonder if I could fake a miracle or something so I could go see him."

I went over and started fiddling with his notebooks.

"I wouldn't. He scared the heck out of me. Practically said I'd be in danger of hellfire if I told anybody that I'm Captain Morris's son."

He pushed me away from his books.

"Really? Why?"

"He wouldn't tell me. And then it got worse when he saw the weird letter and the stupid present."

"A letter? What did it say?"

I got the letter out of my pocket and handed it to him. He read over it and his face showed that he thought it was funny business too.

"This is the weirdest dadgum letter I've ever read," he said. "Who's Antonia and Rose?"

I had to look at the letter again to see what he was talking about. Right there in the middle, it said to hear Antonia and Rose's message.

"Don't look at me," I said. "I ain't never heard of nobody around here by those names. I mean, if it really was 1861, like is scratched out, instead of good old 1961, I'd think he was maybe talking about Antonia Ford and Rose O'Neal Greenhow, the Confederate spies during the Civil War. They leaked information to the south about the Battle of Bull Run and a whole mess of other things. But it ain't back then, so it could be anybody."

He got a funny look on his face.

"When was he in Florida?" He pointed at that part at the top that said *T. Cannon, Springfield, Fla.*

"He wasn't," I said. "He probably wrote it at a bar in Springfield, Alabama, and was so shaky he didn't finish out the first letter. I'm telling you, he was as drunk as a skunk on its twenty-first birthday."

He nodded, but he kept right on staring at it.

"Mind if I hold on to the letter for a bit?" he asked.

"I don't care," I said. "I was going to put it in my keepsake drawer. Just make sure I get it back, okay?"

He put the letter up on his wall with a thumbtack.

"Sure," he said. "Though, what if it ain't really from Tommy? You want to keep it, then?"

ISAIAH CAMPBELL

"What you mean? Of course it's from Tommy. That's his hand-writing. It's his drunk handwriting, but still, it's close enough."

"Okay, but what if it ain't?" he asked.

I hadn't honestly thought of that. Maybe somebody was copying his way with a pen.

"If it ain't from Tommy," I said, "who's it from?"

He shrugged.

"That's what we'd have to find out."

Dadgum, he'd been in secret agent mode for too long. Suspicious of a poor pregnant lady. That just wasn't right.

But, now he had me thinking.

What if?

CHAPTER TWO
GROCERY LISTS

I was standing at the front of the classroom writing on the blackboard. I glanced down to make sure I was wearing pants. I was.

Dadgummit, that meant this wasn't a dream.

It was the first day of school and Mr. Braswell, the brand-spanking-new teacher, was making good on a promise he'd made Mrs. Buttke, my teacher from sixth grade. When she found out he was going to be teaching us, fresh out of college, she went and made sure he was good enough to teach her precious kids. Which was us, I reckon. And apparently he's real good at math and science and English. Heck, he sent us all a letter back in July making sure we all knew about prepositions and how they was the words you wasn't supposed to end a sentence with.

But then she found out he'd just barely passed all his classes in history. And as far as Mrs. Buttke was concerned, history was the most important subject you could possibly learn in school. So she made him promise that he'd have a This Day in History for us every day, just like she had. And, since he wasn't so good at it, he should have one of his students do it for him.

Which meant he was going to have *me* do it. Even though I wasn't no teacher and had trouble talking to more than two people at the same time, somehow she and him both thought putting me in front of a classroom of sweaty teenagers was a good idea.

So there I was, sweating through my undershirt and leaving pit stains the size of Lake Martin, and the day had only just started. Mr. Braswell was sitting on his desk taking a drag on his cigarette. There wasn't supposed to be no smoking in the school, but that's how Mr. Braswell was. He'd already established that he played by his own rules.

My hand was shaking while I copied from my notebook.

August 29, 1756: Frederick the Great invades Saxony and starts the Seven Years' War, aka the French and Indian War.

I put the chalk down, it was real damp from the sweat on my hands. I turned and started back to my seat, but Mr. Braswell stopped me.

"So, tell us, Johnny Cannon, why is this event so significant?"

He could have kicked me in the crotch and held my head under a waterfall and I would have been more calm than I was right then.

"Um, it was 'cause," I mumbled to him, "see, Saxony was neutral, but—"

"To the class, Johnny," he said, the cigarette hanging out of his mouth like James Dean usually had his.

I stared out at the classroom, all them eyes staring up at me. I felt like somebody'd stuffed a bag of cotton in my mouth and then made me swallow it. What made it worse was, that jerk Eddie Gorman, who'd grown about three inches and whose voice had dropped about two octaves, started chuckling at me.

Willie'd told me once, if I was ever in that situation, to picture everybody in the room naked, so I tried that. Bad idea. I had to look at the ceiling to get my brain back in order.

"Why should I care about a man who lived two hundred years ago?" Mr. Braswell said.

I cleared my throat and almost threw up. I closed my eyes and tried to force the words out.

"Music! Running! Beheaded! Cold-blooded!" I said.

"Breathe," Mr. Braswell said. "And don't make us all go deaf."

I nodded and cleared my throat again. Dadgummit, I accidentally hocked up a giant loogie. Without thinking, I spit it in Mr. Braswell's trash can. All the girls said, "Ewww." Oh well, at least it calmed me down a bit.

"See, when Frederick was a kid, he was all into music and art and stuff, and he wasn't the sort to go doing something as cold-blooded as invading a neutral country. And he didn't want to be prince, either, so he and his friend tried to run off to England. But they got caught, and as punishment, the King of Prussia had

ISAIAH CAMPBELL

his friend beheaded in front of him. And I reckon that's when he lost part of his soul or whatever, and that's why later on he didn't care that them folks in Saxony wasn't trying to get involved in the conflicts in Europe. Or that he started a war that would eventually kill over a million people."

The class got quiet. Almost like they was interested.

"Good job," Mr. Braswell said, and I felt all warm. I checked my pants to make sure I hadn't accidentally wet myself. I was fine.

"What lesson can we learn from that?" he asked.

I started to say the answer, but Eddie interrupted me.

"Don't get caught," he said, and a couple of the fellas started to chuckle.

I shot him the evil eye. He shut up.

"Sometimes, even if you're the one that deserves it, somebody else will pay for what you done," I said.

"Great, excellent. I look forward to tomorrow's lesson," Mr. Braswell said. I took a bow, but nobody clapped. I tried to make like I was tying my shoe, then I went back to my seat next to Martha.

"That was great," she whispered, and patted me on my back. Then she wiped her hand on her skirt 'cause it had my sweat on it.

"Now," Mr. Braswell said as he put his cigarette out on his desk, "I sent everyone a letter forewarning you about the big project for this quarter. So, let's hear it. Who did everyone pick?"

I'd read the letter and then forgot all about it. Mainly 'cause it wasn't a new assignment, even though Mr. Braswell was acting like it was. It had been around for almost as long as the school had been in Cullman. The first seventh-grade teacher, Mr. Harris, had started it back when he was teaching the dinosaurs or something, and he'd kept it up until the tornado last year sent him packing. And now Mr. Braswell was keeping it going.

It was the big biography assignment. And every single person who's ever lived in Cullman still has nightmares about it. The mayor even published the grade he'd gotten when he was campaigning for his job. That's how big of a deal it is.

Basically, we had to write a biography of someone that was alive, and we had to do it by interviewing them and everyone we could about them, plus reading and researching and stuff. Rumor has it that there was a boy during World War II that defected to the Nazis just so he could avoid writing it. But then, Mr. Harris made him interview Hitler. I reckon that ain't true, but it could be.

Right after Mr. Braswell asked who we'd picked, all the girls raised their hands. It didn't take too long to figure out that that was how things was going to go in that class. No matter what he asked about, all them girls was going to be primed and waiting to volunteer. 'Cause Mr. Braswell was probably the closest thing to looking like a movie star we'd ever had in our town. He'd played football with Tommy at Cullman High back in the day, and he'd kept his body in shape ever since. Plus he had blond hair and blue eyes and everything else that made girls go gaga. None of us fellas could figure out why he was still single. Maybe he was so busy trying to look good that he didn't have time to spend hunting after girls.

He pointed at Kristen, who hadn't never done nothing in school ever. She stood up and batted her superlong eyelashes at him, but she didn't say anything.

"Whom did you pick for your biography?" he asked her. He liked to say "whom" a lot. I reckoned he was trying to sound British or something. I hear they say "whom" all the time over there.

"Oh, right," she said. "Well, I have decided that I'm going to write about the oldest man in the world, Methuselah."

Mr. Braswell chuckled and dropped his cigarette on the floor so he could grind it out with his heel. Then he pulled out his pack, knocked out another one, stuck it in his mouth, and lit it with a match. All the while, Kristen stood, shifting her weight between her feet, batting her eyelashes at him like they was moths trying to catch the flame.

"Okay," Mr. Braswell said. "I'll give you five points for effort. But, I'm going to subtract five points because you missed the two most important parts of this assignment. One, you have to interview the person you're writing about."

"Oh, I'll call him," she said. "I'm sure I can find his number somewhere. My pastor talked about him on Sunday and he can probably get it."

Mr. Braswell chuckled again, took a long puff on his cigarette, and then blew a little cloud of smoke up into the room.

"That brings me to the other issue. He's dead. You're supposed to write about someone that's alive."

She gasped a little, then sat back down.

"Did you guys know that Methuselah died?" she whispered to me and Martha. There wasn't no point in answering.

"Kristen, you are such a birdbrain sometimes," Martha said.

"Martha," Mr. Braswell barked, "I'm going to assume you have picked someone slightly more alive?"

She stood up and smoothed out her skirt.

"Yes, I did," she said, then she smiled at me. She'd told me that she was going to surprise me with who she'd be writing about. I was going to surprise everybody too, 'cause I wasn't going to write about nobody. Which might not actually surprise anybody, but whatever.

"I am going to write about someone who is very brave and very heroic," she said. "Someone who has dealt with the worst kinds of tragedies and has come out stronger. Someone who has stared death in the face and survived. Someone who has crossed racial borders, overcome his own challenges, and who is now one of the kindest, most sensitive boys in Cullman."

Boy, I sure couldn't figure out who she was talking about. But whoever he was, we'd probably get along real good. He might even make a good hunting buddy.

"I'm going to write about my brother, Johnny Cannon," she said, and then she pointed at me. Everyone turned around to look and then they started clapping for me. Or her, it was hard to tell. Even Mr. Braswell slapped his hands together a few times.

Meanwhile, I was sinking underneath my desk and wishing somebody from China would pop out of a hole in the ground so we could trade spaces. But that didn't happen. Instead I had to sit there and act like I enjoyed the applause like most normal kids would. Which was hard, 'cause it felt more like a firing squad was shooting at me than that people was happy for me. The only person not clapping was Eddie. He was staring at my face and it almost seemed like he could read my mind.

"Who gives two cents about Johnny?" he asked. "Most of his story happened *to* him, and the only reason he survived the little bit he actually brought on himself is dumb luck."

Martha and everybody stopped clapping. She got real mad at him, but I was relieved.

"Oh?" she said. "And I suppose you think *your* story is better?"

He looked at me again.

"You'll never know, will you?" he said.

"All right, moving on," Mr. Braswell said. I glanced over at Eddie and he smiled at me, like he'd just done me a favor or something. I looked back down at my book.

We got through the naming of biographies, and I somehow managed to not get called on, and then Mr. Braswell moved on to teaching about math. But I wasn't quite ready to move on yet, 'cause something was bothering me.

"Where'd you get the darn fool idea to write about me?" I asked Martha.

"Willie suggested it. I wasn't going to at first but—" She started blushing. "I mean, he really made it seem like he wanted to read about you. He's even going to let me use his tape recorder and everything." She stopped talking for a bit and chewed her lip instead. "Anyway, it'll be nice to make something that he'll be interested in." She didn't look at me while she said that. She was busy copying down the math problems Mr. Braswell was writing under my history fact. And chewing her lip still. I wondered if she had a cold sore or something.

"I thought you was going to start helping him with his SuperNegro stories," I said.

"If I can help it, I'd rather do this. They're not really my thing," she said. "But, please, don't tell him."

So weird. She was almost acting like the way girls in movies acted when Rock Hudson would come around. But I didn't figure it was for the same reason. After all, if we was in one of them love stories, then she was *my* girl. And Willie was my guy, like how them romance fellas always had a sidekick. Kind of like Robin, except not such a sissy.

Some folks might have raised the objection that he was black and she was white, but that was just racist. And not worth mentioning, since I'd already disproved it in my mind with that whole romance story argument. Like Willie always said, you can't ignore scientific fact. If there was a Rock Hudson around, it was me. Not Willie. Some things just flat out couldn't never happen.

After school that day, Pa was waiting for me in the truck with Sora. He said we needed to get her checked out at the doctor. I reckoned we was going to go over to Doc Brown's, but we didn't.

Instead, thirty minutes after I got out of school, I was sitting in a strange doctor's waiting room with Pa. We was both as uncomfortable as a Jew on a pig farm, mainly on account that this was the dadgum female doctor. And I don't mean a doctor that was a female. That'd be all right.

No, we was at a doctor that only worked on women. Which meant we wasn't supposed to be there.

But there we was.

Pa was trying to chat up a couple of pregnant ladies that was sitting in there with us, and they was trying to not show on their faces how much they thought he was a kidnapper scouting out prospects. I didn't even bother, I went to try and do some reading. But there wasn't nothing in there that was fit for a boy to look at. It was all about feeding babies and women's body parts and such. It was like being at the library in hell.

I got up from my seat and went over to the window, which had a real good view of the main street there in Cullman. And, since it was the middle of a Tuesday, folks was out doing their business. Lots of interesting things to watch so I could take my mind off all the female stuff that was surrounding me.

Dolly Pickler was out walking her dog and it peed on the fire hydrant right in front of a cop. She hurried to move on before he noticed. There was also some folks coming out of the grocery store and looking at their receipts, arguing with each other over something. Finally, one of them got some change out of her purse and threw it at the other, then she stormed off. Then there was Archie Dean, the town's drunk, who was already off-kilter. He was trying to cross the street and kept timing it right to when he'd step in front of a car. The deputy came and grabbed him real fast, and Archie tried to punch him in the nose.

Basically, just a typical day in Cullman.

But then I spied a scene that took hold of my eyeballs and made me watch. Bob Gorman, the richest fella in town, was standing in front of his auto shop, hollering. And he was hollering at his son, Eddie. And, even though Eddie was probably about as tall as Bob now, he was cowering like a puppy that'd been kicked a few too many times.

Now, there wasn't no making out what Bob was saying or nothing, but judging from the way he was waving his arms and how his face was getting fifty shades of red, you knew there was some choice words getting thrown out. Eddie was wincing from the words, and folks that was walking by tried to look away. Except for those that was breaking their necks to watch.

Just when I reckoned maybe it was time to stop looking at them, Bob snatched a paper out of Eddie's hand and ripped it to

ISAIAH CAMPBELL

pieces. Then he wagged his finger in Eddie's face. All that time, Eddie didn't say much of nothing, just hung his head in shame.

Bob got right in Eddie's face, still screaming. It was almost enough to make me feel sorry for that mole rat. Almost.

Finally, Eddie reached out and pushed his pa away. I didn't blame him none on that, Bob had the worst coffee breath of anyone in town. Still, it ain't right to lay a hand on your own pa. I almost got mad at Eddie for it.

Then Bob punched Eddie in the face.

Just about everybody that was walking around stopped and stared at that, Eddie was holding on to his jaw like it was about to fall off, and my own jaw was halfway to the carpet. Bob must have only then realized all them folks was watching, 'cause he grabbed Eddie and dragged him into his shop.

I wondered if the beating was over or if it was just getting started.

Right then the nurse came out and told Pa that the doctor wanted to speak to us back where he'd just gotten done examining Sora.

We went through the hallways to the room where Sora was sitting on the doctor bed and the doctor was standing next to her, chatting with her. When we came in, he gave us both a smile while he patted Sora's hand.

"Well, I have good news, certainly," the doctor said. "The baby is very healthy, maybe a tad underweight, but overall very strong and healthy."

Pa grinned. "Of course it is. It's Tommy's baby. It's going to be as strong as an ox."

I tried to not think about what Willie'd said, about maybe it wasn't Tommy's baby. I didn't want to spoil the mood.

"There is some concern about Mommy, though," the doctor went on. "She's very underweight for this stage of her pregnancy."

"Really?" I asked. "'Cause she looks as ripe as a Thanksgiving turkey to me." I meant it as a compliment, but it didn't seem like anybody took it that way.

The doctor cleared his throat.

"Anyway, she's malnourished. And, from the stories she told me about her home life, she doesn't have a good support system to go back to. I would recommend that you spend the time between now and her delivery making sure she gets a lot of good food and fluids."

"Her home life?" Pa said.

"She didn't tell you?" the doctor said. He looked at Sora and she looked away. "When her family found out she was pregnant, they kicked her out. She's been homeless for the last four months."

Pa shook his head in disbelief.

"Why would anyone willingly push away their own child?" he asked, then he went and gave her a hug. "Well, you're my daughter now."

She started crying and that made him start crying. The doctor nodded and smiled and tried to hide that his eyes was watering too.

ISAIAH CAMPBELL

But it was like Willie's voice was in my head. What if? I tried to ignore it so I could get as sappy as they was, but it just came across that I had to go to the bathroom.

The doctor gave us some vitamins to give her so she could keep growing the baby real good. He also gave us a list of all the food she needed to be eating. Oh, and he gave us a bill.

Pa paid the bill and we all three headed out to the truck. He handed me the list.

"You know our kitchen better than I do. How much of this do we got?"

I didn't even have to look. Our pantry only had potato chips and peanut butter, and I didn't reckon any of that was on the list. Feeding menfolk is a whole heck of a lot easier than feeding a woman with a baby in her belly. We needed to go grocery shopping.

Going grocery shopping with Pa was always my least favorite chore, mainly 'cause Pa didn't never have no plan when he went for groceries. He'd sort of get an idea in his head while he was looking at noodles that he might like pasta one night, then head over to get some sauce and reckon chili might be better. Then, when he was picking up some onions, he'd change his mind again and we'd have a basket chock full of ingredients to make three quarters of five different meals.

Even though we had a list from the doctor, this time wasn't no different. Well, it was a little different, 'cause Pa kept asking Sora what she thought of things, and she kept saying she didn't have no opinion about nothing, whatever we thought was best. Which was pretty dadgum frustrating, especially when he asked her about macaroni. 'Cause who doesn't have an opinion about macaroni?

"Well, dagnab it," I said, "what kind of food *do* you like? There ain't a whole lot I know how to cook."

She cast a sheepish glance to Pa and said, nearly as quiet as a church mouse, "I don't mind cooking."

Now, why hadn't I thought of that before? She was a girl, after all. Even though she was pregnant, cooking was part of her programming.

Pa jumped on that idea like a barn cat onto a cricket and made me put away all them groceries we'd already picked out, including the three bags of potato chips I'd wrangled. Then we followed her around the store and she took to picking out the weirdest ingredients I'd ever seen someone put in a basket. Things like cabbage and ginger and scallions and just about everything else that I never would have picked as fit for eating in that store.

Then we went down the baby aisle and Pa got the darn fool idea in his head that we ought to start buying stuff for the little tadpole before it was even born. I was just about to finally put my foot down when somebody yelled at us.

"Johnny!" It was Martha. She was there with her ma. As soon as she saw Sora was with us, she dragged Mrs. Macker down the aisle and introduced her.

"Oh dear, Martha was right," Mrs. Macker said, "you're as skinny as a rail."

It was like I was the only one that saw her belly. Was folks just getting blinded by the fact she was Korean or something? 'Cause that would be racist.

"Good afternoon," Pa said, 'cause he believed in keeping the Southern in hospitality. "How's old Gary doing?"

"Still in Montgomery," Mrs. Macker said with a sigh. "He told me last night that the men working on the project just aren't getting it, so he'll have to stay another few weeks."

"Montgomery ain't that far from here," he said. "Why don't he just commute?"

"I don't know," she said, and her face made it look like she wasn't too happy with her own answer. "You should ask him that question."

Pa must have sensed the awkwardness, 'cause he cleared his throat like he only did when things was getting dangerously close to being about feelings.

"Now, you know a lot more than I do on this subject," he said. "What should we start stocking up on so my grandbaby has everything it needs?"

That was the first time I'd heard him call it his grandbaby. It was actually kind of nice, to tell the truth. Mrs. Macker seemed relieved that the subject had changed too.

"Formula," Mrs. Macker said. "Lots of formula. Your little bundle is going to be hungry."

Sora touched her chest. "I thought—"

"Usually they give you a shot of Delestrogen to dry them up, since formula is more consistent with the vitamins and minerals your baby needs," Mrs. Macker said. All of a sudden she seemed less like Martha's mom and more like a doctor or something. "As I used to always warn young mothers, there are some side effects, like nausea, headaches, swelling, and changes in your menstr—"

"Mom!" Martha said, her face as red as a tomato. I was glad she'd stopped her, 'cause my ears was burning.

"Sorry, old habits from a life before my own baby was born," Mrs. Macker said, and patted Martha's hair, then she went back to being a mom. "You'll also need to get some diapers. After all, as much as they eat, that's how much they—"

"Can I go look at the comic books?" I asked.

Pa nodded. He was real intent on listening as they was discussing which diapers was best and all that jazz, and I hurried to get away from there. It had only just struck me that there was going to be an actual crying, pooping baby in our house. And that thought terrified me something fierce.

I went to the rack and looked to find a comic I hadn't read yet. Which was practically impossible 'cause I read them every single day. So I picked up one I'd already read and tried to see how good I remembered it.

I got to the fourth page when Sheriff Tatum arrived, and it didn't look like he was there to buy milk or anything. He was looking for

Sam, the grocer. They went and started talking in the corner, which was just a few feet from me. And, since the comic book wasn't very interesting at all, I aimed my ears at listening to them.

"Okay, tell me what's missing," Sheriff Tatum said, and he opened his notebook to scribble in.

"Two dozen cans of baked beans, a case of hot dogs, three packs of bread, and a box of cigarettes."

"And it was all stolen this morning?"

"Yes sir," Sam said. He wiped his forehead with his apron. "The truck came in from Montgomery and while I was paying the driver, somebody took it."

Sheriff Tatum grabbed an apple off one of the racks and started eating it. Sam scrunched up his eyebrows but didn't say nothing, 'cause you can't never say nothing to the sheriff.

"Sounds like a vagrant," Sheriff Tatum said. "Probably already moved on, if I had to guess. But I'll go looking in the woods and see what I can stir up."

"Will you let me know what you find?"

"If there is anything, sure." Sheriff Tatum put his notebook back in his pocket. "Otherwise, well, I wouldn't want to waste your time."

"But—"

I didn't get to listen no more 'cause Pa started hollering for me. He and Sora was in the checkout line with two baskets and a buggy full of stuff. I went over to see what he wanted.

"I ain't got enough cash for all this," Pa said.

"If you're aiming to put it all back, you can do that yourself," I said.

He laughed. "No, just run out and get the spare cash from the truck."

He kept a couple of fifties under the seat, in case of emergency. I never thought grocery shopping would be an emergency, but I reckon things change when there's a baby on the way. I went out to get the money.

I went around the block to where we was parked and fished out the two fifties. I started back to the grocery store, but then I saw someone sitting in the alley next to Gorman's Auto Shop. It was Eddie, and from the looks of it, he was crying.

And you can't un-see things, no matter how hard you try. I learned that lesson when my grandma walked through the house in just her underwear. Try as you might, some things will stay with you till the day you die.

And, when it comes to folks crying in alleys, once you've spied it, it's on you to do something about it.

After a few seconds of debating, I remembered that he'd helped get me out of hot water in school, so I went over to where he was and tapped him with my foot. Maybe it was a little harder than I intended, but it's the thought that counts.

"What?" Eddie said, rubbing his leg.

"You all right?" I asked. I noticed that his jaw was sprouting up a real nice bruise from where Bob had socked him.

He sniffed real hard, wiped his eyes, and made his voice sound as tough as he could.

"I'm fine."

I reckoned that was the end of that, so I turned to walk away. Then something in my gut stopped me. Maybe it was my conscience. Or the potato chips I'd had for breakfast. Either way, I turned back to him.

"You know, there's a lot of things you deserve, since you're such a nasty person," I said to him. "Getting tarred and feathered, boiled in oil, run out of town wearing a dress, just a whole mess of stuff." Then I took a deep breath, 'cause the next thing I was going to say was going to take a lot out of me. "But you sure as heck didn't deserve to get punched in the face by your pa. No kid does."

He nodded.

"Thanks."

"Don't mention it," I said. "Ever."

I went to walk off, feeling right good about myself. But then he must have felt something in his own gut too, 'cause he stopped me.

"Johnny?" he said.

"Yeah?"

"Have you ever wished you wasn't related to your own dad?"

Now, Eddie probably thought he was talking about Pa, and the answer to that question was no, I hadn't never wished that. But I knew the truth, that my real father was that scoundrel Captain

Morris. And there wasn't a day that went by that I didn't look in the mirror and hate every part of me that came down from him.

"Sometimes," I said.

"What do you do about it?"

I had to think about that for a bit.

"Ain't much you *can* do about it. Blood's blood."

He looked down at the ground again and I got scared he was fixing to cry.

"But," I said, "just 'cause you got a polecat's blood in your veins don't mean you got to smell like him. Remember that."

He grinned and seemed a little relieved by that.

"Thanks," he said. He sat quiet for a second, then he looked at me real funny. "Remember back when we used to hang out?"

"Yeah," I said. Once upon a time he'd been the only friend I had, back before me and Willie got close and such.

"Whatever happened?"

"Life changes," I said. "People change."

"Yeah," he said. "It stinks. 'Cause things don't ever change for the better."

There wasn't no arguing with that. In fact, for the first time in a long time, I remembered how much him and me was alike. Which was a problem.

I kicked him in the leg again just to keep the universe balanced. That was better. I turned and ran off.

I got back to the grocery store, we got it all paid for, and then we loaded up the truck and headed home. When we got there, the other two Caballeros were waiting for us on our porch. And Short-Guy, of course. Or, to keep with the theme, *hombre pequeño*. Which Carlos told me means Short-Guy.

"We need to have another meeting?" Pa said when he got out of the truck. Short-Guy nodded. Pa turned to me. "Go ahead and unload the groceries."

Him and them other fellas went into the living room and I started carrying in all the bags from the truck. Sora sat in the kitchen and watched me put everything away.

"Dang, why'd we get so much tuna?" I asked. We must have bought eighteen cans. And they weighed a ton. Oh well, it was getting my muscles bigger, I guess.

"I've been craving tuna," she said. "And macaroni."

I put all them cans on the shelf, then Willie's voice in my head slapped me across the face and I turned to look at her.

"Wait, I thought you said you didn't have no feelings about macaroni."

She blinked a few times like she was thinking real hard.

"I didn't. But the baby did, and when you mentioned it, I knew what it was it wanted."

I wasn't sure if that made sense or not, 'cause I wasn't no doctor, so I let it slip on by. I'd ask Willie about it later.

I just about got all the groceries onto the shelf when Pa called me into the living room. He pointed next to him on the couch.

"I really think this is a bad idea," Short-Guy said.

"I don't care," Pa said. "This involves him. And I ain't going to hide things from him again. I think we all can say that was a bad idea last time."

My stomach started knotting up again.

"What y'all talking about?" I asked. "You in trouble again?"

They all laughed, but not like they thought it was funny, but like you do when you ask a fella that just got bit by a bear if it hurt. Like you do when you just heard the biggest understatement of the year. And my stomach turned into a double square knot.

"I need you to go to a meeting with me tomorrow," Mr. Thomassen said. I waited for him to explain, but he didn't do it.

"When? After school?"

"Actually, I'm going to pull you out of school for it. We have to meet someone in Birmingham."

My mouth was going dry. I looked over at Short-Guy. As usual, his face didn't give me no answers.

"What's going on?"

Pa put his arm around me and I felt a little better.

"You know how we've been doing some stuff as the Three Caballeros?" he asked.

Mr. Thomassen stopped him.

"I think it would be better for him to find out at the meeting," he said.

Pa didn't look too happy about that, but he was a military man, so he nodded and shut up.

"No worries," Carlos said. "Everything is under control."

My mouth was even more dry. Like I'd tried to eat a Sahara pizza or something.

"Can I go get a glass of water?" I asked.

"Sure," Mr. Thomassen said. "Provided you'll go to the meeting with me."

I nodded and headed into the kitchen. Sora wasn't in there, but I reckoned she went upstairs to her room or something. I grabbed me a glass and tried to think about something besides the fact that my stomach was tearing apart. I looked over at the shelf of groceries and started counting things, just for the heck of it.

I got to the tuna and only counted twelve cans. I went over and moved some things around, but I couldn't find hide nor hair of the other six cans we'd bought.

I heard the front door slam and them fellas drive away. Pa came in and gave me a big hug.

"I'm sorry I can't tell you anything more," he said. "I want to, but I got to trust the men that know better than me about these things."

Them tuna cans had successfully taken my mind off everything else completely.

"How many cans of tuna'd we buy?" I asked, and pulled out of his hug.

He blinked a couple of times.

"I don't know, eighteen maybe?"

"There's only twelve."

"Oh, then maybe we only bought twelve."

I looked around at the bags of groceries.

"I think we're short a bag, too."

He went and opened the fridge to get himself a Coke.

"Well, we can probably go get it from Sam tomorrow. He's real good about keeping track of those sorts of things."

"No, I mean we brought the bag here, but now it's gone."

He popped the cap off his bottle and took a sip.

"What are you trying to say? Somebody came in here and stole our tuna?"

"Maybe," I said. "Or maybe Sora took off with it."

"Johnny," he said.

"Look, Sam was just telling the sheriff that somebody stole some groceries from him this morning. And now we done had some of ours go missing."

"And you think Sora stole from Sam, too?"

Okay, that sounded stupid.

"No, I ain't saying that, I'm just saying it's a strange turn of events."

He put down his Coke and put his hand on my shoulder.

"Everything's going to be okay," he said. "You don't need to worry about this meeting."

Of course that's what he thought it was about. 'Cause it would make perfect sense that I was taking my fears about a meeting with Mr. Thomassen and some stranger and taking it out on our groceries.

But I wasn't. I was ate up over tuna. And over Willie's voice that was yelling in my head. And over Sora.

And maybe over that meeting, sure.

Definitely over the meeting.

My stomach went back to its square knot.

CHAPTER THREE
ONE IN A MILLION

It was a little before lunchtime and me and Mr. Thomassen was sitting in front of the big window at Nicole's Diner, which was just on the outskirts of Birmingham. We could see the railroad tracks from where we was, and the train coming through a tunnel that was made for it in the side of a hill. It was real pleasant, almost like looking at a painting or something. Except that I was jittery and nervous and not sure what to do with my hands at all. So it was exactly like looking at a painting.

Mr. Thomassen was sipping on some coffee and looking over the menu and I was halfway through my fourth Coke. And we'd only been there for fifteen minutes.

"So, when is this fella going to get here?" I asked.

"He'll get here when he gets here," he said. That was a waste of a conversation.

"And you ain't going to tell me even a smidgen of something to prepare me for this here meeting? What if I slip up and say something stupid?"

He tried to hide a smile.

"I have a feeling my chances are better the less you know," he said. "There's not very many stupid things you could say right now that would make this whole thing go south."

Didn't make me feel no better. I looked around the room and tried to find something that would make me feel less like I was about to nose-dive into the Grand Canyon.

"What'cha think about that wall they built in Berlin?" I asked after I spied a headline. Apparently the Soviets was building a wall and separating Berlin, Germany, into two sides, one that would be for us folk to visit and the other that was just for the Commies. And they did it without warning nobody, so there was whole families that was separated, kids from their parents, brothers from their sisters. Maybe forever.

"It makes sense," he said. "It's almost impossible to coexist with your enemy. Especially when they'd very much like to see you dead."

I nodded. That rang true with history, for sure. Which reminded me.

"Hey, did you know today is the day the Germans beat up the Russians during World War One? It was the Battle of Tannenberg, see, and they was—"

"Oh look, they're here," he said, and I forgot all about the Germans.

THE STRUGGLES OF JOHNNY CANNON

I could see through the window three black LeSabres with Florida license plates pull into the lot and park. Then a whole mess of fellas in suits, most of them built like battleships, got out and came into the diner. They spied where we was sitting, then they went around and talked to the other folk that was sitting at other tables. Then those folks all cleared out of the diner real quick. Finally it was just me and Mr. Thomassen. And he never stopped sipping his coffee.

Then a white Rolls-Royce with maroon fenders came rolling in, the nicest dadgum car I'd ever seen. It had Florida plates too. It parked, the driver got out and opened up the back door, and an older fella wearing a white suit got out and came into the diner. I couldn't help but stare at him, with his thinning gray hair and his tinted glasses that brought out the dark moles that was scattered along his cheeks and neck. He spoke to a couple of them big fellas, they nodded, and then he came to our table.

"I thought we were going to meet alone," he said to Mr. Thomassen. His voice sounded like somebody that had smoked one too many cigars. He smelled like it too.

Mr. Thomassen put down the menu.

"I couldn't find a babysitter," he said. "But he's my understudy. There's nothing you could say to me that he can't hear, or that he won't hear later. So let's talk."

He motioned for me to move around next to him, so I did, and then the old fella took my seat. I hurried and grabbed my Coke to make sure he didn't get no ideas.

"What's his name?" he asked Mr. Thomassen.

"This is Johnny, and that's all you need to know."

The fella nodded at me.

"I hope you're as honest as he says, Johnny," he said. "For your own sake."

Now, I ain't so sure how they do things in Florida where that fella was from, but in Alabama you don't get a name from somebody without giving one back. I reckoned he forgot.

"I didn't catch your name, mister," I said.

He chuckled.

"Cute kid," he said.

"This is Santo. Santo Trafficante, Jr.," Mr. Thomassen said.

"And me and your boss here go way back," Mr. Trafficante said. "How long has it been, Chuck?"

I looked at Mr. Thomassen.

"Chuck?" I asked.

"That's my name," he said. "Charles Thomassen. You know that."

Nope, I sure didn't. I didn't reckon I was going to take part in calling him Chuck, either. Just didn't sit right with me.

"Anyway," Mr. Thomassen said, "it's been a long time. Since my first year in Havana, if I remember correctly."

I looked at Mr. Trafficante.

"You was in Havana?"

That set him to laughing.

"Kid, I practically ran Havana back in the good old days."

I had a bad feeling I knew what that meant. Back before Castro ousted Batista as the leader of Cuba, Havana was like a compost pile for the mob and gangs. Which meant, if Trafficante ran it all, then he was definitely bad news. I decided to keep my trap shut.

"And what are you up to now?" Mr. Thomassen said.

"Cigars," Mr. Trafficante said, real fast. "And other side businesses. But cigars is what I pay taxes on. Anyway, this isn't meant to be a social visit. Let's get down to—"

"And your family?" Mr. Thomassen acted like he hadn't heard that last part. "How's your son? And Nell? Why, I haven't heard from her in years."

Mr. Trafficante gritted his teeth.

"My son is gone and Nell is dead. I thought you knew that."

"I did," Mr. Thomassen said before he took a sip of his coffee. "I just wanted Johnny to be caught up to speed."

Mr. Trafficante stared at him and his eye twitched a little, which was really weird and made me stare, which made him stare back, which made me feel like I was going to pee my pants.

"Can we start talking business now?" he asked.

I raised my hand. Him and Mr. Thomassen both looked at me like I was crazy.

"Can I go to the bathroom?" I asked.

Mr. Thomassen glanced at Mr. Trafficante.

"The kid's got to take a leak," Mr. Trafficante said. "So let him."

I got up and headed to where the restrooms was and one of them big fellas followed me, even came inside with me.

I went over and unzipped, then realized he was standing right behind me.

"You don't got to watch me. I won't make no messes," I said.

"I'm just making sure there's no funny business."

"I try to avoid being funny when I'm peeing. Otherwise the walls get all messed up."

He laughed but didn't move an inch.

I got done with my business and flushed. I started toward the door but he stopped me.

"Wash your hands, you animal," he said.

"Why? I didn't pee on them."

He curled up his lip and grabbed my wrists. He pulled me over to the sink and squirted some soap into my palms. He rubbed my hands together and whistled through the ABCs, then he turned on the water and rinsed them off. He picked up the towel, dried my hands, and used the towel to turn the doorknob.

I went on ahead of him back to the table. Things had gotten more heated since I left.

"Don't try to tell me you don't know anything about the Three Caballeros," Mr. Trafficante said. "It has your fingerprints all over it."

Mr. Thomassen wasn't drinking his coffee anymore. Instead he had both hands on the table, more tense than I'd ever seen him.

"I don't know what you're talking about," he said. "And more than that, I don't know why you're concerned. Based off what you've told me, they're only targeting the Cosa Nostra. Which, last time I checked, didn't include the Trafficante family."

Mr. Trafficante popped his knuckles as I took my seat back next to Mr. Thomassen.

"No," he said, and shot me a look. "But it does include the Bonannos and the Giancanas, and they've started to complain."

"To you?" Mr. Thomassen said. "Why would they come to you?"

"Because, you idiot, they recognize a Cuban operation when they see one." He leaned in over the table. "And I recognize one of yours when I see it, too."

I looked at Mr. Thomassen to see if he was scared. I'd be scared, that was for darn sure. But he didn't look an ounce nervous at all. Instead he reached for his coffee cup.

"Would one of your goons mind topping me off with some decaf?" he asked.

Mr. Trafficante almost spit fire out as he nodded to one of his fellas.

"Now," Mr. Thomassen said, "you've had your chance to talk to me. Let me talk to you."

Mr. Trafficante sat back in his seat and quieted down a bit. As soon as they brought Mr. Thomassen his coffee, he added a little cream and sugar and took a sip.

"I already knew about the Three Caballeros," he said. "I'm not saying that I'm one of them, or that I'm affiliated with them, but I know about them. And I can tell you right now that they aren't interested in you."

"I wasn't concerned about—" Mr. Trafficante started.

"Let me finish." Mr. Thomassen put his cup down and his face changed and even I got a little scared of him all of a sudden. "They aren't interested in the Trafficantes at the moment. From what I hear, these days you are as much a patriot as I am."

Mr. Trafficante studied his face for a second and nodded.

"So this is about patriotism for you?"

"For the Three Caballeros, from what I understand, yes," Mr. Thomassen said. "It's about keeping this nation from becoming the cesspool Havana was. Keeping the hands of the Cosa Nostra from holding power in the government. Because we saw what happened in Havana once people got sick of you and your family. They brought in the Commies to clip your wings."

Mr. Trafficante reached into his pocket and pulled out a cigar. He lit it and took a couple of puffs while Mr. Thomassen sipped his coffee. I didn't much know what to do, so I started using the spoons as drumsticks and played a beat on the table. Mr. Thomassen snatched them out of my hand real quick.

"So you're saying I should stay out of it?" Mr. Trafficante finally said.

"No, I'm saying you should get out of it."

"But I'm not in it. Like you said, my wings are clipped. The Three Caballeros haven't got any beef with me, remember?"

"Not yet," Mr. Thomassen said. "But there's a matter of a price tag I've been hearing about."

Mr. Trafficante's eye started twitching again. He slammed his hand on the table.

"That doesn't have anything to do with you. Or with the Three Caballeros."

"Oh, but it does. Because it stinks of the old days in Havana, of exactly what they're trying to prevent."

"That's because it came out of the old days in Havana."

"Then get rid of it," Mr. Thomassen said. "Leave it back there."

"I can't," Mr. Trafficante said. "I won't. Some things you can't leave in the past."

"Come on, Santo."

"He killed the woman I loved, Chuck," Mr. Trafficante said, and I thought I almost saw a tear come out of his twitching eye. "Dr. Morris killed Nell. I'll never let that go."

I felt like somebody done slapped me across the face. Dr. Morris, Captain Morris, my actual father, killed his girl? I started to slip down in my chair, but Mr. Thomassen grabbed my leg and squeezed it real hard, so I didn't.

"But what if he's already dead?" Mr. Thomassen said. Which he was, Captain Morris had been shot by my pa and he was as dead as a doornail.

ISAIAH CAMPBELL

"Whoever told you about the price tag didn't give you all the details, did they?" Mr. Trafficante said. "Morris has a kid running around out there somewhere, from back when he was still in Havana. So, even if Morris is dead, I want his blood on my hands. And I don't care if it's his or his kid's. I want to hold his heart in my hands and break it like he broke mine."

I started to reach up and cover my chest, not even thinking, but Mr. Thomassen squeezed my leg again so I didn't.

"Well, for your sake, I hope you never find him," Mr. Thomassen said. "Because I'd hate for the Three Caballeros to add your name to their list of enemies."

"And, for your sake," Mr. Trafficante said, "I hope they don't do that. You and I are friends. And friends make the worst enemies."

Mr. Thomassen smiled and sipped his coffee again. Mr. Trafficante looked at me.

"So, what about you? What do you do?"

My heart started beating so hard I reckoned he could hear it from where he was. I was real worried I was going to say something that would show him I was Captain Morris's son and all that. So I decided to go in the opposite direction.

"Well, I sure don't go around killing nobody, that's the truth."

He started laughing at me.

"Wow, you're one in a million, aren't you?" he asked.

"I reckon so," I said.

Mr. Trafficante took a puff of his cigar.

"Where you from, kid?" he asked.

Mr. Thomassen almost dropped his cup of coffee. His hand dropped down on my leg and he started to squeeze it.

"Oh, I'm from Cull—" I sputtered for a second 'cause Mr. Thomassen had just about cut off the blood to my foot. "Clarksville, Tennessee. Same as Mr. Thomassen here."

Mr. Thomassen let up for a bit.

"Tennessee?" Mr. Trafficante said, then he shot Mr. Thomassen a look. "You came all the way down here from Tennessee?"

"Yup," I said. "What can I say, folks in Tennessee, I mean *us* folks in Tennessee, just really love this Birmingham air. Reminds me of living in Havana a little bit."

Mr. Thomassen squeezed my leg again, so hard this time that I reckoned some leg juice was going to come out in a bit.

"You're from Havana?" Mr. Trafficante said. "Tell me, have *you* ever heard of the Three Caballeros?"

I gulped about as loud as a frog gulping a horsefly.

"Nope," I said. Which would have been fine if I'd have left it at that, but for some reason my brain figured there needed to be more said. "I mean, y'all been talking about them, so I've heard of them just now. And maybe before, but I don't got no idea who they are. Or what they're doing. Well, I reckon I have an idea, but it ain't worth me mentioning."

Mr. Trafficante chuckled and looked at Mr. Thomassen's face. Mr. Thomassen was trying to not show any emotion, even though I

ISAIAH CAMPBELL

could tell from his eyes and the fact that he just about had removed my kneecap through my jeans that he was panicking.

"I think we're done," Mr. Thomassen said.

"I think we are. For now."

And with that we all got up and went our separate ways. I limped a bit, on account of needing knee replacement surgery now and all, but other than that, I was just glad to be out of there.

We got into the car and drove about a block down the road, then Mr. Thomassen pulled over, put the car in park, and just started shaking.

"Why?" he asked. "Why did you tell him you were from Havana?"

His hand trembled as he pulled his hanky out of his pocket and started wiping off his forehead. He was breathing real hard, too.

"I—I don't really know," I said. "It just slipped."

He slapped his steering wheel.

"Well, it can't!" he said, and his face looked like he might be inclined to kill me or something. I shrunk back in my seat.

"I'm sorry," he said, and shook his head. He calmed back down and started shaking again. "It's my fault. I should have prepared you."

He pulled back out onto the road and headed home. We didn't say nothing else as we went, he looked like he was thinking, and I was too busy having a panic attack.

"I need to talk to your pa and Carlos," he said. "I'm going to drop you off at the Parkinses', okay?"

I nodded 'cause I didn't feel like arguing with him at all. Besides, I hadn't seen Willie since Sunday, so it'd be nice to visit.

There was a whole mess of cars there when he dropped me off, and I recognized most of them from going to the church services in Colony. They must have been having a function at their house or something. Which probably meant that Willie was stuck bored half to death and my visit would be real appreciated. And also meant there'd be plenty to get my mind off of Santo Trafficante.

I went up and the front door was open, so I headed on inside. All the deacons and their wives from the church was gathered in the living room, listening to the radio. I went to the kitchen, where Mrs. Parkins and Willie was making a tray of snacks for everybody. Willie did his schooling at home, which basically meant he had to do more chores than the rest of us.

"Hey, how's it going?" I asked. Mrs. Parkins smiled at me.

"Going well," she said, and she kissed my forehead. "Going very, very well." She carried the little tray of sandwiches out into the living room and left me in there with Willie. He was slicing cheese.

"What was that about?" I asked.

"It's a big day today," he said. "It's all over the news. Ain't you heard?" He picked up his tray and carried it out there too. I followed him. The radio was telling the story they was all so happy about.

"And, as the day is drawing closer and closer to its conclusion, there have not yet been any reports of incidences inside Grady High. It would

appear that all nine students have been able to attend their classes and
even eat their lunches in peace and equality."

I leaned over to Willie.

"Seriously, what's going on?"

"It's happening in Atlanta," he said. "Nine black students went to school at an all-white high school. It's integration. And there ain't been nothing bad to happen with it."

"Not like last year," Mrs. Parkins said. "Remember poor Ruby Bridges, down in New Orleans?"

I hadn't never heard of it, so I shook my head.

"Six years old, she enrolled in the school down there and they practically tortured her. People threw bricks at her as she went inside the schoolhouse, grown women tried to poison her food, some stood outside with black baby dolls in coffins. The marshals had to take her in, and she couldn't even sit in a classroom with the other students."

"Holy cow, I wouldn't have gone back," I said.

"But now, just a year later and we have integration happening in Georgia without none of that," she said. "It's a miracle is what it is."

Reverend Parkins stood and came over to us.

"And a miracle we'll have here soon, I believe. Alabama isn't as far behind as people think."

She put the tray down and went back into the kitchen, and the way she did it showed that she wanted to say something else but couldn't 'cause she knew it wasn't a woman's place to say it in front of all them people.

"What's wrong with her?" I whispered to Willie.

"It ain't nothing," he whispered back. "She's been bellyaching to Pa that she'd like us to pick up stakes and move up north somewhere, 'cause folks here ain't so happy with a black family living nearby."

"Y'all are thinking of moving?" I asked. That hit me like a sack of bricks.

"No, we ain't going to move. She gets on these kicks every time something hits the news about the race problems around here. We just got to ride it out. Like Pa says, Alabama ain't that far behind."

Mrs. Parkins came back out with a pitcher of lemonade.

"By the way, Johnny," she said, "Willie told me you have a visitor that's about to have a baby. How is she?"

I shrugged. How are you supposed to answer a question like that?

"Still pregnant, so I guess about as good as can be expected."

She nodded like that was the perfect answer. Women was weird.

Willie grabbed my arm.

"That reminds me," he said. "Come on."

He dragged me into his bedroom and pulled the letter that was supposedly from Tommy off the wall.

"I was thinking about what you said, about Antonia and Rose being spies, and it got me to thinking, what if Tommy was being a spy when he wrote this letter?"

"That don't make no sense," I said. "He was a pilot, not a spy."

"No, I don't mean like a literal spy." He put the letter on his desk and started looking at it more closer. "I mean, what if he was thinking like a spy. What if he wrote it in code?"

Well, that sounded more interesting, but there was a problem.

"But Tommy wouldn't have no reason to write me in code."

"Right, but what if he *did*?" He pointed at something on the letter. "I mean, look at how many times he wrote 'first letter.' He wrote it five times."

"I don't know, I think maybe he was just drunk. He'd written me before, so that ain't even true."

"Right, so maybe it's a clue," Willie said. "What happens if we just take the first letter of the words and try to read them?"

I looked at the letter. I could tell that wasn't going to work just by the first sentence.

"It says 'wmfl.' That don't mean nothing."

He nodded but kept looking at it.

"Okay, but what if we start here at the paragraph that says 'Knowing every elected politician'? 'Cause, look, this sentence that's standing all by itself doesn't have no period. Almost like it's leading into whatever this paragraph is saying. 'But what I really need to say is' what?"

I looked at it again.

"It starts with 'Knowing,' so *K*. Then 'every,' so *E*. Then another *E*, then a *P*. So 'Keep.'" I was starting to see what he was saying.

"Then *Y*," he said. "And *O. U.* Then *R.* Your. Then *B. L. O.* Uh, let's see. *O.* Then *D.*"

We looked at each other and both said it at the same time.

"Blood."

Dadgum. The hairs on the back of my neck was starting to raise. Willie real quick underlined the first letters of the rest of the paragraph.

Satisfies As Failure Elevates Failure, Rusting Our Men. Hear Antonia + Rose's Message

I read it, and my voice wasn't able to go above a whisper.

"'Keep your blood safe from harm.'"

We both stared at the letter like it was a snake that had fallen asleep on his desk. He folded it back up and pinned it back to his wall, then he sat down on his bed.

"So, what do you think he meant?" he asked.

I thought for a bit.

"Maybe he's talking about the price tag," I said.

"The what?"

Even though it was probably the sort of thing I was supposed to keep secret, I went ahead and told him all about the meeting and Santo Trafficante and the price tag on Captain Morris and everything.

When I was done, he sat down on his bed and let out a whistle.

"Wow. This is serious," he said. "For real, this ain't good."

"Yeah, but maybe it ain't as bad as we're thinking," I said. "I mean, as long as nobody finds out about me being his son, I'm probably safe."

He didn't look too convinced.

"And here I thought Captain Morris was the biggest bad guy we'd ever meet," he said. "Ain't that just how it is?"

"What you mean?"

"Like in the comic books, the hero goes and he beats the bad guy and everybody thinks it's all amazing. But then he finds out the bad guy he beat was just the messenger boy or something, and he's got to fight an even scarier, bigger, meaner bad guy in the next comic."

"Except I ain't ever going to have to fight Mr. Trafficante," I said.

"As long as he don't ever find out the truth about you," he said.

"Exactly."

"But that's why I'm worried," he said. "'Cause if there's one thing I've learned, it's that the truth has a pesky way of getting found out, whether you want it to or not."

I tried to brush him off, but deep down, I knew he was right. Lies never last as long as you want them to, and the truth never stays buried no matter how deep you dig the hole.

Except for this time. Hopefully.

CHAPTER FOUR
TOM AND HUCK

It was only lunchtime on Friday, but it was already a really bad day.

First of all, I'd overslept, which meant I didn't get to eat no breakfast, so I was about ready to faint when it was time for me to do the This Day in History thing for the class. Then, while I was telling them all about how September 1 was the day that Narcissa Whitman and Eliza Spalding became the first white women to cross the Rockies back in 1836, I got all mixed up and said they rocked the Crossies and everybody laughed their heads off.

Which then meant I failed the math pop quiz 'cause I couldn't stop thinking about it. And then I missed hearing Mr. Braswell call my name for extra credit, so I missed that, too.

And now it was lunchtime, and it should have been perfect, but it wasn't. I was sitting at a table alone with Martha, and it was sort of like how I'd always wanted it to be. Except she had Willie's tape recorder and she was getting ready to ask me all about my life's story.

And I just wasn't feeling up to doing no storytelling.

It was also tuna surprise in the lunchroom, which was icing on the cake. I couldn't catch a break at all that day. Oh well, at least we had a three-day weekend, thanks to Labor Day on Monday. And there'd be a fireworks show. Maybe I'd get blown up or something.

I sat there, poking my food with a fork, and I was so hungry I almost was willing to eat it. Martha got the microphone set up in front of me and was fiddling with the tape.

"Okay, I think I've got this set up now," she said. "Are you ready?"

"I guess," I said. "Why can't you do your biography on somebody else? Like your ma or something?"

She laughed.

"My mom? Yeah, I'm going to do a biography on the single most boring person that's ever lived." She shook her head and started the tape recorder. "I mean, if I want to learn how to bake cookies or dress so I don't attract boys or something, sure. But otherwise, no. There's not any good reason to do a biography on my mother."

"I'd do one on mine, but she's dead," I said. Sometimes, if I played the dead mom card, I could get out of stuff like this interview.

"Don't even try it, Johnny," she said. "We're doing this interview because you want me to get a good grade. Right?"

I let out a really long, painful sigh.

"Fine, fire away. In fact, if you could shoot me in the head, that'd be great. Put me out of my misery."

"Golly, and they say *girls* are overdramatic," she said. She pulled out her notebook and flipped to a page where she'd made up a list of questions. Looked like there was Willie's handwriting on it too. I was beginning to wonder if he was working with me or against me.

"Okay, I guess let's start at the very beginning. What's your earliest memory?"

"Well, there was one time when I got up at four in the morning to go fishing. I think that's probably the earliest."

"No," she said, and she tapped the pencil on her notebook for a couple of seconds. "What's the first thing you can remember about your childhood?"

"Ain't I still in my childhood?"

"I'm beginning to think so," she said. "Look, everybody remembers something from when they were little, and it's the thing that sort of sets up the stage for the rest of your life. Like, for me, the first thing I remember is when I was three and my cousin's dogs attacked my teddy bear. My mom saw me crying and she turned the dining room into an operating room. Even had me wear a mask, and she did surgery on my bear. She sewed him back together and even put a Band-Aid on his chest."

"And that set the stage for your whole entire life?" I asked. "A fake surgery?"

She was getting frustrated, I could tell, 'cause she breathed real hard out of her nose.

"Yes, because I always know my mom will fix anything, no matter how big or small it is. Now, what's yours?"

I had to think real hard. It was difficult, 'cause my memories wasn't exactly set out in a proper timeline in my brain, but they was sort of lumped together like a box of photographs that don't got no dates on the back and you ain't real sure what order they go in. And, since there wasn't no way I could figure out which one was the earliest, I just grabbed the first one I could think of.

"I guess it was when Tommy left home in Guantánamo to move up here with Grandma, back around '53," I said. "I remember crying real hard about it and running to Ma, and her just crying too. And the whole time, Pa was begging him or anyone to explain why he was doing it, but nobody would. And he left."

"Wow," she said, and she made a few notes. "Did you ever find out why he left?"

"Yeah, he'd figured out that Ma was cheating on Pa."

"Oh, yeah. Right. With Captain Morris."

I real quick reached over and turned off the tape recorder and then I snatched the pencil out of her hand.

"Hey!" she said. "Don't be a jerk."

"You can't say that name, the Captain's," I said. "And you sure can't put him in this biography."

"What in the world are you talking about?" she asked. "He's part of your story, so I have to. Why are you acting so weird about it?"

I didn't want to tell her 'cause girls get real scared about things, and plus they can't keep no secrets.

"It's just . . . ," I said. "I don't want that part of my story getting told."

She studied my face.

"What if I don't use his name?" she asked.

"Nope, won't work. You just got to not tell that part."

She rolled her eyes.

"Then why am I even writing a biography on you if I can't tell your whole story?"

"I don't know," I said, maybe a little louder than I should. "Why are you? I didn't ask you to do it."

She got real quiet, but not like you do when you feel bad, but more like you do when the only words you can think of is cusswords.

I stood up.

"You know what, I think Willie needs his tape recorder back," I said, and I grabbed it and packed it up.

"No he doesn't," she said, and she tried to get it back from me. "He said I could use it."

"Well, he's my blood brother, and I'm saying he needs it back. Like now."

"Okay, fine, I'll take it back to him after school," she said.

"No, he needs it now," I said. "*I'll* take it on up to him."

That got everybody in the lunchroom looking at me, but it didn't much matter. I needed to go talk to Willie 'cause I was starting to realize just how hard it was going to be to keep my blood safe from harm, like Tommy'd warned.

I went outside and found a bike nobody was watching. I'd return it before anybody noticed. I put the tape recorder in the basket and rode the bike on back to the Parkinses' house.

Their car was gone when I got there, so I hoped he was home. I went to the front door and banged on it, partly to get somebody to come open it and partly to get my stress out. So it was real loud.

The door swung open and Mrs. Parkins stood behind it. Holding a shotgun. Aimed at my chest.

I threw my hands up in the air and she saw it was me, so she lowered it.

"What in tarnation are you doing?" I asked.

She looked out at the yard, like she was checking to see if anybody was hiding in the bushes, and then she let me come in. Willie was sitting on the couch with his sister. They both looked as freaked out as I was.

Mrs. Parkins closed the door and stood behind it, shotgun pointed at it again.

"Mama, can Johnny and I go to my room?" Willie said.

She nodded.

"Just stay away from the windows."

We hurried and went down the hall to his room. Once we got inside, I just about lost my mind.

"What in the name of all that is good and holy is your ma doing with a shotgun in your living room?"

"Pa bought it for her after that whole Captain Morris thing," he said. "And I taught her, same way you taught me."

"I don't recollect teaching you to stand armed and ready at the door to kill the mailman."

He laughed at that.

"She ain't. Not usually," he said. "But there was an incident in Colony that Pa's checking into and it's got her freaked out."

"What you mean 'an incident'?"

He sighed.

"We reckon it's on account of that integration that happened in Georgia. Folks want to make sure the black community here doesn't go getting any fancy ideas."

"What happened?"

"There was a lynching," he said.

I felt my heart drop into my ankles.

"Oh no," I said. "Who'd they go after? How come I haven't heard nothing about it?"

"They didn't lynch no humans, that's why you haven't heard nothing."

"Then what'd they lynch?"

"Dogs," he said, and his voice got real sad. "They went through Colony and stole every single dog out of all the yards, and then they strung them up. Off the roof of the schoolhouse, so all the kids got to see them when they showed up this morning."

There wasn't nothing either one of us could say right then, it was just too horrible a thing to think about. After a bit, he went on.

"My pa went down to check on things. Russ Conner is in a bad way, he was the first one to get to school and tried to cut them all down before the little kids showed up. Got six down, but then it got to him. He went home and ain't come out of his bedroom since."

"You going to go down there and talk to him?" Russ was one of Willie's good friends. Plus he had a mean left hook, which I knew from experience. To think of him hiding under his bed or something, it just wasn't right.

"Wish I could, but Ma's convinced this is all part of the Klan's plan to hit us again. That's why she's guarding the door. And why she won't let me go get involved."

"Dang," I said. "This probably doesn't help too much on convincing her that Cullman's a decent place to live, does it?"

"You don't have no idea," he said.

We heard a car door slam outside and we both jumped.

"Papa's home!" Mrs. Parkins hollered, which made us both relax. We went back out to the living room and Reverend Parkins came in. The first thing he did was give his wife a big hug, then his kids. Then me, which was a little weird.

"Sheriff Tatum is down there now," he said after that. "He's going to investigate."

"Yeah, right," Mrs. Parkins said. "I'm sure he'll trace the blame to some drunk Tigger from farther south."

Now, just to be clear, she didn't say "Tigger." She said another word that I ain't supposed to say but I reckon she can 'cause she's black. So, whenever folks say that word, I substitute in "Tigger." Although, if Tigger ever did get drunk, I'll bet he'd cause a whole mess of trouble. But not like what had happened in Colony.

"Coretta," Reverend Parkins said. "Language."

Mrs. Parkins stormed off to put her gun away in her bedroom. Willie went over to his pa.

"How's Russ doing?"

"Not good," Reverend Parkins said. "He and his grandma are going to go up to Memphis, stay with some relatives for a little while till this whole thing blows over."

"Really?" I asked. "They're leaving?"

Mrs. Parkins heard me.

"That's what we need to do too," she said as she came back into the living room. "Because nobody here is going to take care of us."

"I think you're wrong," he said. "Sheriff Tatum has some leads, he said."

"Really, like who?"

Before Reverend Parkins could answer, or maybe while he was and I just didn't pay no attention, a tow truck drove up onto the yard.

Bob Gorman's tow truck.

Bob got out, adjusted his suspenders, and came up to the Parkinses' front door. I was the only one that saw him coming, and I opened the door before he knocked so he didn't get a gaping hole shot through his chest.

"Oh, there you are," he said. "Some folks in town said they saw you taking little Molly Turner's bicycle about an hour ago."

I looked over at the bike I'd ridden. I hadn't noticed them tassels hanging off the handles. I'd just thought it was pink 'cause it was out in the sun too long.

"So you came up here to fetch me?" I asked.

"No, I was coming up here anyway, so Mr. Turner asked me to fetch the bike." He peeked inside. "Is the preacher-man here?"

Reverend Parkins came over to the door and held out his hand to Bob.

"Mr. Gorman. To what do we owe the honor?"

Bob glanced at the hand, gritted his teeth, and shook it.

"Well, I wanted to chat with you about the recent turn of events," he said. I was real glad that he qualified that by saying "recent," 'cause there was a whole mess of events Bob had been involved with from a bit further back. From trying to burn down the Parkinses' church to beating the pulp out of the Reverend to helping Captain Morris capture and torture Willie. And that was just in one night.

"You mean the dog killings?" Reverend Parkins said. "I appreciate your concern. Sheriff Tatum is investigating. He's actually been quite supportive ever since the incident earlier this summer."

I don't know if Bob realized that incident was the one he'd worn a bedsheet to, but he let that sweep on by. He actually seemed more taken aback by the killings.

"There were some dog killings?" Bob said. "I hadn't heard anything about it. I imagine it was gang related. Such an epidemic in the, uh, colored community. But, it's funny that you'd mention Sheriff Tatum, 'cause that's why I'm up here to talk."

He took a deep breath like somebody might that's about to dive into a deep pool. Then he crinkled up his nose, so I reckoned that pool must have been of sewage or something. He shook his head and started in on what sounded like a speech he'd done rehearsed.

"Sheriff Tatum is going to announce his retirement next week, which means we'll be electing a new sheriff this year. It's believed by many that this election might be heavily influenced by the colored vote." He coughed and cleared his throat. "So, I wanted to come here and say that I hope you'll influence your people to vote for the best man for the job. Even if he ain't a Republican."

"I appreciate your good citizenship, Mr. Gorman," Reverend Parkins said. Mrs. Parkins came up behind him and touched his shoulder. Bob looked like he didn't feel that was the answer he wanted.

"After all, the man who's sheriff has a lot of power, and usually has a powerful memory, too," he said, and took a step closer to being inside. "And if he remembers your support, he might be more apt to overlook your people's shenanigans."

"Thank you for stopping by," Reverend Parkins said and extended his hand again. But Bob Gorman wasn't done. He grabbed Reverend Parkins's hand and pulled him in close.

"But, if he doesn't get your support, he'll be powerful sure to remember that, too." He shot a look at the rest of us that was in the living room. "Trust me on this, there could be a lot more than *dogs* that get hurt if the wrong man gets elected."

Speaking of dogs, they was both standing there like two pit bulls staring each other down over a T-bone. And, even though Tommy'd done warned me to protect myself and all that, this looked like the kind of thing that needed to be stopped even if it might mean a bloody nose.

"How's Eddie doing?" I asked.

Bob let go of Reverend Parkins's hand and straightened out his shirt over his belly.

"He's fine," he said. "As usual."

"So, if you run for sheriff, what'll that make him? Sheriff Jr.?"

"Now, now, it's premature to start talking about candidates," he said. He forced a wink at Mrs. Parkins that he probably thought would look friendly but instead came off as serial-killer-ish. "But I wanted to do my part to prepare you people for what's coming. It's the neighborly thing to do."

"Then why are *you* doing it?" I asked, and he shot me a look like he was fixing to bite me on the butt. Good thing he *wasn't* a dog.

"I appreciate you coming by," Reverend Parkins said again.

Bob nodded and started to walk off. He stopped and looked back at us.

"You ought to be careful who you're hanging around with," he said. I wasn't sure if he was talking to me or them, but his point was made.

"Yeah," Willie said from inside, "we'll be real careful to not hang around with any of those Gormans."

Bob didn't hear that, I don't reckon.

After he left, Mrs. Parkins grabbed Reverend Parkins and hugged on him real hard. Reverend Parkins looked shook up, but he held his wife and rubbed her back real good and took to

ISAIAH CAMPBELL

telling her that there wasn't nothing to worry about.

"We've got to move," she kept saying.

"Now, now," he kept saying. "We don't have anything to worry about."

"Do you reckon he's going to run for sheriff?" I asked.

"He didn't say he was," Willie said.

"Yeah, but the things he didn't say meant a whole heck of a lot more than what he did," I said. Reverend Parkins nodded in agreement, but he didn't say nothing 'cause I think he was trying to keep Mrs. Parkins from freaking out.

"We should all pray," he said. "And take Mr. Gorman's advice, as ill-intended as it was, to heart. We should vote for the right person and pray that the right person, whoever he is, will defeat Bob Gorman in the election."

All of a sudden, I didn't feel too safe having that letter so far away from me, even if it was safely in Willie's room. Especially if the wrong fella was about to be the sheriff, I needed to protect myself as much as possible.

"Hey, I reckon I'm going to take the letter with me," I said.

Willie looked confused at first, but then he understood, 'cause he could read my mind I reckon, and he got the letter for me. I folded it up and put it in my pocket.

I stayed up there for another couple of hours, shooting the breeze and being funny to try to cheer Mrs. Parkins up. Then I remembered that I was supposed to be at school. I hurried and headed back into town just in time for Mr. Braswell to inform me that I was going to get detention 'cause I'd skipped out of school. Which was fine by me for two reasons. One, staying in detention meant I didn't have to worry about spilling my blood or the beans about Captain Morris. And two, detention was run by the best teacher we'd ever had, Mrs. Buttke.

Detention was held in the lunchroom, but they didn't serve no food, so if you was hungry it was pretty bad. That day, when I walked in, I realized that it was going to be even worse for me. 'Cause, sitting in the back corner, right behind the kid from sixth grade that liked to put his boogers on the girl that sat in front of him, was Eddie. And he was sporting a black eye. It didn't take me but five seconds to guess who'd given it to him.

There's only been a handful of things in my life I've ever really regretted doing, like spitting on a roller coaster when Martha was riding behind me when I was ten or trying to siphon gas and drinking a quarter of a tank when I was eight. And I had a feeling that going over and sitting next to Eddie in detention that day was going to be added to that list. I should have stayed away, but for whatever reason, I felt like it was what I was supposed to do. I don't rightly know why.

I plopped down next to him and he slid away from me on the bench.

"Where'd you get the black eye?" I asked.

"Ran into a door," he said.

"A door with knuckles?"

He glared at me.

"Yup," he said.

"Ahem," Mrs. Buttke said. "Mr. Cannon and Mr. Gorman, if you two are trying to make me feel nostalgic about last year, I assure you my memories aren't nearly fond enough. Now stay quiet and work on your homework."

Eddie seemed real relieved at that and he buried himself into his math. I probably should have done the same, but me and math never did have a real keen relationship, so I took to drawing stick men fighting with swords instead.

After a bit, Mrs. Buttke finished off a big mug of coffee and excused herself to go to the restroom. Which is always the cue in detention for everyone to take a break and raise Cain. The Miller twins went right back into the same fight that had got them into detention in the first place, something about ducks and geese and which one was faster. At least I think that's what they was debating. It was hard to tell with them wrestling all over the floor while they was talking. I think Cory was going to lose the argument, though. Natalie had a mean right hook.

Meanwhile, Cody Fannon was back to lighting matches and watching how long he could hold them before he had to blow them out. I don't know why he got detention over that. It ain't like he was catching nothing on fire besides his own fingers. And if he wanted to burn his hand off, that was his own business.

I decided it was a prime good time to try and talk to Eddie again.

"So, how's things going with your pa?"

He didn't look up from his math.

"Fine," he said. "How's things going with yours?"

"Fine," I said. Yeah, that was deep. Oh well, back to my stick men. Maybe I could give them guns and liven up their battle.

I looked over at Eddie's paper. He was doodling Nazi swastikas on it.

"Um, you really shouldn't draw them," I said.

He looked up.

"Why? Pa says the swastika's been around for a lot longer than folks think, like a thousand years. It used to be a good luck symbol. It meant that great things was going to happen."

"Sure," I said. "But now it just means being a Nazi."

He scratched through them symbols, which I was glad for, and then he looked over at my paper. He watched me drawing for a bit before he finally spoke again.

"Does your pa ever play games?" he asked.

"Um, I don't know," I said. "You mean like checkers?"

"Sure."

"Yeah," I said. "Don't most everybody?"

He nodded and then went back to figuring out a math

problem. He scribbled through a couple of numbers and then tapped his eraser on the paper.

"Does he ever lose?" he asked.

That made me laugh.

"Yeah, most all the time. He's an egghead when it comes to gadgets, but with games he ain't got the brain for it. I can beat him any day of the week."

"Really?" Eddie put his pencil down on the paper and leaned into our talking. "What does he do when he loses?"

"He laughs," I said. "He rubs his hands through his hair and says, 'But can you dance the polka?' Every time. He thinks he's hilarious."

Eddie leaned back and let that sink in.

"Wow," he said.

"Why, what does your pa do when he loses?"

He looked away and touched his face, right under his eye.

"He don't lose," he said. "At nothing."

I looked down at my stick men. One of them was stabbing the other with the sword straight through the head.

"You ain't never beat him?"

"He don't never let me," he said. "I came close one time with Monopoly. I got Boardwalk *and* Park Place, and he was down to his last bit of money. But then he remembered that I'd sassed him over breakfast, so he whupped me and sent me to bed."

"And that's the only time you ever came close?"

"That's the only time I ever wanted to."

He closed his math book and stared straight ahead for a bit. I was waiting for him to say something, and it looked like he was waiting for the same thing. Like he had something itching to come out but he wasn't sure if he was ready for all the mess that him saying it was going to make. Finally he looked back over at me.

"You and me, we used to be friends, right?" he asked.

"Yeah, I reckon," I said. "At the time, I guess you was my best friend, mainly 'cause I didn't know no better."

"Like Tom and Huck, right?"

"I guess so," I said. "Wait, was I Tom or Huck?"

He rolled his eyes.

"Ain't it obvious? I sure ain't Huck, and you're the one with a Tigger friend."

"You shouldn't say that," I said.

"Say what?"

"Tigger," I said. Course, I didn't want to say the real word, so I actually *said* "Tigger."

"I didn't say 'Tigger,'" he said. "I said 'Tigger.'" He said the real word. "Mark Twain put it in the book, it ain't meant to be disrespectful."

"Yeah, well, someday when you write a book, you can say that word all you want and nobody won't say nothing. But around me, don't say it."

"Okay," he said. I was real surprised by that. I didn't expect him to see my point. "But anyway, what if I told you I found something that I can only share with my Huck Finn?"

My ears perked up. Maybe he was going to start spilling about Bob, and about his life, and about his story, and all the things like what I couldn't spill on account of my blood needing to be kept safe and such. Maybe listening to somebody else talking would make it easier for me to keep my trap shut.

"I'd say you better spill it," I said.

He started to talk, but then Mrs. Buttke came back into the room. He set his head down on top of his book. After she broke up the Miller twins and sent Cody to the nurse for his third-degree burns, she came over to where we was at and put her hand on his back.

"Are you feeling all right, Edward?" she asked.

"No'm," he said. "Can I go?"

She took a look at his black eye.

"Are you sure?" she asked.

He nodded.

"Go on home, then," she said. "Take the long weekend and get better."

"I reckon I need someone to walk me," he said. "Can Johnny go with me?"

She shot me a real suspicious look.

"I don't think that's wise," she said. "Perhaps you should go to the nurse instead."

While she wasn't looking at him, Eddie grabbed his pencil and shoved it in his mouth till it tapped the back of his throat. Then he turned and puked all over the floor.

"Oh my gosh!" Mrs. Buttke hollered. "Yes, Johnny take him home. Now!"

I jumped up and grabbed our things. Eddie was acting real faint and weak and he leaned on me as we went out the door. The whole time, Mrs. Buttke was barking down the hall for the janitor to hurry up and how some got on her shoes and all that. I looked at Eddie's face, he didn't even have a smile. He was the best actor I'd ever seen.

Once we got outside and was clear of the door, he stood up off of me and started laughing.

"Come on, let's go to my dad's shop."

"I ain't so sure that's a good idea," I said. "Me and him ain't on the best of terms right now."

"He's not there. He's out buying more fireworks for Monday," he said. Bob liked to make the folks in Cullman love him by putting on our annual fireworks show, but he did it for Labor Day 'cause he could get the fireworks at a discount if he waited. I used to complain that we didn't have no fireworks on the Fourth of July, but when I said something to Willie, he said he didn't care 'cause it wasn't his Independence Day anyhow. So I reckoned we could all be happy with it on Labor Day.

Eddie took off running down the street and I was amazed at

ISAIAH CAMPBELL

how fast he went. He used to be so tubby and slow. It was like watching a completely different person. Maybe he *was* different. There was only one way to know for sure.

I followed him, running with both our backpacks banging against my butt. We got to the outside of his pa's auto shop and he fetched the key from his back pocket. He opened the door and headed straight through the front into the big garage, which had all the lights out 'cause apparently everybody'd gone to help Bob load up the fireworks.

"Feast your eyes on this," he said. He flipped on the light switch.

It was like a car hospital in there, there was three cars up on lifts or opened clean up, all of them being worked on or taken apart for parts. There was puddles of oil under some of them, one had a drip of gasoline so bad you could smell it from the doorway. It was real neat, but it wasn't worth puking all over the lunchroom floor.

The next thing I noticed was that the walls was already lined up with stacks and stacks of fireworks boxes. Bob'd be moving them and the extras he was out getting all down to the railroad tracks near Smith Lake on Monday for the show, since no trains ran on Labor Day. Getting to see them all beforehand was neat. And a little scary, since all them explosives was so close to all that oil and gasoline. But still, not vomit worthy.

Then I saw it. The last car in the shop, parked down there at the end. It was cherry red with fancy white stripes. And definitely worth hurling over.

"Is that a Corvette?" I asked.

"It ain't just any Corvette," he said with a grin. "It's a brand-new 1962 Corvette convertible. 327 V-8 engine, 360 horsepower if you drive it right, and it can get over 100 miles per hour." That was a lot of numbers I didn't know nothing about, but they sounded real impressive.

"Who in Cullman owns a Corvette?" I asked. "I reckon that'd make the front page of the paper or something."

"It's my dad's," he said. "He just got it, and he ain't wanting folks to know about it. He won it in a poker game down in Birmingham."

I nodded, standing in awe of that beautiful sleek car like I was seeing the face of God Himself right in front of me with custom rims.

"But," he said, "that ain't what I want to show you. We got to go driving."

Before I could even process what he was saying, he ran over to the desk and fished out a key chain. Then he went and opened up the garage door that was right behind that Corvette. He headed over to the driver's door, then he stopped.

"No, you know what, this might be the only chance you'll ever get to drive something like this," he said.

"Wait, what?" I asked. "What you mean?"

He tossed me the keys.

"You drive, I'll ride. We got to go outside of town so I can show you my thing."

Now, I ain't stupid and I know there's a big difference between driving your own pa's truck to go fishing and driving another man's Corvette to go joyriding, and I know it ain't something you're supposed to do, and I recognize that if I'm ever talking to other kids I'm going to tell them this story different so they don't get any ideas.

But, Eddie had a point. This really *was* probably the only chance I'd ever get to drive one. So I jumped in behind the wheel.

I said a quick prayer that there wasn't no law anywhere around, which I probably didn't need to 'cause Sheriff Tatum had stopped caring since he was going to retire. Then I peeled out of that garage like James Dean and we left a swirling cloud of dust that probably scared some of the folks that had survived the tornado. We both couldn't stop laughing and giggling while I pushed that little car to go as fast as I possibly could while we flew down the road and out of Cullman. I ain't going to say we hit ninety, but I ain't going to deny it either. I also ain't going to deny that I maybe drifted across the road and almost into a ditch one time, which made me drop our speed down to around sixty.

He pointed out which way to go and we drove along until he told me to pull over.

"Wait, you're wanting to show me something here at Snake Pond?" I asked.

He hopped out.

"Yup," he said. "And it's a Tom and Huck kind of something."
He ran into the trees and disappeared.

Now, not everybody called that place Snake Pond. In fact, I
think on the map it's called Fellows Lake or something like that.
But all the kids in Cullman knew what it really was. It was too
ate up for any fishing and too shallow for swimming, so it didn't
deserve to be called a lake. Instead, we all called it Snake Pond.
It don't take too many guesses to figure out why we named it
that. One time, I counted twelve water moccasins that was having a pool party just in one corner of the water.

I thought about sticking with the car and letting him be the
one that died from a snakebite or something, but then I figured
if Bob reported it stolen, I'd be spending most of my days in jail,
so I'd better leave the scene of the crime. I got out and followed
him.

I caught up with him just as he was coming to the edge of
the trees.

"Okay, you ain't gonna believe what I'm about to show you,"
he said. He led me out of the trees and into the clearing that was
right at the edge of the water.

And there it was. And he was right, it was a Tom and Huck
sort of thing.

It was a tent. A white pup tent, set up by somebody who
either didn't know there was snakes everywhere or didn't care.
There was a few other things scattered around too, like some

food cans and the remains of a campfire. Also there was a mirror and a razor next to the tent.

Eddie grinned like a possum.

"Cool, huh?" he said.

"Whose is it?" I asked.

"I don't know. I only found it last night and nobody was up here. Maybe the fella that built it is laying off in the woods, dead by a water moccasin or something. Come on, let's look at it."

We went and looked around the tent, watching our step so we didn't accidentally wake up no snakes or nothing. I looked inside, where there was a sleeping bag and a whole mess of supplies. Like a carton of cigarettes, a mess of baked beans, and six cans of tuna.

"Holy cow," I said out loud. "I think this is the fella that's been stealing groceries."

Eddie didn't pay me no never mind and felt the campfire remains.

"It's still warm," he said, just as excited as a kid at his birthday party. "That means whoever this is was here recent."

"And might be coming back soon," I said. His grin got even bigger.

"Yeah, wouldn't that be something?" He went into the tent. "Oh, cool!" He came out and was waving his newest discovery around in the air.

It was a gun.

"Tarnation, Eddie!" I said. "Put that back and let's get the heck out of here."

"What? If I got it, then he don't." He went back in and kept rummaging through the things. I went back to feeling nervous and watching my feet for snakes.

I went over to the mirror with the razor next to it. There was also a little can of shaving soap and a bottle of aftershave. Almost without thinking, I sniffed of the aftershave.

Wintergreen. Real familiar wintergreen.

Then I spied the mirror and what was down there in the corner of it.

It was a picture of Sora.

I grabbed that picture and looked at it real close, just to make sure. She looked less skinny in the face. Maybe less pregnant, too. I looked on the back, it was dated 1960.

I started to feel sick to my stomach.

"I think we ought to leave," I said.

He popped his head out of the tent.

"What? No way, this is our big Tom and Huck adventure," he said.

"No it ain't. We ain't Tom and Huck no more," I said. "We're Johnny and Eddie, and we ain't got no business being out here."

His face soured and he got real mad at me.

"Fine, get on and run. I don't care," he said as he went back into the tent. "But leave me the keys so I can get home."

I nodded even though he couldn't see me and I dropped the keys next to the mirror on the ground. I put Sora's picture in my pocket and ran off through the trees to the road. I had to get as far away from there as possible.

I walked about a mile or two down the road to our hill. I was trying my best to stop feeling like I needed to sleep for the next few months until everything blew over when I heard a honking coming from behind me. Carlos's truck passed me and stopped on the side of the road. He hollered out the window.

"¿Qué pasa, amigo?"

"Hey, you headed up to my house?" I asked. He nodded. "Could you give me a ride?"

"Any day of the week, my friend," he said. I got in and we headed up the road. He whistled a song that I'd heard him play before on his trumpet, in another one of them mental photographs I had in my head, back when he would wear a white suit and a red flower and he had a whole band behind him in Mr. Thomassen's club. And Ma would dance.

"How was school?" he asked.

"I don't know, it was school, I guess." I eyed his face real good. "How's the Cosa Nostra?"

He grinned like he always did when I started talking about stuff I wasn't supposed to know about.

"They're nervous, I believe."

"What is 'Cosa Nostra' anyway, Spanish? It sounds Spanish."

He'd been giving me some Spanish lessons off and on, which was real nice. I still couldn't figure out why there was so many llamas in Spain, but other than that I was catching on.

"It's Italian," he said. "It means 'Our Thing.' But it sounds similar to the Spanish. What would 'Our Thing' be *en español?*"

I thought for a second.

"*¿Nuestra Cosa?*" I asked.

"*¡Bravo!*"

"But what is it?" I asked.

"*Las cinco familias. Los italianos de Nueva York y Chicago,*" he said real fast. Sometimes he forgot that I wasn't like Mr. Thomassen. When they'd get to talking, they'd mix up Spanish and English together all the time.

"What?"

He snapped his fingers in the air for a second while he tried to translate himself in his head.

"The Sicilian Mafia," he said. "From New York and Chicago. And other places as well."

"You mean like Capone?"

"Cuh-pown," he said. "Is that Italian?"

"Yeah, I think he was. He was a gangster from Chicago."

"Then, yes, like Capone," he said.

"So you Three Caballeros are fighting against the Mafia?" I asked, and my heart started racing. "Are y'all crazy?"

He laughed and I reckoned maybe he was.

"Nosotros no le caemos bien," he said. "We're pains in their butts. We're simply making it as difficult as possible for them to be successful in this country."

We pulled into our driveway.

"No worries, *amigo*," he said. *"No se puede hacer tortilla sin romper los huevos."*

I didn't take the time to try and figure that out, 'cause I was too busy being worried. I got out and went inside to maybe lie on the couch and watch some TV or something to get my mind off of things.

But the couch was occupied. Sora and Martha was sitting on it with Willie's tape recorder set up in between them and Martha was holding the microphone.

I'd caught Martha midsentence. She hurried and shut off the tape recorder.

"Hey, Johnny," she said. "About time you came home."

"What are you doing?" I asked. She winced when I said it, either 'cause I'd said it really rude or 'cause girls just don't like getting asked to explain themselves.

"I have to interview people for your biography," she said.

That stupid biography. It was going to be the death of me. Literally.

"So, why you interviewing her?" I asked. "She don't know me."

This time Sora winced. I was batting a thousand with the ladies. Must have been that Cannon charm.

"You'd be surprised, actually," Martha said. "Tommy told her a heck of a lot."

I looked over at the mantel where stupid Robin was perched, like a goblin just laughing at me. Tommy hadn't told her enough.

"Where's my pa?" I spit out.

"In his shed in the backyard," Sora said. I turned and hurried through the house toward the back door, tripped over a fancy rug that didn't have no business being there, and knocked over a vase I didn't recognize, full of flowers that belonged outside and water that would have been better fit for drinking. Sora must have been decorating. Martha tried to hide a giggle but didn't do a very good job with it.

I hurried out the door and went to Pa's radio shack. I stopped short of knocking 'cause I could hear him and Carlos talking to somebody over the radio.

"*—the trucks leave for Chicago tomorrow night,*" whoever they was talking to said.

"And did you find out what I asked you about?" Pa said.

"*Yeah, though I don't know how—*"

"Just tell me," Carlos said. "Rats or beetles?"

"*The big guy is scared of rats,*" the fella said. "*But I don't get what that does for you.*"

"Simple," Carlos said. "When the truck arrives in Chicago and they open it up, they will be greeted by hundreds of rats that have chewed holes in all their bags."

"And pooped in all their drugs," Pa said with a chuckle.

"*You know they're going to kill you someday, right?*" the fella said. "*When they find out who the Three Caballeros are, they'll put your kidneys in their trophy racks.*"

"Which is why they aren't going to find out," Carlos said. "Or they might learn some other facts about you that will make them much, much angrier."

I was listening real hard, my heart just about ready to blow up in my chest, and that's why I jumped when the screen door slammed behind me.

Martha marched out of my house and came over to me. I moved away from the shack so she wouldn't hear none of what was being said.

"What is wrong with you?" she asked. She seemed mad enough to cuss.

"Why are you up here talking to Sora?" I asked. "And why are you so all-fired interested in finding out my story?"

"You won't tell me anything," she said. "We're supposed to be friends, but you won't even give me a straight answer about the things that happened when you were a kid."

"Because I don't want folks knowing all that stuff."

"But it's all part of your story," she said. "It's not like you can deny it."

"But, see, that's the problem," I said. "To you, that's what it all is. Stories. But for me, they ain't stories, they're memories.

And they're memories I ain't figured out how to deal with yet."

She looked at my eyes like she wasn't sure if I was being sincere or not.

"And anyway," I said, "Sora ain't got no business telling them at all. She wasn't a part of any of it, so she don't know."

"But she does know," she said. "Tommy told her a lot. A lot that I didn't even know. Like how you were still getting surgeries after you moved here to Cullman, and how you wore a catheter until second grade."

"And you think I want you to know that stuff?" I asked, and I could feel my cheeks turning red.

"She told me other stuff, too," she said. "Not embarrassing stuff. Stuff from *before* your accident."

I started panicking.

"You didn't ask her about Captain Morris, did you?"

For some reason, that made her even more mad.

"You asked me not to, didn't you?" she said. "Do you really think I would do that? Why don't you trust me?"

I didn't know what to say to that, or to anything else, so I did something that probably ain't smart to do, especially to the girl you're hoping to woo.

"I'm going hunting," I said, and I turned to walk away.

She grabbed my arm.

"Are you for real right now?" she asked.

"Why don't you go interview Willie, too?" I asked. "Get as

much information from him as you can before his ma makes them move off to Michigan or something."

She let go of my arm and her eyes got big.

"What's that supposed to mean?"

"Oh, you don't know?" I was sounding real nasty, but I didn't much care. "See, I guess while you was so busy trying to dig up all my secrets, you missed the fact that Mrs. Parkins is trying to get them to get out of here on account of all the segregation and Bob Gorman running for sheriff and such."

"Willie might be moving?" she asked. She suddenly looked ready to cry.

"Yeah, but don't you worry. We'll always have the memories for you to poke at and write papers about."

With that still hanging in the air, I turned again and ran off, leaving her standing there looking as lonesome as a lost kitten. I got my gun and went on out into the woods. Alone.

I had a feeling I might need to get used to that.

CHAPTER FIVE
SACRAMENTS

That Sunday morning, I was all ready to head on down to Colony and see how them folks was handling things, but Mr. Thomassen called us early and insisted we come to church in Cullman. Which didn't matter one way or the other to Pa, but going to that church for me was always the worst part of my week. It was dull and boring and it smelled like old folks and hymnals. I decided to wear my school pants instead of my church pants out of protest. It made me feel a little better.

Bob Gorman was one of the head deacons, which meant I had to see him every time we walked through them doors, 'cause he was always greeting folks at the front. That was going to make it real uncomfortable when we got there, but I reckoned I could slip by him and go get a head start on my nap in the back.

But he had a different idea.

We got to church that morning nice and early, so Pa could hit the altars for a good while 'cause he wanted to have a little talk with Jesus and pass on messages to Ma. And maybe Tommy, if him and Jesus was finally on speaking terms. Which was a long shot, but Pa reckoned a slim chance is still a chance, so he did it anyway.

Bob grabbed me by the arm before I even got all the way through the front doors.

"Boy, why don't you come help me set up the sacraments?" he asked, and before I could answer, he dragged me through the church to the kitchen. I wasn't exactly sure what the sacraments was, but I reckoned it was a fancy word for a whipping. Maybe with a sack of mints or something. I really hoped it didn't hurt as bad as it sounded. And that they wasn't peppermint. I hated peppermint.

He cornered me against the yellow wall next to the refrigerator. I got myself ready for the impending beating. I tried to figure which hand he was going to use to sacrament me first and which pocket he was going to pull the sack from.

"What was you doing up at them Tiggers' house?" he growled in my face. He didn't look to be ready to start sacramenting, so I relaxed a bit.

"They're my friends. What was you doing up there?" I asked.

"Pretty sure I made my intentions crystal clear."

"Yup, I'd say you did."

Right then, Pastor Pinckney came in.

"What's going on in here, Bob?" he asked.

"Just getting the grape juice to set up the sacraments," Bob said. I tried to figure how juice was going to play into it. Maybe he was going to pour it in the wounds or something. Sacraments sounded brutal. "This young fella volunteered to help me."

I was waiting for Pastor Pinckney to jump in and tell him we didn't do that sort of thing at church, or at least that Bob ought not to waste the grape juice from communion on sacramenting me, but he didn't say nothing about it.

"Well, the trays and cups are in my office. Ethan is in from seminary, so I thought I'd let him officiate."

Bob got the bottle of grape juice from the fridge and started toward the pastor's office. I reckoned we wasn't going to be doing no sacramenting now, so I started back to the sanctuary to find my sleeping spot. Bob stopped me.

"We ain't done talking. Come with me."

We went into the pastor's office, which had a great big oak desk with all sorts of items from around the world placed on it that Pastor Pinckney'd gotten from visiting missionaries. No shrunken heads, though. Which made all them boring missionary sermons seem like a real waste. There was also about four or five bookshelves with all them books he needed to write his sermons, including a joke book, which I didn't reckon he'd ever read in his life.

And, in the corner, there sat Ethan Pinckney, still just as skinny and nervous as he had been when he used to run around in high school with Tommy. It was funny, I hadn't thought about them days in a long time. Ethan, Tommy, and Mark, or as we called him now, Mr. Braswell, used to go around raising hell all over the county, usually as sauced as a rack of ribs, and almost always with five or six girls in tow. But you wouldn't know it to look at Ethan now. He was wearing his pa's preacher robe and trying to memorize his lines from the Bible. His hair was slicked back and his face was clean except for a caterpillar mustache under his nose. And he was talking real pretty-like.

"For I have received from the Lord that which also I delivered unto you . . . ," he said, then he double-checked his Bible for the next part.

"Pipe down, Ethan," Bob said. "We've got to get the sacraments ready."

Ethan nodded and didn't look worried about me getting pummeled one bit. Which meant he'd make a great preacher someday. He lowered his voice and took to whispering.

"For I have received from the Lord that which also I delivered unto you . . . "

Bob pulled the brass communion trays out from under Pastor Pinckney's desk and started pouring grape juice in the little cups. Oh, so that was the sacraments? Jeepers, the Bible needed to have a glossary or something. Not that I'd read it, but still.

"Did they say anything after I left?" he asked.

"Sure," I said. "Folks don't usually stay quiet for too long."

"Well, what did they say?"

"What's it to you?" I asked.

"THAT THE LORD JESUS," Ethan said, "THE SAME NIGHT IN WHICH HE WAS BETRAYED . . ." He checked his Bible again.

"Did they say who they're going to vote for?" he asked.

"Last I heard there wasn't no candidates yet," I said. "Unless you're saying you're running."

"TOOK BREAD: AND WHEN HE GAVE THANKS, HE BRAKE IT . . ."

"I ain't said nothing official yet," he said. "But did they mention that? Do they think I'd be a good sheriff?"

"AND SAID, TAKE, EAT: THIS IS MY BODY, WHICH IS BROKEN FOR YOU . . ."

"I don't know," I said. "The sheriff is supposed to do a whole lot less lawbreaking than I reckon you're used to."

"THIS DO IN REMEMBRANCE OF ME." Ethan had his eyes closed, trying his best to say it all from memory.

"I don't know what you're talking about," Bob said.

"Well, there's all that stuff with the Klan, plus them dogs in Colony."

"What do I care what happens in Colony?" he asked.

"I don't know. What *do* you care about?"

"AFTER THE SAME MANNER ALSO HE TOOK THE CUP, WHEN HE HAD SUPPED, SAYING . . ."

"I ain't exactly following you, boy."

"THIS CUP IS THE NEW TESTAMENT IN MY BLOOD . . ."

"Just seems to me you're spending a whole heck of a lot of time running around to get votes, and not nearly enough time taking care of what's already yours."

"THIS DO YE, AS OFT AS YOU DRINK IT, IN REMEMBRANCE OF ME."

"If you're talking about Eddie—" he said.

"I am," I said. "And you ought to pay heed to him too."

"FOR AS OFTEN AS YE EAT THIS BREAD, AND DRINK THIS CUP . . ."

"What's that supposed to mean?"

"I don't know," I said. Then I got some gumption I don't know where it came from. "Maybe if you was punching him in the face a little less and going hunting with him a little more, he wouldn't be going off and joyriding in your new car."

"YE DO SHEW THE LORD'S DEATH UNTIL HE COMES." Ethan gave a big sigh 'cause he finished, then he cleared his throat and started again. "FOR I HAVE RECEIVED FROM THE LORD—"

"Dammit, Ethan!" Bob hollered, and hit the desktop like he was killing a bug. Knocked over the bottle of juice and it spilled. Not much on the desk, though. Mainly just all down my pants. 'Cause that's how my life goes. "If you're this nervous about doing the ministry, maybe you ain't in the right profession."

Ethan blinked three times and I was pretty sure he was fixing to cry.

"I'm sorry," Bob said, and cleared his throat. "What I mean is, don't be nervous. Just imagine everybody naked and you'll do fine." He picked up the bottle of juice. "This one's empty now. I'll be back."

Ethan watched him go like a dog watches its master walking after it's been beat.

"I wouldn't recommend the imagining folks naked thing," I said, looking around the office for a towel or something I could dry off with. He had one he was sweating into that he offered me, but I turned him down. "It can cause more problems than it can fix."

Right then Mrs. Forker, Kristen's mom, who Tommy always said had a body that belonged on the side of a bomber, came in to fetch some church bulletins. Ethan watched her rummaging around in Pastor Pinckney's desk for a bit.

"Yeah, I reckon you're right," he said.

The organ started playing and I hurried to get to the bathroom so I could dry off and then find myself a seat. Pa was sitting next to Mr. Thomassen on the second row, which was about seven rows farther up than I had aimed to sit. I enjoyed the back row 'cause the cushion on the pew was nice and fluffy and the ushers didn't hardly ever check to see if you was sleeping.

Anyway, right as the service was starting there was a whole mess of commotion, people hemming and hawing at the back of the sanctuary, but since we was so far up and Pa had his arm around me, I couldn't turn to see what was going on. I didn't reckon it was the Holy Ghost, 'cause stuff like that only happened in black churches or the occasional Pentecostal one. When they wasn't playing with rattlesnakes.

I sat there during all them hymns trying to figure out what had gone on, but I shouldn't have wasted my time, 'cause I found out soon enough. After the offering, Pastor Pinckney got up with a special announcement.

"As many of you have heard, Sheriff Tatum is retiring soon," he said. "A great deal of speculation has been going on about who the next candidates will be. I am pleased to tell you that one candidate has chosen today as his time to officially toss his hat in the ring."

Folks in the sanctuary gave a little clap, which was weird 'cause folks didn't normally clap for nothing at that church.

"However, the privilege of introducing this man does not fall on me," he continued. "Instead, I am privileged to introduce to you a very special guest who has come to give his endorsement to the candidate, and he will join me on the platform now to introduce the man to all of you. Please welcome, all the way from Birmingham, the Commissioner of Public Safety for that fair city, Mr. Bull Connor!"

The whole place blew up in applause and I spun around to see it. Sure enough, out from the very same back pew I'd wanted to claim for myself was the man himself, with a white shirt that matched his hair and a black tie that matched his glasses, and with fat rolls under his neck that jiggled when he walked. He came marching up the aisle of the church like it had been built just so he could step in it.

Now, in case you haven't heard, or in case you need a refresher, Bull Connor was one of the most notorious fellas from Alabama.

Segregationists loved him, 'cause he was famous for saying things like that black folk would have equal rights over his dead body and such. Integrationists hated him. And Willie didn't mince no words, he called him a fascist without a shred of hesitation. And I was inclined to believe him.

Which was why it made sense that he and Bob Gorman was buddies.

Bull got up on the platform and didn't even approach the microphone. Didn't need to, his voice was as loud as a tornado siren.

"Thank you, Brother Pinckney. And thank you, fine, fine citizens of this here Cullman County," Bull said. "I don't think anyone, anyone at all, truly realizes just how important the business and politics of this area are to those of us down in Birmingham. When the law is weak, when the people believe they can get away with murder, when the blacks are allowed by the law to mingle and interact with the whites, even in a small hamlet such as this, it creates ripples, which affect even the largest of metropolises."

People all around us started nodding and agreeing. I wondered if maybe they hadn't heard what he said about blacks and whites. I mean, really, that was the dumbest thing ever. But nobody seemed to care. I was beginning to understand how come Hitler was successful. People didn't care much what you said exactly, just how loud you said it.

"And that is why," he said, "I am glad to introduce a candidate after my own heart. A man committed to keeping the integrity of the law, of separate but equal treatment of races, and of ensuring this happy little town can remain as pure and untarnished as possible. So I'd like to introduce my pick for the next sheriff of Cullman County, Bob Gorman."

Everybody clapped again, real hard this time. Bob stood up and made his way to the platform, strutting like a rooster that had plenty of hens in his henhouse. I leaned over and whispered to Mr. Thomassen.

"I wonder if the Three Caballeros could do something about that?"

He pinched my gut and I didn't say no more.

Bob went into a real long speech that I didn't bother listening to and then, when he was done, he posed with Bull for some pictures for the paper. And then we still had the rest of the service to get to. Dadgum, I sure wished I was in Colony. Or even back home answering some of Martha's interview questions. That's how bad it was.

The worst of it all, unfortunately, was when Ethan got up to do communion. He was so nervous, he muttered real quiet and stared down at the Bible the whole time. About midway through the passage, Bob said to his wife, real loud, "Well, I sure hope the Lord can hear him."

Then Ethan started crying. Just like that, right up there on the platform, in front of God and everybody. A grown man bawling like a baby. It was the worst thing I'd ever seen at church.

Ethan went running off the platform and back to his pa's office and Pastor Pinckney got up and finished the communion. Then he reminded all of us about the Labor Day picnic out at the park, which none of us needed reminding about, and said that Bull Connor was going to be the guest of honor for the fireworks. Fantastic. There wasn't no way anybody from Colony would be coming if that was the case. And I had a bet with Willie that I'd beat him at horseshoes.

When the service was over, I tried to find Ethan, but he wasn't nowhere to be found.

Instead, I found Eddie by himself around the back of the church. He'd caught a mess of crickets and he was popping their back legs off. He offered me a couple, but I was still planning on licking the grape juice off my fingers later, so I declined. Still, I was grateful for the offer, 'cause that meant he wasn't sore at me for leaving him out at Snake Pond.

But, from the looks of his face, he was sore about something. That was for darn sure.

"So, your pa is going to run for sheriff," I said.

"No, my pa is going to *be* the next sheriff." He let one of them crickets hop up his arm.

"You excited?"

"I don't care." He flicked the cricket on the ground and stepped on it. "I ain't going to be here nohow."

That made me take a pause.

"What you mean?"

He looked me in the eyes. "You can't tell nobody."

"Of course not," I said.

He nodded. "I'm running."

"You mean like Otis Davis at the Olympics or—"

He blinked at me a couple times. "Like I said before, we're Tom and Huck," he said. Then he finally got a half smile. "Which, since I'm the one running off, I guess that makes *me* Huck."

Which made me Tom. Which meant I got Becky. Okay, this wasn't the time to dwell on that. Back to the conversation.

"You're running away? To where?"

He shrugged. "The woods first, I reckon. Then maybe up to New York or something. Anywhere I can go that ain't here. That ain't with my pa."

I couldn't say I blamed him.

"Look, why don't you go stay with a relative or something? Tommy did that, he went and lived with our grandma for a while."

"My dad would find me and bring me back. And I ain't living with him no more. I can't."

The air around us got quiet, even though folks was laughing and carrying on congratulating Bob around at the front. Where we was, in that moment, you could hear a pin drop onto a dandelion. Eddie and me stood there, breathing the same air, and I wasn't really sure what I ought to say next.

"It ain't safe," I finally said. "Them woods, you saw that tent.

That fella had a gun. There's all sorts of dangerous folks out there and you're going to be by yourself."

"I'll be fine," he said. "I'm good at making friends."

"No you ain't. I'd say you might be the worst at it of anyone I've ever known. Besides myself."

"That's 'cause I'm here, in Cullman. 'Cause of my name and such," he said. Then he grinned. "Trust me, I'm one in a million."

"Them ain't the kind of odds you gamble on," I said, but he wasn't going to change his mind.

We stood back there just sort of being, not really doing, and I reckon part of me was wondering what in tarnation life without Eddie was going to be like, and realizing that most of my friends would probably be real happy to hear he was leaving, and not sure why I was as sad as I was. Finally Pa came and fetched me, and Bob came to get Eddie, and we all went off to head home.

While we was driving, Pa curled his nose up and rolled down the windows for some reason.

"What's that smell?" he asked.

I took me a second to know what he was talking about. "Oh, that's my pants," I said. He shot me a look. "I got grape juice on them."

He looked at my lap. "Ain't them your school pants?"

"Yup."

"Well, you best get them over to Mrs. Parkins after lunch so she can wash them. I ain't gonna ask her to do it on Labor Day," he said, and I got plumb confused for a bit.

ISAIAH CAMPBELL

"Ain't we going there for lunch?" I asked. "I can give them to her then."

"No, Sora is cooking a big lunch for us."

That didn't seem like a good idea. "Is it all right for her to be cooking in the kitchen, what with the baby and all?"

Pa laughed. "She'll be fine," he said. "Cannon babies are the healthiest kind. And women are built for this kind of work, carrying babies and cooking meals."

I didn't really think that would fly if I said it to Martha, but since I was going to get a meal out of it, I didn't reckon I'd argue too much.

We got to the house and Sora had a feast fit for the king of Korea ready for us. Which meant it wasn't suitable for even the hungriest kid in Kentucky. And they keep them hungry up there.

She had a bowl of rice, which was fine except it was plain white and sticky and didn't have no beans or nothing mixed in. There was also another bowl of something she called "kim chee," which looked and smelled like rotten cabbage with pickle juice thrown on it. Then there was some green stuff, and some black stuff, and a plate of hot dogs.

"Those are for you, Johnny," she said with a smile. "Tommy told me you probably wouldn't ever like any Korean dishes."

I was grateful to Tommy for that, though I didn't reckon she'd have needed any special insight to figure that out. I sat down, grabbed three of them hot dogs, and covered them in mustard. Pa started making himself a plate of all the other junk and we got to eating.

After we all munched away for a while in quiet, I realized something.

"Pa, did you go to the store without me?"

He shook his head, his mouth full of rice.

"Then where'd we get these hot dogs?" I asked.

Pa swallowed.

"We probably already had them," he said. Sora didn't say nothing.

"No we didn't," I said. "Trust me, if we'd had hot dogs in the house, they wouldn't still be in the house by today. I'd have eaten them as a midnight snack a while ago."

"Okay, so she borrowed them from the Parkinses," Pa said, and he looked sort of embarrassed. "Why are you making a big deal out of it?"

"Or somebody got them for her," I said, then I looked at Sora. "That's what it is, ain't it? Somebody brought you them hot dogs, didn't they?"

I was just primed to pull out that picture I'd found at the tent and ask her if she was communicating with that fella who was stealing groceries and such, but Pa decided to change the subject.

"So, Sora . . . ," he started. "You haven't ever told us how you met Tommy."

That frustrated me, but I knew when my ears was getting close to being boxed, so I piped down. She looked relieved.

"I first met Tommy two years ago, actually, in Mobile," she said. "He was there working and taking language classes—"

"Language classes?" Pa said, and he couldn't help his disbelief from sounding. Tommy had enough trouble with English, adding on another language might have made his head explode.

"Yes, he wanted to be ready before he got deployed."

"Oh, right, to—" Pa stopped himself.

"Korea," she said real fast. Maybe a little too fast, I reckon. "He needed a—uh—a tutor in Korean, so he hired me. We met at my parents' house twice a week."

Pa looked at me like he was getting suspicious. For good reason, what with the Korean lie being told like it was truth. But maybe Tommy's cover just had to be that good or something. I decided to keep listening before I passed judgment.

"So then what happened?" Pa asked.

"As we had lessons, he told me more and more about his home and his family. And with every story, I began to have feelings for him. But, of course, I couldn't say anything with my mother listening to us. She would not have approved. Didn't approve."

Pa nodded. The story sounded good, even if it was unbelievable.

"But then, one day, while we were talking, there was some smoke in the house and we ran outside. My mother went to call the firemen and left Tommy and me alone in our front yard."

"Was there a fire?" Pa asked.

"Oh yes," she said, and blushed. "Tommy had set fire to a

wastepaper basket in the bathroom. He hoped it would help us get away from Mother."

Pa chuckled at that.

"Sounds like Tommy."

Sure did. If I had a nickel for every time he almost burned down the house to get out of doing the dishes, I could buy the Yankees. Well, maybe not the Yankees, but I could sure buy the Phillies.

"Anyway, I thought it was the perfect time to tell him about how I felt, but he beat me to it. He asked me to go out on a date with him. And after that, even when he went back to Cullman, we still kept dating. In secret, of course. But, whenever he came back down to Mobile, we would find ways to get away with each other. All the way up until April. Right before he left for Korea."

And there she went with the Korea business again. Didn't make no sense, and I could tell Pa wasn't having it. But he didn't have it in his blood to call out a woman, so instead he stood and picked up his plate.

"Well, I've got a lot of work to do, so I reckon I'm going to head back out to my shack. Thanks for lunch."

He went out the back door and left me and Sora staring at each other. I had two more hot dogs to go or else I would have left too.

As soon as he was out of earshot, Sora leaned as good as she could across the table and whispered to me.

"Can you keep a secret?" she asked.

"Sure," I said.

ISAIAH CAMPBELL

She looked over her shoulder out the window to make sure Pa was in his shack.

"Tommy never went to Korea."

No kidding.

"Really?" I asked. "How do you figure?"

"He told me right before he left. Korea was a lie, a cover story. He actually went to Nicaragua, but he made me swear to not tell anyone, especially your pa. We made up the story about the Korean classes so I wouldn't blow his cover."

Dang, she knew more than she let on.

"What did he do down there?"

She took a deep breath. "Have you heard about the Bay of Pigs invasion?"

"A little."

"That's what he did down there. He trained the Cubans to prepare them for the invasion." Her voice got all sad. "That's probably how he really died."

How'd she know all that?

My face must have shown how confused I was 'cause she reached across the table and grabbed my hand.

"I know, it's a real shock. But I'm sure he would have wanted you to know," she said. Then she smiled. "He always said you weren't just his brother, you were his closest friend."

And that did it for me. Got me right in the throat. I couldn't listen no more or else I'd make a danged fool of myself. I got up and left a perfectly good hot dog waiting to get eaten.

"I got to run my pants to Mrs. Parkins," I said, then I went upstairs, changed into my jeans, and carried my folded-up pants out the front door as fast as I could.

I got down to the Parkinses' house in time to catch the tail end of dinner, which was good 'cause I was still powerful hungry. There was only one problem. They had company. Specifically, they had the Mackers over. Well, Mrs. Macker and Martha. Mr. Macker was still in Montgomery.

Sitting next to Martha was a little like President Kennedy sitting next to Nikita Khrushchev. It was cold and quiet between us, even though the whole table was talking to each other and laughing as hard as ever. We was in the middle of a Cold War.

After everybody got done eating, I asked Mrs. Parkins if she'd mind getting my pants good and clean. Mrs. Macker looked sort of funny when I asked that and said it was time for her and Martha to head on home, which was fine by me, 'cause I was getting tired of straining my ears to hear if Martha might eventually apologize or something. Which she didn't, by the way.

Mrs. Parkins took my pants to go wash them, and me and Willie went to work on some SuperNegro stories in his room. He wanted to talk about the letter, or about the Gormans, or about Martha or something. But I wasn't up to it. I needed to get away into the world of Mercury and them aliens he was hunting.

After a little while, Mrs. Parkins knocked on the door right at the best part of the story just like she always did and Willie had to turn off his tape recorder.

"Doggone it, Ma," he said. "What do you need?"

She opened the door.

"Johnny, this was in your pants pocket. I don't reckon you want me to wash it, do you?"

She handed me that letter. There was a great big purple stain on it from the grape juice.

"Oh, thank you, ma'am," I said. I took the letter and tossed it over by the tape recorder. She left us alone 'cause that's what a good ma knows to do when your boys is working on something important like a SuperNegro story.

Willie picked up the letter.

"What's this?" he asked, and pointed to the purple stain that was at the bottom.

"Oh, some grape juice spilled on me. Ain't nothing."

"No, not the stain," he said, and he held the letter out closer to me. "This." He was pointing at the edge of the stain where there was some letters that hadn't been there before. They was bright white against the purple of the grape juice. They said:

solitary fort is

"What in tarnation—" I said. He looked at the letter again.

"Oh, of course," he said, and he slapped his forehead. "Invisible ink."

"Huh?" I asked. "That's a real thing?"

"Sure, you just mix up baking soda and water, then you write your message with like a toothpick or something, and it don't show up unless you heat it up. Or paint it with grape juice."

He hopped up and went to his kitchen, then he came back with a bottle of Welch's. He poured it on a rag and wiped it all over the letter. And, sure enough, a whole nother message came shining through.

If a solitary fort is a Scottish lake,
Then what is its resident?
JVSJN IND KQUZT

Me and Willie stared at that message for a bit, both of us trying to make heads or tails of it.

"You think it's the first letter thing again?" I asked.

He shook his head.

"No, it don't work out. Plus that last line is obviously a cipher."

"A what?" I asked.

"A cipher. A code where you substitute out the letters in your word for other letters."

A lightbulb turned on in my head.

"Like the decoder rings?" I asked. "Tommy was always into that kind of stuff. He had the Captain Midnight decoder ring, the Little Orphan Annie decoder ring, even the Ovaltine decoder ring. He loved them things, collected them since he was four."

The way them decoder rings would work was that there was a little disk with the alphabet on it, set to turn inside of a rim that had the alphabet on it again. You'd turn the ring around and then make your message by substituting the letters on the inside for what you had on the rim.

"Then it makes sense that's what he'd do, don't it?" he said.

"It shouldn't be too hard to figure it out," I said.

Boy was I wrong.

We spent the rest of the day working on that line, substituting letters this way and that to make it work. But it just wouldn't do it. We literally used all twenty-six letters as the substitute for *A*, but no matter which way we did it, it didn't make no sense. Finally, Willie snapped his pencil in half.

"We're doing this all wrong," he said. I looked over at the paper he was working on. He'd only been doing the middle section of letters, the *IND*.

"What do you mean?"

"There's only so many three-letter words," he said. "So I've tried every single one I can think of to get a hint of what the substitute would be. But it don't work out. If I say the *IND* is 'and,' so *I* equals *A*, it don't let it stay as 'and.' Same as if I do 'but' or 'the' or any other three-letter word."

It was getting dark outside and we was both tired, so I didn't feel up to pointing out how silly he was sounding.

"So, what does that mean?"

"I don't know," he said. "Short-Guy gave me a book about cryptography. Maybe I'll look and see what it says." He let out a great big yawn. "Tomorrow."

I looked at his watch. It was well after eleven. I didn't have to get up early 'cause of the holiday, of course, but Willie told me his ma decided to make him get caught up on some of his English assignments. Willie always said that doing your school at home was the worst thing that could happen to a kid. And he'd had polio, so that's saying something.

I went home and thought about reading a comic or two, but my brain wasn't too keen on letting that letter sit by itself. Instead, even after I got washed up for bed, while I was snug as a bug in a rug under my covers, I couldn't fall asleep. Them letters from that coded message was swimming in my brain and begging for me to work on it. And I tried to not do it, but after a couple of hours of staying awake staring at my ceiling, I couldn't take it no more. So I got up and started trying to break the code again.

It wasn't no use, of course. I didn't have the brainpower I needed, especially that long after midnight. But I couldn't fall asleep, either. Finally, I had one of them ideas that you really only get after midnight when you're still awake but you shouldn't be. I decided to go ask Tommy.

The whole house was asleep when I went down and got the

keys from the back room and took off in the truck to the cemetery. All the way down there, I was praying that the ghosts would have maybe taken the night off since it was a Sunday and all. I really just needed to talk to Tommy alone. Even though he wasn't there. So maybe it was just about being alone myself.

When I got to the cemetery, I realized that wasn't going to happen.

CHAPTER SIX
CAMPING BUDDIES

There was two trucks and a car parked outside the cemetery when I got there. And when I say they was parked, I mean that whoever'd driven them there had enough sense to keep from hitting each other and to put their trucks in park before they got out.

When I got out of my truck, I could hear some voices coming from inside the gates, singing at the top of their lungs. And not the pretty kind of singing like you'd get at church or on the radio. They was singing the kind of songs that only came bubbling from the bottom of a bottle of Jack Daniels. I knew, 'cause that was the only kind of singing Tommy used to ever do.

Now, it probably would have been a good idea for me to turn around and head on back home. Try to get some sleep or something and let them fellas mess themselves up alone. But of course that ain't what I did. Instead I snuck into the cemetery, hoping to find whatever fools was raising the ruckus and keeping them poor dead souls from resting in peace.

As I made my way around some of the bigger tombstones, I finally figured out that them crazy fellas was having a party in the graveyard and they was having it over in the Cannon corner. I wondered if they knew they was drinking over my grandma. She'd probably appreciate them pouring some out onto the ground for her.

I made my way over to where I could see them fellas and where they was at, and when I did, both of those facts stopped me dead in my tracks. 'Cause them fellas was having their little party over at Tommy's grave. And them fellas was Mr. Braswell, Ethan Pinckney, and—

It took me a second to figure out where I knew the last guy from, and then I realized. It was the fella that had driven Sora to the graveyard. I looked back at the car. Sure enough, it was a gold Buick LeSabre.

I stepped out into the moonlight 'cause I couldn't quite see if there was anybody else up there with them. Then Ethan spotted me.

"Hey!" he hollered. "Hey, there's the—the—uh—" Then he took to giggling.

Mr. Braswell turned and saw me. He cussed.

"Johnny Cannon, what in the"—he cussed again—"are you doing here? You've got school in the morning."

"No I don't, tomorrow's Labor Day," I said. That set Ethan to giggling real hard.

Sora's driver looked at me.

"Hey," he said, and he swung the bottle of Jack in the air. "You're the kid that gave my girl"—he hiccuped—"my friend a ride out of this place, aren't you? Come on over here. I never got the chance to really show you my appreciatitude."

I wasn't scared of drunk fellas, thanks to all them times with Tommy. I'd learned that they was real easy to push over if you needed to. Or if you just needed a good laugh. I walked up to Tommy's grave.

"What are y'all doing here?" I asked.

"Having a reunion of the All-Winners Squad," Mr. Braswell said.

Ethan hiccuped and nodded.

"The what?" I asked.

"Ah, not so good at history as you thought, huh?" Mr. Braswell said with a sneer. "Well then, let me educate you. After all, that's my job, right?"

"And my job is to administer the sacraments," Ethan said, then he started crying again. Sora's driver went over, patted him on the back, put the bottle of Jack in his mouth, and tilted his head back to help him drink. After a long gulp, Ethan coughed up half of it, then nodded and said, "Thanks."

Mr. Braswell went and put his hand on Tommy's tombstone.

"When me, Tommy, and Ethan were kids, we found a box of my dad's comics in my attic. And in there, we found the greatest two comics that have ever been created."

"Action Comics number one, the first appearance of Superman?" I asked, getting real excited. "Or Detective Comics number twenty-seven, the first appearance of Batman. Or both, oh my gosh, you guys found both, didn't you?"

"No, idiot," Mr. Braswell said. I wondered how many times he'd felt like saying that when he was teaching and sober. If he *was* sober when he was teaching. "We found All Winners Comics numbers nineteen and twenty-one." He grinned like he expected me to wet myself or something.

"Never heard of them," I said.

He groaned.

"See, this generation has no clue about the important things in life," he said. "Those were the comics that had the greatest superhero team ever created, the All-Winners Squad. Captain America, the Human Torch, Sub-Mariner, Whizzer, and Miss America."

"Human Torch was my favorite," Ethan said. "He was a robot."

"How could he be the *Human* Torch if he was a robot?" I asked. "Shouldn't he be more like the Robo-Torch or something?"

"Anyway," Mr. Braswell said. "We read those comic books over and over and over again together. And we decided we were going to be the new All-Winners Squad." He patted Tommy's gravestone. "Tommy was Captain America. I was the Human Torch."

"I was Whizzer," Ethan said. I looked at his soiled pants. Yeah, that nickname made sense.

"And we were as thick as thieves," Mr. Braswell said.

I glanced over at Sora's driver.

"Apparently so," I said. "Was this here stranger the Sub-Mariner?"

Mr. Braswell stumbled over and put his arm around the fella's neck.

"We didn't know him back then," Mr. Braswell said. "But we do now. This man is Rudy."

Rudy gently pushed Mr. Braswell off of him and pulled out his hanky to wipe off the sweat that Mr. Braswell had left behind. He reached out his hand to shake mine.

"Well, I'm Johnny Cannon," I said. "Captain America's little brother."

"He's his sidekick!" Ethan hollered. "He's Bucky!"

"No, I ain't nobody's sidekick," I said. "I'm just Johnny."

"Well, Just Johnny," Rudy said, "it's nice to finally meet Tommy's brother. And nice that Captain America brought this team together."

Ethan and Mr. Braswell both nodded like he'd just said something profound. I waited a second to see if it would sink into my brain, but it didn't.

"What's that supposed to mean?" I asked.

"Your brother," Rudy said. "He connected us. Just like good ol' Scott Rogers—"

"Steve Rogers," I said.

"Right, just like Steve Rogers, Captain America himself, did for the All-Winners Squad."

Ethan stumbled forward and embraced Tommy's gravestone.

"Thank you, Cap," he said. Them other fellas laughed.

I wasn't laughing.

"You're saying you was mixed up with Tommy?" I asked Rudy.

"Oh, yeah," he said. "We became friends in Mobile last year. Drinking buddies, even."

Mobile. Why was everything coming up from Mobile?

"Why was you in Mobile?"

"I was checking on a military operation for my father's business. Tommy was involved and we quickly became close."

"A military operation?" I asked.

"The Bay of Pigs invasion!" Mr. Braswell blurted out. "Our own Captain America flew in the Bay of Pigs invasion."

"And he died doing it," Ethan said, rubbing the gravestone like it was a dog or something. "Can you believe it?"

Of course I could, but I couldn't let on.

"Really?" I asked. I tried to get my sad eyes on. It was easier since it was so late.

"Oh, gee," Mr. Braswell said. "That's a lot for you to take, isn't it?" He grabbed the bottle of Jack from Rudy and came over to me. "Here, have a sip."

He shoved the bottle in my mouth and tilted it up in the air, and before I knew it, my mouth was full of that disgusting, burning, halfway-to-poisonous junk.

Worst. Teacher. Ever.

As soon as his back was turned, I spit it out all over the ground. And my shirt. Rudy noticed but didn't say nothing.

"So," I said, and wiped my mouth off. Wished I had some water to drink or something. "Why was the Bay of Pigs invasion any of your pa's business?"

"Let's just say he has a professional interest in seeing Cuba liberated," Rudy said. "But I'd really rather not talk about it. I'm done working for him, and I'm not about to get involved again."

What was that supposed to mean? I tried to move past it.

"Then why are you here?" I asked, hoping them other two fellas didn't notice. They was both singing again in front of Tommy's stone. Something about all the girls they'd loved before or something. "Keeping tabs on her?" I pulled out that picture of Sora I'd found at the tent by Snake Pond and showed it to him.

He looked really shocked and grabbed the photograph.

"That's a really long story," he said. Then he put the picture into his back pocket, pulled out a flask, and took a sip. "But right now? Right now I'm helping the Whisper over here—"

"The Whizzer," I said.

"Right, the Whizzer . . . forget about his troubles and see that he'll live to pray another day."

Ethan fell back against the ground, covered his eyes, and groaned.

"Ugh, I screwed up the sacraments," he said. "Y'all don't have any idea how big a deal that is. I mean, I'm probably cursed now. And not just me, but my kids, too. It's like Deuteronomy 5:9 says, God visits 'the iniquity of the fathers upon the children unto the third and fourth generation.' So even my grandkids are screwed."

"That's a lot like what my father says," Rudy said. "'The children shall pay for the sins of their fathers.' That's his motto, I believe."

"That's a pretty creepy motto," I said. "I hope he didn't say it while he was holding you in the hospital."

"My father is a pretty creepy man," he said. "However, thankfully, he wasn't around when I was born. So I at least had a few months before I inherited his brand of creepiness."

"God, I hope that verse isn't true," Mr. Braswell said. "My grandfather was arrested for public lewdness. I'd hate to get pinned for that myself."

I think Rudy was about to say something, but right then, Ethan puked all over Tommy's gravestone. Mr. Braswell started laughing like a maniac. He pulled Ethan up to his feet once he was all done.

"Well, you hurled first, so that means you're driving," he said. "Let's get going. I have to make an appearance at the Labor Day shindig tomorrow and my hangover's already going to be worse than death."

Ethan mumbled something and his eyes started drooping. Mr. Braswell slapped his face a few times.

"Come on, wakey-wakey." He grabbed the flask from Rudy's hand and poured some into Ethan's mouth. Ethan's eyes jerked open. "There we go," Mr. Braswell said. "Down the ol' rain pipe."

He went to hand the flask back to Rudy, but Rudy told him he could keep it. Then Mr. Braswell and Ethan staggered off down the hill to the truck. Ethan fumbled with his keys a bit and turned on the engine. Mr. Braswell rolled down his window.

"See you at the lake tomorrow, Johnny!" he said. Then he raised up, pulled down his pants, and showed off his bare backside. He kept it hanging out the window while Ethan made a cloud of dust as he drove off down the hill.

I suddenly remembered the motto the teachers at school had decided on that year, *Training the Leaders of Tomorrow*.

Rudy chuckled.

"Well, I think I'll be going too." He pulled his keys out of his pocket, couldn't quite keep hold of them, and they went flying through the air. They landed in Ethan's vomit. He cringed.

"So, I'm walking." He started to stumble down the hill.

I closed my eyes. I needed to learn to keep my big mouth shut, I knew that. I knew I shouldn't do things or offer things or be there for folks the way I had been lately. But I wouldn't be a Cannon if I did what I knew I should do all the time.

"Would you like a ride?" I asked.

"No, I'll be fine," he said. "I'm in a tent just five miles from here. Of course, you already know that, don't you? Anyway, I can walk it."

"Or I could drive you," I said. "Ain't no skin off my teeth."

It only took a little more convincing until he gave in and got into my truck. We started down the road. And, just like Tommy used to be, he was awful chatty with all that whiskey in his system.

"So, what do you remember about Cuba?" he asked. Tommy must have told him.

"Not much," I said. "Just the bad stuff, mainly."

He sighed.

"That's too bad," he said. "But there's got to be something you remember that's good. What about *Batidos*?"

Batidos was like a milk shake in Cuba. And he was right, that was a good memory.

"Heck yeah," I said. "*Batido de Trigo* was my favorite thing in the whole world. I'd drink them by the dozen when I could."

"Mmm, mine was *Batido de Guanábana*." He sighed. "What about the dancing? And the music? And friends? Surely you had friends."

I shook my head.

"I remember dancing, but if I had any friends they done got erased from my brain." I thought for a second. "But, wait, you was in Cuba?"

He nodded.

"Lived there all the way up until Castro's chumps drove my family out," he said. "Cut my teeth on the banana trees."

"And now you're here," I said. "And you still ain't told me why you're tracking Sora like a dog."

"I made a promise," he said. "And I'm working to keep that promise."

"A promise to who? To Tommy?"

He nodded.

"And Sora," he said. "A promise to keep her safe."

I stared up at the road that was getting shined on by the headlights and mulled that in my brain for a bit.

"It's pretty plain and clear from your outfit and your car that you got money. Why are you stealing groceries, then? Why not just go in and buy them?"

He groaned. "My father has eyes everywhere. And I need to make sure he doesn't find me. Because once he's found me, he won't let me get away again so easily."

"Well, if you've been taking care of her so blamed good, why is she so skinny?"

"Feeding a pregnant girl is hard," he said. Brother, he could say that again.

"Well, I got to say that your promise to Tommy and Sora must have been a powerful strong one," I said. "To get you staying in a tent out in the middle of nowhere. Stealing groceries and risking getting arrested or dragged back to your pa and all that. Don't reckon I'd do it."

He stared out the window at the darkness.

"I'm trying to avoid paying for the sins of my father. To find penance for the scars on my soul. So, yes, it is a powerful strong promise."

I shivered. That didn't sound good.

"Which sins you talking about?"

"Take your pick," he said. Then he pointed up ahead of us. "You can park up here."

I pulled over and he went to get out. He had one leg out of the truck and then he looked back at me.

"You want to come see my tent? Or, see it again, I guess?" His eyes was halfway closed. He pulled a mint out of his pocket and put it in his mouth, then he offered me one.

In case you're wondering, there's only one right answer to give to somebody if they ask you if you want to see their tent. You tell them no. Just like that. If you want to add a kick to the knee or a sock in the jaw, that's up to you. But no matter what, you ought to always say no. Saying anything else is dadgum stupid.

"Sure, I guess," I said. Never said I was smart. Plus, like he said, I'd already seen his tent, so it was different. "But then I got to get on home."

I got out and followed him. He almost toppled flat over into a pile of weeds that probably was hosting a family of snakes. I went and let him lean on me and we walked through the woods. He still smelled like wintergreen, but with whiskey thrown in. Wasn't the worst thing I'd ever sniffed, but it wasn't apple pie either.

We made our way through the trees to the clearing and headed toward his tent. There was a lantern on inside of it and what looked like another person, sleeping.

"You brought somebody with you?"

"No," he said, "I picked up a straggler."

He opened the flap to the tent and kicked the sleeping bag as he went and collapsed on the other side. The person sleeping jumped up. He wasn't wearing nothing but his skivvies.

"Eddie?" I said.

"Johnny?" he said.

"Oh good, you two know each other," Rudy said as he pulled his blanket over top of himself. He started to say something else, but the whiskey finally set in, and instead he went to snoring.

"What are you doing out here?" I asked Eddie. "Where's your clothes?"

"I told you, I'm running away," he said.

"From your pants?"

"No," he said, blushing.

"Why are you with him?"

"'Cause we're"—he looked over at Rudy and his voice got

softer—"kindred spirits. We're both running from the sins—"

"Of your fathers, got it," I said. "But I got a feeling you'd be better off running on your own than camping out with him. Your pa isn't going to take too kindly to you running off in the first place, let alone hanging with a vagrant. And when Rudy finds out your pa is up for sheriff, well, I reckon he'll want to be as far away from you as possible."

As soon as I said that, he pushed me out of the tent and shushed me.

"Listen, about that, I need you to keep a secret for me. Just from Rudy, if you ever talk to him again."

I didn't figure I'd be talking to Rudy much more after that night, so I said I would.

"Okay, see, I might have lied to him when he asked me who my father was," he said.

"Probably smart," I said. "Though I don't reckon you can keep that lie up if you stick around here any longer."

"I know, I know, but listen," he said. "Here's the deal, at first he wasn't aiming to let me stay with him, so I needed to come up with some reason he might want me to stick around."

"And?"

"And after you left me here on Friday, I went through his journal and stuff and I came across some entries that he was looking for a fella."

"Okay, so?"

"So, if you're ever talking to him again, my name ain't Eddie Gorman. It's Eddie Morris. And my father is Captain—"

"Richard Morris," I said, and my gut clenched up something fierce.

"Yeah, how did you know?" he asked.

I peeked back into the tent and could see Rudy breathing real hard in his sleep and I wondered if he was dreaming about the reward money Mr. Trafficante had put on the Morris blood. On my blood.

"Word spreads fast," I said.

"Well, anyway, as soon as he heard me say that, he said I needed to stay with him and to not go nowhere or nothing. Said it was for my own good." He grinned a big fat grin. "So, from now on, I'm Captain Morris's son."

That'd make my life quite a bit easier. But it might not be the best turn of events for Eddie. And, since I'd already done stopped hating him and started caring about whether or not his life went off okay, I couldn't let him walk into a bear trap like that.

"Listen, you can't ask me how I heard about this, but I think it ain't exactly safe to be Richard Morris's son at the moment."

"On account of the price tag on his head?" he asked.

"Yeah," I said, and I eyed him as suspiciously as I ever had. "How'd you know that?"

"Rudy told me," he said. "Said that's exactly why I needed to be right by his side, 'cause that was the only way I could guarantee that I'd be safe from anybody that might be hunting for me."

I peeked back in the tent again at Rudy, grinning while he snored like he was dreaming about finding Shangri-La or something.

"But wasn't he hunting you?"

"Sure, but he was after me to keep me safe from them folks that's aiming for me," he said. "Well, for the Morrises, but whatever."

I really hoped he was right. I sort of thought it might just be easier to spill the truth, but I wasn't sure. It was one of those situations where you feel like the kid who saw the magician practicing before the birthday party and you knew all about the trapdoor in the box and such, but you wasn't sure if you wanted to say nothing 'cause you didn't want to be that guy that messed up the magic show. Especially when you was the one that might get sawed in half. I decided to keep my big mouth shut.

We talked a little more about his lies and about what he and Rudy was going to do and whether they was going to stick around for a bit or not. He didn't know nothing, to tell the truth, so it was a waste of spit and wind. Finally, I decided it was time to go home. I was heading out the camp when he stopped me.

"You got to swear you won't tell nobody."

"Sure, whatever," I said.

"Johnny," he said, "I'm serious. You saw what my pa did to me before, and that was him trying to restrain himself. Trust me, if he finds me now, well, I ain't so sure he'd know how to hold back." His eyes almost started tearing up. "From here on out, I'm a Morris, not a Gorman. And you didn't see me out here at all."

He was scared. There was something about it, something about him being as scared as a little kid, without one ounce of meanness or even a shred of a prank or nothing. I hadn't never seen it on him before. So I swore I'd keep it secret, and not just any old oath you'd take on the schoolyard. I took an Alabama blood oath, the sort that only gets paid back once you've burned in hell for a few years. That was serious business.

I wondered how long you had to burn for lying about who your father was. Hopefully not as long. I probably already had a few centuries' worth of sins saved up that I'd have to simmer in brimstone over, I sure didn't need no more.

I went back to the truck and headed on home.

do nothing but go to school and then sit in your
ll only be doing homework in here too. No comic

to head out of the room.
vell made me do it," I said. He stopped in his tracks.
he asked. "Used to hang around with Tommy and

Mark did it. He forced me to drink."
bed me by the arm.
r you're lying or Mark is going to be out of a job."
't lying, so I hoped Mark had his résumé ready to go.
agged me downstairs and put me in the truck. Didn't let
sh my teeth or fix my hair or nothing. I was still in my
g shirt, though he did let me throw on pants and my shoes,
I was thankful for. Then he drove us real fast into town and
to Mr. Braswell's mom's house. But she wasn't there. She and
ybody else was out at the one place I sure didn't want to be
t then.

They was all out at Smith Lake Park for the Labor Day picnic.
nd, 'cause he was fixing to embarrass me in front of every single
erson that lived in or around Cullman, Pa drove us out there so
he could give Mr. Braswell a piece of his mind.

The whole way there, I was begging and pleading with him to
turn around and head back home. I tried bargaining with him,
offering to spend the rest of my days working in our house, even

CHAPTER SEVEN
SPARKS FLY

It was right before five in the morning, and I was powerful
grateful that I could sleep all day. Before I laid back down,
I wrote a note and pinned it to my door asking Pa to let me
sleep until at least after lunch, and then we could head over to the
picnic.

He must have gotten my note, 'cause he didn't come into my
room until late. But, when he did finally come to wake me up, he
did it by turning my mattress over and dropping me on the ground
like a flapjack with a fly cooked into it.

I jumped up, hopping mad.

But he was even madder. He was furious.

"What is this?" he asked, and held out the shirt I was wearing
before I went to bed, which I'd thrown on the floor right next to
the door.

"It's my shirt," I said. I still wasn't ready to stop scowling at him.

"I know it's your shirt," he said. Then he pointed at some stains going down the front. "I mean this. What is this? And don't try to lie your way out of this, I know whiskey when I smell it."

Ah, dang. I stopped my scowling and started stuttering.

"It's . . . It's . . . it ain't like what you think," I said.

"Oh, sure." He threw my shirt at me. "It ain't never like what I think, is it? Ain't that just what Tommy used to always say? And then we'd find out he'd beaten some poor soul to a pulp, or he'd wrecked somebody's car, or he'd been out with some girl and couldn't remember her name."

I peeked out at the hallway. Sora stood, dazed, with her mouth open. She saw me looking, so she ducked away.

"Yeah, that's how it used to be with him, but it ain't with me. I ain't aiming to be like that."

"Of course you ain't," he said. "But that don't mean you ain't going to hit it if you keep on going."

"You don't understand."

"Okay, fine." He sat on my desk. "Tell me, did you or did you not go out after bedtime last night?"

I took a deep breath.

"Yes sir, I did."

"What time did you come home?"

I closed my eyes. This wasn't going to be good, but lying would be worse.

"About five."

He looked like [...] couple seconds befo[...]

"Were you alone o[...]

"I was with people, [...]

He held up his hand [...]

"Was there drinking in[...]

I took another deep brea[...]

"Yeah, there was, but—"

"Don't you 'but' me," he said [...] "Now, you answer this question [...] drink anything yourself?"

I looked at that finger and reme[...] smacked Pa's hand away for doing it. [...] could do that then. I did now.

"Well, it really depends on what you n[...]

Pa got real mad at that and smacked my [...]

"Damnation! Don't you go splitting hairs [...] a single, solitary drop of whiskey make its way [...] you taste alcohol? How else can I say it?"

Unfortunately, there was only one honest answ[...] tions.

"Yes," I said, "but that ain't a fair line of questions[...]

He stood up, his face fallen down like an old barn.

"You're grounded," he said. "No more hanging aro[...] Willie or Martha, no more hunting or fishing, none of it.

You ain't going t[...] room. And you'[...] books."

He started [...]

"Mr. Bras[...]

"Mark?"

Ethan?"

"Yeah. [...]

Pa grab[...]

"Eithe[...]

I was[...]

Pa d[...]

me bru[...]

sleepin[...]

which[...]

over [...]

ever[...]

rig[...]

tried threatening to tell folks his most embarrassing story, when he sleepwalked and thought the trash can was the toilet and we all woke up to the worst smell there'd ever been, but it didn't do nothing. He was bound and determined to ruin my life, and there just flat wasn't no stopping him.

The park was so full that people was parking on the road, and we pulled up behind about twenty-five cars. Which meant we was going to be walking from the far end of the park over to where everybody was congregating. Me still in my pajama shirt and my hair still matted from my own drool. I ain't never wanted to die so bad in my life.

We marched along the grass, Pa stabbing the ground with his cane like he figured he was knocking the devil in the head or something. The park was a sea of noisy people, but as soon as we stepped foot in it, the sea parted and we walked along on the dry ground of silence. Every single pair of eyes snapped on us and followed us as we moved deeper and deeper to find Pa's target.

We passed Martha and Kristen, sitting on a blanket, watching some fellas from our class playing Frisbee. Or they was until we passed by. Then they was watching us. Which is why I've always hated Frisbees, 'cause they can't keep folks' attention for nothing.

There was folks over barbecuing, and I was afraid they was going to burn their weenies 'cause they stopped tending to them. Some folks was playing volleyball and one fella got an easy point 'cause the other team noticed us first.

Finally, we got deep in the heart of the crowd and found Mr. Braswell. He was standing with a whole mess of girls, just gabbing away like he knew they all wanted to be his girlfriend. He was in swim trunks and didn't have no shirt, which made all them girls keep glancing at his chest. He had on big sunglasses and was holding a beer in one hand and his cigarette in the other. He didn't see us coming.

Poor fella.

Pa got up behind him and picked up his cane like a baseball bat. Then he swung it and whacked the drink right out of Mr. Braswell's hand, all the way over onto Doc Brown's backside.

Mr. Braswell spun around, cussing and sputtering like a drowning sailor. His sunglasses slipped off in the ruckus and it was pretty amazing how bloodshot his eyes was.

"Mr. Cannon? What the"—cussword—"are you doing?"

"Mark, what's this I hear about you getting my boy drunk last night?"

All the people around us gasped like they was watching Perry Mason and he'd just pointed out somebody had a gun hidden in their pillow.

Mr. Braswell rubbed the bump that was rising on his hand from Pa's cane.

"I—I—" he stammered. "I honestly don't know what you're talking about."

Dadgum liar.

ISAIAH CAMPBELL

CHAPTER SEVEN
SPARKS FLY

It was right before five in the morning, and I was powerful grateful that I could sleep all day. Before I laid back down, I wrote a note and pinned it to my door asking Pa to let me sleep until at least after lunch, and then we could head over to the picnic.

He must have gotten my note, 'cause he didn't come into my room until late. But, when he did finally come to wake me up, he did it by turning my mattress over and dropping me on the ground like a flapjack with a fly cooked into it.

I jumped up, hopping mad.

But he was even madder. He was furious.

"What is this?" he asked, and held out the shirt I was wearing before I went to bed, which I'd thrown on the floor right next to the door.

"It's my shirt," I said. I still wasn't ready to stop scowling at him.

"I know it's your shirt," he said. Then he pointed at some stains going down the front. "I mean this. What is this? And don't try to lie your way out of this, I know whiskey when I smell it."

Ah, dang. I stopped my scowling and started stuttering.

"It's . . . It's . . . it ain't like what you think," I said.

"Oh, sure." He threw my shirt at me. "It ain't never like what I think, is it? Ain't that just what Tommy used to always say? And then we'd find out he'd beaten some poor soul to a pulp, or he'd wrecked somebody's car, or he'd been out with some girl and couldn't remember her name."

I peeked out at the hallway. Sora stood, dazed, with her mouth open. She saw me looking, so she ducked away.

"Yeah, that's how it used to be with him, but it ain't with me. I ain't aiming to be like that."

"Of course you ain't," he said. "But that don't mean you ain't going to hit it if you keep on going."

"You don't understand."

"Okay, fine." He sat on my desk. "Tell me, did you or did you not go out after bedtime last night?"

I took a deep breath.

"Yes sir, I did."

"What time did you come home?"

I closed my eyes. This wasn't going to be good, but lying would be worse.

"About five."

He looked like I'd stepped on a kitten or something. He took a couple seconds before he said another word.

"Were you alone or with people?"

"I was with people, but it—"

He held up his hand and stopped me.

"Was there drinking involved?"

I took another deep breath.

"Yeah, there was, but—"

"Don't you 'but' me," he said, then he put his finger in my face. "Now, you answer this question honest or so help me. Did you drink anything yourself?"

I looked at that finger and remembered a time that Tommy'd smacked Pa's hand away for doing it. I didn't understand how he could do that then. I did now.

"Well, it really depends on what you mean by drinking."

Pa got real mad at that and smacked my desk, loud as a pistol.

"Damnation! Don't you go splitting hairs with me! Did a drop, a single, solitary drop of whiskey make its way over your lips? Did you taste alcohol? How else can I say it?"

Unfortunately, there was only one honest answer to those questions.

"Yes," I said, "but that ain't a fair line of questions."

He stood up, his face fallen down like an old barn.

"You're grounded," he said. "No more hanging around with Willie or Martha, no more hunting or fishing, none of it. No TV.

You ain't going to do nothing but go to school and then sit in your room. And you'll only be doing homework in here too. No comic books."

He started to head out of the room.

"Mr. Braswell made me do it," I said. He stopped in his tracks.

"Mark?" he asked. "Used to hang around with Tommy and Ethan?"

"Yeah. Mark did it. He forced me to drink."

Pa grabbed me by the arm.

"Either you're lying or Mark is going to be out of a job."

I wasn't lying, so I hoped Mark had his résumé ready to go.

Pa dragged me downstairs and put me in the truck. Didn't let me brush my teeth or fix my hair or nothing. I was still in my sleeping shirt, though he did let me throw on pants and my shoes, which I was thankful for. Then he drove us real fast into town and over to Mr. Braswell's mom's house. But she wasn't there. She and everybody else was out at the one place I sure didn't want to be right then.

They was all out at Smith Lake Park for the Labor Day picnic. And, 'cause he was fixing to embarrass me in front of every single person that lived in or around Cullman, Pa drove us out there so he could give Mr. Braswell a piece of his mind.

The whole way there, I was begging and pleading with him to turn around and head back home. I tried bargaining with him, offering to spend the rest of my days working in our house, even tried threatening to tell folks his most embarrassing story, when he sleepwalked and thought the trash can was the toilet and we all woke up to the worst smell there'd ever been, but it didn't do nothing. He was bound and determined to ruin my life, and there just flat wasn't no stopping him.

The park was so full that people was parking on the road, and we pulled up behind about twenty-five cars. Which meant we was going to be walking from the far end of the park over to where everybody was congregating. Me still in my pajama shirt and my hair still matted from my own drool. I ain't never wanted to die so bad in my life.

We marched along the grass, Pa stabbing the ground with his cane like he figured he was knocking the devil in the head or something. The park was a sea of noisy people, but as soon as we stepped foot in it, the sea parted and we walked along on the dry ground of silence. Every single pair of eyes snapped on us and followed us as we moved deeper and deeper to find Pa's target.

We passed Martha and Kristen, sitting on a blanket, watching some fellas from our class playing Frisbee. Or they was until we passed by. Then they was watching us. Which is why I've always hated Frisbees, 'cause they can't keep folks' attention for nothing.

There was folks over barbecuing, and I was afraid they was going to burn their weenies 'cause they stopped tending to them. Some folks was playing volleyball and one fella got an easy point 'cause the other team noticed us first.

Finally, we got deep in the heart of the crowd and found Mr. Braswell. He was standing with a whole mess of girls, just gabbing away like he knew they all wanted to be his girlfriend. He was in swim trunks and didn't have no shirt, which made all them girls keep glancing at his chest. He had on big sunglasses and was holding a beer in one hand and his cigarette in the other. He didn't see us coming.

Poor fella.

Pa got up behind him and picked up his cane like a baseball bat. Then he swung it and whacked the drink right out of Mr. Braswell's hand, all the way over onto Doc Brown's backside.

Mr. Braswell spun around, cussing and sputtering like a drowning sailor. His sunglasses slipped off in the ruckus and it was pretty amazing how bloodshot his eyes was.

"Mr. Cannon? What the"—cussword—"are you doing?"

"Mark, what's this I hear about you getting my boy drunk last night?"

All the people around us gasped like they was watching Perry Mason and he'd just pointed out somebody had a gun hidden in their pillow.

Mr. Braswell rubbed the bump that was rising on his hand from Pa's cane.

"I—I—" he stammered. "I honestly don't know what you're talking about."

Dadgum liar.

"Yes you do," I said. "You and Ethan was drinking together last night and you made me take a swig of Jack Daniels."

The crowd gasped again. There ain't too many scandals in Cullman, so this was as big as Elizabeth Taylor stealing Debbie Reynolds's husband. I got half a smile that died as soon as Pa saw it.

"Is that true, Mark?" Pa said.

"Look, I'll admit I was drinking last night," Mr. Braswell said. "With Ethan. He'd had a rough time at church yesterday and he needed some consoling, so he came over to my house and we had a few glasses of Scotch." He stopped and looked back at me, almost like he felt like he was forgetting something. "But then I went to bed."

One of them girls came and grabbed his arm and started looking at the bump on his hand like she was worried it might be broken.

"You're a liar!" I said. "You and Ethan was at the cemetery getting plastered at Tommy's gravestone."

"Wow, that's an active imagination you have," he said. I peeked at the crowd again. They was hanging on every single word. But I realized real quick that I was a kid and he was the teacher. Which meant I was probably going to lose the argument.

"You was with Rudy," I said, trying one last time at the truth.

"I don't even know who you're talking about," he said. He looked at Pa. "I'm sorry, this sort of thing happens. A kid wants to find someone to take the heat off and their teacher seems like the likeliest of candidates. So, no hard feelings, sir."

Pa was changing from being mad at him to believing him, I could tell that by his eyes. He was probably fixing to apologize for beating him with his cane, too. Which meant Mr. Braswell was better at telling lies than I was at telling the truth. So I decided to change plans and play the game his way. 'Cause there wasn't a better liar in all of Alabama than Johnny Cannon.

If I couldn't blame it on Mr. Braswell, I had to pick somebody that everybody would believe would do wrong like that. And there probably wasn't nobody in Cullman folks liked to judge more than Eddie Gorman. Now, I'd swore that I wouldn't tell where he was at, but I didn't say nothing about telling I was with him. See, you got to find them loopholes if you're going to take an Alabama blood oath. Otherwise you'll probably get lynched on your own words.

"Fine," I said, and tried to act relieved that I was finally spilling the beans. Adults loved it when they felt like you'd changed your wicked ways. "It wasn't Mr. Braswell. It was Eddie. I was out with Eddie and he made me drink some whiskey."

"Eddie!" a voice boomed from the other side of the crowd. I looked over to see who it was.

It was Bob Gorman and Bull Connor.

Dadgummit.

They came rushing through the crowd at us.

"You were with Eddie last night?" Bob grabbed me by the collar of my sleeping shirt. "Where is he? What is he doing?"

Bull Connor pulled him off of me. "Calm down, Bob. Calm down."

"What's going on?" Pa said.

"Bob's son, Eddie, ran away," Bull Connor said real loud so everyone could hear. The whole park gasped even louder. This was the best day of the whole year for folks in Cullman. Too bad nobody was taking pictures.

"Where was he?" Bob said. "Where did you and he go to drink? Is he okay? Did you leave him passed out somewhere?"

Sheriff Tatum made his way over to us.

"What's going on?" he asked. "Do we need to get up a search party?"

"That's a good idea," Bull said.

"Johnny said Eddie was at the cemetery," Pa said.

Bob shot me a look.

"Okay. Round up every available man," Bob hollered. "We're going to find my son, and we ain't going to stop until he's back home."

"But what about the fireworks?" Mr. Braswell said.

"Boy, I reckon fireworks is the least of our concerns," Bull said. "We need to start looking over every inch of this county. He couldn't have gotten very far."

Bob grabbed Pa by the arm.

"Pete?" he said. "Can I count on you?"

Pa nodded.

"Sure, sure. Yes, I'll help you. Of course. Let me just take Johnny home first."

"But he was with Eddie. He might know better where to find him."

Pa glared at me.

"No, I reckon he's been as much help as he'll be. I'll take him home and set him in his room and then I'll meet you and whoever else at the cemetery."

"So there's not going to be any fireworks?" one of the girls with Mr. Braswell said.

Mr. Braswell took a look at Bob's eyes, which was practically shooting flames out of them.

"Nope," he said. "None that we want to see. Let's move this party back to my house."

Edith Braswell, Mr. Braswell's mom, stepped in and grabbed him by the ear.

"You told me you didn't do no drinking last night," she said. "There ain't going to be no more party for you at my house. Let's go."

I almost laughed, watching a grown man get dragged by a little old lady out to her car, but then I spied Bob again. He was frothing at the mouth.

"So, what you going to do when you find Eddie?" I asked.

He cracked his knuckles and ground his teeth for a second.

"I will make sure he never gets the darn fool idea to run off like this in his head again. Even if I have to beat the spit out of him."

I could almost feel them hellfires tickling at my toes.

"Look, I'll bet I could lead the manhunt," I said. "Show y'all all the places I reckon he went. Like, he said he was going to head over to the library. We could all go over there. And maybe pick up a book or two while we're at it. They say all the answers can be found in books."

Pa grabbed hold of my arm real tight.

"Nope, you're going home. Sora can watch you."

He dragged me back out of the park, with everybody watching us twice as hard, and made me get back into the truck. And I should have been mad about getting grounded and everybody thinking I was a stinking drunk and the fact that I wasn't ever going to be able to show my face around town again. Any other normal kid would have been mad at that. But I wasn't. I was worried instead.

I had a bad feeling if Bob had his way, Eddie's blood was going to be on my hands.

CHAPTER EIGHT
LOST THE KEYS

Did you know that when folks ain't quite sure what they ought to say, they'll usually clear their throat or cough? It's like they're trying to make folks believe the reason their brain ain't working is 'cause they caught tuberculosis or something. And then maybe folks'll run off 'cause there ain't nobody that wants to catch tuberculosis, no matter how nosy they are. Which is also why folks cough so much in church. They're hoping the preacher will quarantine himself.

I was sitting at the dining room table and Sora was watching me, clearing her throat like she'd just come in from a dust storm. Meanwhile, I was stewing away, trying to figure out how to sneak out and get to Rudy and Eddie before the town posse caught up with them.

Which was stupid, 'cause there wasn't neither one of them that was a decent enough fella to risk getting grounded for the rest of my life over. But there also wasn't neither one of them that was bad enough to deserve what Bob was primed to give them. It was one of them moral dilemmas, like when you're powerful hungry but you just saw *Bambi* in the theaters, so you can't bring yourself to shoot the deer in front of you. But then you remember that Bambi's ma was probably feeding that hunter's family real good, so you shoot the deer anyway. It was like that.

"You don't got to watch me," I said. "I ain't going nowhere."

"I don't mind," she said. "Pa asked me to, so I'm going to do it."

So she was going to play the game. Me and Tommy used to play it all the time. We'd know the other one had a secret, and so we'd keep playing dumb to all the lies they'd tell until they was so frustrated they'd finally spill it. But I didn't have time for that game, so I reckoned I'd just go ahead and put my cards on the table.

"Rudy's with him, you know," I said.

She took a quick breath. She wasn't expecting to hear his name from my lips. That was for darn sure.

"Rudy?" she asked. "Who's that?"

"Don't even try," I said. "You can't out-lie a liar. I don't know what he is to you, but I sure know what you are to him. And if Bob finds Eddie with him, he'll have Rudy's hide as a rug in his shop. Won't even think twice."

She stared at me for a couple of seconds and then she stood up. "Take me to them."

"Wait, what?"

"Take me to them. We need to warn them."

She didn't get no arguments from me, so we got up and headed out. Pa had hitched a ride with Bob, so we took the truck and drove on down to Snake Pond.

When we got to the tent, the campfire was working to get a pot of water boiling. Eddie was tending to it.

"Hey," I said as I went over to him, "we got—" Then I noticed what was sitting next to him in the dirt. "Wait, what are you cooking?"

"Snake stew," he said. "My grandma got the recipe in Sweetwater, Texas."

"With water moccasin?" I asked. "That'll kill you."

"No," he said, and he picked up a bag of snake heads. "You just cut it low enough so you don't get no venom. Plus it all cooks out anyhow."

Sora finally caught up with me, 'cause pregnant women is slow.

"Where is he?" she asked.

No sooner had she said that when Rudy popped out of the tent.

"Sora?" he said, then he ran to her and hugged on her, and she hugged him back, though she didn't seem as enthused as he was about it. The whole thing would have been weird any day of the week to be honest, but considering the baby that was in between them was Tommy's, it seemed downright sinful.

I cleared my throat and Rudy let go of her.

"You're supposed to be gone," she said. "I thought you said you'd leave on Friday."

"I was going to," he said, then he glanced over at Eddie. "But then I found him."

She looked over at Eddie and then back at him.

"Him?" she asked. "*He* is him?"

He nodded and grinned.

"But, I thought—" she said. He stopped her.

"Let's go talk in private," he said. They went off and headed to a place in the trees that looked like a good spot to die of snake poison.

"They're talking about me," Eddie said. I looked over at him and he stirred the pot. "They're excited about me being Morris's son."

"Your pa is looking for you," I said. "And, knowing him, he's going to find you. Both of you."

He stopped stirring and started staring at me with real scared eyes.

"He wouldn't look for me out here, though. Right?"

I looked back over at the spot that Sora and Rudy had snuck off to.

"I don't know," I said. "I hope not. But he's got a posse out hunting you."

He cussed. Then he cussed again.

Before he could get out a third one, I decided that I needed to know what they was talking about.

"Hey, I'm going to go pee," I said.

I headed over and tried to get as close to those two as I could without getting heard or nothing, and then, 'cause I actually did have to pee, I went ahead and started watering some of them weeds.

"Are you absolutely sure?" she asked. "I mean, he doesn't even look like—"

"Yeah, I know," he said. "But he knows things."

"What kind of things?"

"Like about Havana. And about the club. And—"

"Okay, so it's him," she said. "So, what now?"

I got done peeing and zipped up. It was funny, when I was a kid with Tommy and we came down to Snake Pond, he'd always told me not to pee near the water. I couldn't remember right then why, though.

"Now we try to get word back to my father," he said. "And maybe—"

He kept on talking, but I stopped listening, 'cause I remembered why Tommy'd told me never to pee down there.

Snakes like it when folks pee near them. 'Cause pee attracts rats, and snakes like rats more than ice cream.

And right then, a big, fat water moccasin came slithering to check out the mess I'd just made and see if any nice juicy rats had showed up for a drink or two.

I've faced down some pretty dadgum scary things in my life, even stood toe-to-toe with Che Guevara after he broke my nose, but there ain't nothing that sends me into a frantic worse than snakes. Especially poisonous ones. And doubly especially when it's sniffing my toes and figuring out that I am the source of that sweet-smelling liquid it knows is going to fetch it a nice meal.

I went from zero to screaming in two seconds. Which only made the snake even more curious. I reckon there ain't much screaming down in the snake pits.

That snake started darting around me, hoping, I guess, that it'd get me to stop doing the screaming it wasn't liking so much, which shows just how small snake brains are, 'cause all it did was make me scream worse than I did during *Psycho*.

Rudy came busting through the woods to see what all the commotion was about. I pointed at that snake that was getting ready to bite me. Without another word, Rudy reached around to his back and pulled out that gun Eddie'd found before, and he shot the snake right in the head. It flopped up into the air and around in the dirt a few times, but then it gave up the ghost.

"You can stop screaming now," Rudy said.

I closed my mouth.

Sora came over to us.

"What just happened?" she asked, then she saw the snake.

"Nothing a little firepower can't fix," Rudy said.

"Yeah," I said. "Too bad you probably got Bob's posse heading this way now."

"Bob's posse?" he said, and then he looked at Sora. She went ahead and told him what all'd happened and such, and he got real serious real fast.

"Okay, I guess that's our cue to hit the road."

"'Our' meaning you and Eddie?" I asked. "Or 'our' meaning you and Sora?"

Sora shot me a look.

"Him and Eddie, of course," she said. "I'm here for the long haul. That's what Tommy would want."

That seemed to fire a dart at Rudy, though he recovered pretty fast. He went back to their campsite and started packing up.

"But, the stew is almost ready," Eddie said. "Why are we leaving so soon?"

"We'll have time to eat," Rudy said. "Let's just get all this loaded up in my car and then—"

He smacked himself in the forehead.

"My car is still at the cemetery."

Well, that wasn't good.

"That's where the posse is starting their search," I said. "Which means they found your car."

"I locked it, though," he said. He dug into his pockets for his keys.

"They're still in a puddle of Ethan's throw-up," I said. He groaned.

"Do you think you could go get it?"

Sora and Eddie both looked at me and I laughed.

"Are you out of your mind?" I asked. "If the posse is still at the graveyard and I show up, I'll be grounded till two years after college or something. Why don't you go get your own danged car?"

"You're the only one out of all of us that could get it without raising suspicion," he said. "I show up and they're there, they're going to want to ask me questions, maybe even throw me in the jailhouse so they can be sure I'm being honest. Eddie shows up, well, you know what would happen with that."

"What about Sora?" I asked.

She looked a little shocked.

"I guess I could."

"No," Rudy said, pretty stern-like. "No, she's not getting dragged into this. You have to do it."

"I don't got to do nothing but—" I started to say, but then I saw Eddie's eyes. It was one of Bob's favorite sayings, that you didn't have to do nothing but stay white and die. But it was wrong. Bob was wrong. And he hadn't never done nothing good for Eddie.

"Fine," I said. "I'll do it."

With a whole batch of fresh-baked cusswords rattling around

in my mouth, I drove on over to the cemetery so I could fetch his dadgum LeSabre. As I got closer, I could see a mess of cars, including Mr. Thomassen's Cadillac and Carlos's truck. Plus there was the sheriff's car, and a bunch of other ones that had been out at the lake all parked slipshod all over the place. So I circled around and parked on the other side of the hill, then I hiked up to see if I could sneak in and get them keys from in front of Tommy's grave.

When I finally found my spot, I spied Rudy's car, but there was a problem. It was hooked up to the back of Bob Gorman's tow truck.

Mr. Thomassen, Pa, and Carlos was all standing close enough that I could hear what they was saying, and they was joined pretty quick by their favoritest CIA agent, who must not have had nothing better to do than to stick around Cullman and make it harder for me to be comfortable breathing.

"I found these over in a pile of vomit," Short-Guy said. He was holding a set of keys with a pair of pliers.

Mr. Thomassen shook his head.

"So what do you think that means?"

Short-Guy shrugged.

"If I had to put the pieces together as I see them now, with Eddie missing, this car that's been abandoned and is missing plates, and now a set of keys in vomit, I'd say we're looking at a gang crime."

Oh, dang. That was a whole heck of a lot more interesting than the truth.

"Ain't that a bit of a stretch?" Pa said.

"Not at all. It's fairly common in the underworld to transport small items by swallowing them. A nice car with no plates is obviously stolen, probably towed here on the back of a truck, set to be sold on the black market. Perhaps the driver and the buyer were meeting here to make a deal, then Eddie stumbled on them right when the driver brought up the keys."

"And now Eddie is either kidnapped or dead," Mr. Thomassen said.

Short-Guy nodded.

"But Johnny said he was with him," Pa said.

"Probably left just in time," Short-Guy said.

"But why go through the trouble of getting the keys up if you aren't going to take them?"

"That's the question," Short-Guy said. "There's what looks like a safety deposit key and maybe a key to a commercial lock on here. I'll need to analyze them and see if we can find out what they all go to." He looked at Pa. "Did you install that piece of equipment I gave you?"

"The one that transmits pictures over the radio waves? I'm working on it."

"So, which one of us is going to break it to Bob that Eddie probably isn't going to be found anytime soon?" Mr. Thomassen said.

"I will," Short-Guy said. "That's what my badge is for."

He turned to head over to Bob, who was finishing securing the LeSabre to the tow truck. I headed down to our truck so I could get out of there before anybody saw me.

I got back to Rudy's camp just as they was eating their snake stew. I went and sat down next to Eddie.

"Don't know how you expected me to get your car anyway," I said. "I'd have had to leave my truck up there."

"You didn't get it?" Rudy said between chews.

I told them about what had happened and Rudy stood up and tossed his bowl of stew out into the woods.

"Well, I guess we're stuck here, then, aren't we?" he said.

Eddie had a piece of snakeskin that he must have not peeled off very good sticking out of his mouth. He slurped it down.

"Wait, why are we stuck here?" he asked. "I know how to get cars out of my dad's shop. And he showed me how to hot-wire, too, so we don't need your keys."

"No, we need my keys," he said. He looked at Sora. "My keys are the most important thing."

She stood up and touched her belly. "No, not the most important thing," she said, then she grabbed me by the wrist. "Let's get back before Pa does. Or else losing some keys will be the *least* important problem Rudy has."

He didn't seem too happy with that, but I couldn't argue with her logic, so we got back into our truck and headed up to the house. And the whole way there, I was praying that Pa and them others hadn't quite made it home yet. 'Cause there's only one punishment left after being grounded, and that's getting your butt beat so bad the eggs in the fridge feel sorry for you.

We pulled in and nearly ran over a bush on my way to getting the truck right back into its own tire ruts. I just about had a heart attack when I saw that somebody was on the porch, but it turned out it was Willie, so we didn't need to call no ambulance or nothing. He was sitting on a green chair Sora had Pa get from the store. As soon as we walked up onto the porch, he got up and offered it to her. She walked on past and into the house.

"What you doing here?" I asked.

"Got done with my homework, so I came up here to talk at you," he said. "And to see if Short-Guy was going to be around anytime soon. Thought I might pick his brain about that letter. How was the Labor Day thing?"

I started to tell him, and I even got started filling him in a bit on Rudy and how he was the mysterious stranger, but then the caravan of the Three Caballeros showed up on the road coming up to our house and I had to stop before I was done.

"Look, I can't finish the story right now, but if they know I wasn't here, I'll be picking out my harp and wings, so you got to act like I was here when you got here."

"You was," he said with a grin. "We've been throwing rocks at squirrels for the last two hours."

That's why we was blood brothers.

The whole gang of them fellas came up to the porch, which I reckon meant they needed to change their name to *Banda de los Caballeros*, but then again, what do I know? When they got over to us, Willie did his part to make sure nobody got suspicious.

"He was here when I got here," he said.

Short-Guy shot me a look and I reckoned I was sunk. Thank the Good Lord that Pa was in egghead mode.

"Hey, Willie, glad you're here," he said. "Have you heard anything about SSTV?"

Willie's eyes lit up like they only did when he was fixing to get into an egghead discussion with someone.

"You mean slow-scan TV, like what Copthorne Macdonald wrote about?"

Pa nodded, and he and Willie got sucked into a weird tunnel of science that left all the rest of us feeling stupid and staying quiet.

"They've been using it on the Sputniks to send pictures down to Earth," Willie said.

"Yup," Pa said. "Though I didn't know there was dogs in space."

They both giggled at that and the rest of us smiled like we thought it was funny, even though it really wasn't.

"Well, anyway, I got one in my shed," Pa said.

"You got one?" Willie's eyes got as excited as I do when I find a good deer that's just sitting and staring away from where I'm hiding with my rifle.

"Yeah, but I'm having trouble connecting it."

"What's wrong?"

"The photomultiplier tube is disconnected and I can't figure out where it goes."

"Copthorne put it in his article, I think it's on the first page."

"I don't got that article. Do you have it?"

Willie tapped his forehead.

"Sure do. Right here."

"You want to come help me?"

"Like sodium wants to share ions with chlorine."

"Are you positive?" Pa said, and then they both started laughing all over again. The rest of us didn't even try to laugh at that one. When jokes are that brainy, it only makes you look stupid to act like you understood it.

They went off together, Pa using his cane and Willie using his crutch, and my first thought in my brain was how much Willie took after Pa. But then I remembered that Willie wasn't even related to Pa, so that didn't make no sense. Then I remembered that I wasn't related to Pa either, so maybe it did.

Short-Guy tapped me.

"Do you have anything to eat in this house?"

We went inside and I started to make them all ham sandwiches, but Carlos saw that I had some leftover pork roast in the fridge and got super-inspired, so he made them into Cuban sandwiches instead. Which really only meant that he added the roast on with the ham, buttered the bread, slapped on mustard, Swiss cheese, and pickles, and then he grilled it like a grilled cheese sandwich, only he smashed it as flat as it'd get with a spatula. Short-Guy and Mr. Thomassen acted like it was the best thing they'd ever had in their entire lives, but I'd had french-fried coon with gravy before, and that was a pretty heavy contender. Still, it was a danged good sandwich, regardless.

Sora was lying down, so we saved her a sandwich and then we all went out to the shed to see how they was coming along with the egghead project. Pa and Willie had gotten it all ready to go and was playing with it, joking about how they was sending their own faces into outer space so the Martians would know there was intelligent life on Earth.

Short-Guy handed Willie the keys to get set up for taking pictures and then he called his folks back at the CIA place to tell them he was about to send them some images that needed to be analyzed. He told them he'd dug them out of vomit, which was when Willie yelped and tossed them across the shack, and then I finally started laughing. I was the only one.

I looked outside and spied Sora, standing at the back side of the house, smoking a cigarette. I hadn't never seen her smoke before, so I reckoned this was a special occasion, and not a happy one. I left them fellas and went to see what was going on with her.

"So when you smoke," I said as I walked up behind her, "does the baby smoke too? 'Cause I can just imagine some smoke rings getting puffed in your belly."

She looked at the cigarette and dropped it on the ground. "What do you want, Johnny?"

"What's going on with you and Rudy?"

She ground the cigarette with her heel. "What makes you think there's anything going on?"

"I don't know," I said. "I ain't exactly used to the whole boy and girl thing, so I'm probably as far off base as Willie Mays before he steals second. But it sure seemed weird the way you two was hugging and such. I mean, Tommy's only barely been dead for a couple months and you're already hugging on other fellas?"

She let out a big sigh. "How old are you?" she asked.

"I'm thirteen," I said. "What's it to you?"

"I have a rule in my life," she said. "I don't take relationship criticism or advice from anyone under the age of nineteen."

"That's a Tommy quote, ain't it?"

She smiled. "Yes it is," she said. Then she looked at my face real close. "It's strange, I actually thought at first that *you* were the one Rudy is looking for."

I coughed. "What you mean?"

"Well, ever since Tommy told me about the accident—"

"He told you about that?"

"Yes," she said. "He told me how you were with your mom and your aunt in the car and it killed both of them."

Well, that was a lie.

"Okay, so what about that made you think I was who Rudy was aiming for?"

"He said your mom was there to meet someone. And then I met you and could tell you weren't related to Pa. But you're definitely related to Tommy, so the traits you two share must be from your mom. And the traits you don't must be from somebody else."

I felt a lump in my throat starting up.

"So you thought I was—"

"It doesn't matter anymore," she said, then she closed her eyes and sighed. She held her hand on her belly like she was waiting to feel something, so I reckoned it was a kick. She must have gotten it, 'cause she smiled and moved her hand away. "Rudy found him, so that's that."

The way she said what she said made me feel like there was a whole lot more trouble yet to come from whatever "that" was.

"What's he going to do with him?" I asked.

She shot me a look. "Are you friends with him?"

"Depends on the day of the week."

"Then please trust me that his plans are for the good of everyone concerned," she said. "But I'm hungry. I'm going to go feed my baby that sandwich Carlos made."

She turned and went back inside the house and left me standing there, trying my best to decide what exactly the line was I was staring at and which side of it I wanted to be on.

Then Pa called me back over to the shed and, like she said, I reckoned that was that.

CHAPTER NINE
CLOSE SHAVE

School was the worst on Tuesday. Everybody was talking about what had happened the day before. Most of the kids was talking about how mad they was about not getting no fireworks, and I couldn't blame them for that. Others was talking about how big of a drunk I was turning out to be, which I could have blamed them for, except if I'd have been them, I'd probably be saying the same thing. Funny thing was, not very many of them was talking about Eddie being missing. Not even Mr. Braswell. Of course, he was as mad as a hornet at me, so he didn't say nothing to me at all the whole day. Not even when I did the This Day in History thing. Which was a shame, 'cause it was all about how, back in 1863, the US threatened the British that they'd declare war on them if they helped out the Confederates in the Civil War. And it showed the lesson that you got to be real careful whose side you pick in things.

I probably needed to learn that lesson.

Anyway, I even had trouble keeping my mind on history or school or anything else, 'cause all I could think about was the job Rudy had given me when I'd snuck back out to talk to him the night before. He said I had to steal his keys away from Short-Guy. And, even though I protested like crazy, I couldn't argue with his logic. Out of all of us, I was probably the one that could get the closest so I could get them out of his pocket. If he was keeping them in his pocket. Which he probably wasn't, but still. It couldn't hurt to try. Or, actually, it probably could. But I was committed, so I was trying to come up with a good plan.

Around noon, the paper showed up at the school, and then there was a whole other thing for folks to get riled up about. And it was probably the worst timing for an article in newspaper history.

The article was announcing to the community that Sheriff Tatum had decided he'd be retiring and that Bob Gorman was going to be running for the position. And right next to that article was a letter to the editor from none other than Reverend Parkins himself. In it he talked about how nice Sheriff Tatum had been to the folks in the black community and how he'd helped them restore the steeple on the church and even laid the cornerstone for a new recreation center in Colony. And he ended the letter by encouraging folks to elect another sheriff of the same caliber. Which wouldn't have been that big of a head turner if not for his last sentence, which was the doozy. It said:

Elect another man of fine morals, not a man of means. We have enough Gormans in this county, but Tatums are hard to find.

Now, I happened to know for a fact that he'd written and submitted that letter on Saturday, before anyone knew that Bob was going to freak out and Eddie was going to run off or anything like that. But the paper didn't decide to run the letter until today, and it served to get folks more fired up against Reverend Parkins than to get fired up about Bob. It was like they blamed Reverend Parkins for all the things that went wrong on Labor Day. And that was a real bad thing, 'cause folks in Cullman was already against the black folk. But this got them set to fetch their guns.

Which probably meant that Mrs. Parkins would be even more set on moving away from town.

When school was all over, I rushed out the door 'cause I figured, if you're going to get shot in the face by a CIA agent, you might as well get it over with. Martha stopped me just at the sidewalk.

"Hey," she said, "I think we need to put aside our differences for a little bit. This whole newspaper thing is going to push the Parkinses out of Cullman forever."

Put our differences behind us? I wasn't sure women knew how to do that, but I reckoned I could give it the benefit of the doubt.

"Well, it's really just the timing that's all wrong, really. That

ISAIAH CAMPBELL

letter would have been better if it'd hit before Eddie ran off."

"Exactly," she said. "So what we need to do is remind people that Bob is still just as bad a guy whether his son is gone or not."

Wow, that was low, even for a girl. I shook my head and tried to sidestep her.

"Don't you walk away from me again, Johnny Cannon," she said.

"Look, it ain't right. We should just let it alone. The poor son of a gun just lost his kid. He's having enough trouble without us trying to make him look bad to people."

"It's not like Eddie died or anything," she said. "He ran away. Because Bob is a bad person. I don't see what the issue is."

That made my stomach feel like it was doing a cartwheel.

"But, ain't that dirty politics?" I asked. "I mean, dragging a fella through the mud when he's already been knocked down for the count?"

"Didn't you listen to Mr. Braswell?"

Nope.

"Sure, but I've forgotten what he said."

"He told us that Machiavelli quote, 'The end justifies the means.' So it's okay."

Well, now I really wished I'd been listening, 'cause I would have loved to have let Mr. Braswell know how wrong he was. That was something me and Mrs. Buttke used to have fun talking about in detention, about all the things folks claimed people said but they didn't really say. And that Machiavelli quote was one of her favorites.

"Machiavelli didn't say that," I said.

"Mr. Braswell said he did."

"Well, he's wrong. Mr. Braswell also said that Vice President Johnson would maybe make a pretty good president, and we all know that wouldn't be true."

She didn't say nothing to that, so I reckoned that meant I could keep on going.

"But Machiavelli did say something else, he said, 'Men judge generally more by the eye than by the hand, because it belongs to everybody to see you, to few to come in touch with you. Every one sees what you appear to be, few really know what you are, and those few dare not oppose themselves to the opinion of the many.'"

That had been Mrs. Buttke's favorite quote for me. She said it to me every time I'd start to whining about folks that was staring at my scars.

"Okay, so?" she said.

"So that means if you ain't going to put in the time to really get deep with somebody, it ain't right to claim you know all about them. Even if everybody else claims they do. This stuff between Eddie and Bob, it's a lot more complicated than making headlines and getting folks to change their votes."

She shrugged.

"So?" she said. "The important thing here is that the Parkinses are in trouble and this is the way to help them. By making Bob look bad to everybody."

"Why are you so hung up on helping the Parkinses? They'll be fine, they always are."

She looked at me in disbelief.

"I can't believe this," she said. "Our best friend is in trouble and you don't want to jump in and help?"

Well, now that made me a little mad.

"Our best friend?" I said. "*Our* best friend? He's *my* best friend, plain and simple. You've got all your best friends lined up behind you, all them girls you hang out with and talk about boys and all that nonsense, but Willie's all I got. The only other fellas that came close before him was Eddie, which ain't saying much, and my brother. And he's dead. So don't go acting like you get to lay claims on Willie as your best friend. You have your girls, but he's the only best friend I got."

She looked hurt by that.

"Glad to know where we stand with each other," she said, then she turned to storm off.

Well, at least I got her out of my way. I'd probably hate myself later, but it was effective in the moment. I started to head along to Mr. Thomassen's.

She stopped and turned back around.

"You're a pig, you know that?" she said.

She was either talking about how I smelled or how I ate, that was for sure.

"You and I, we're friends," she said as she came back over to me. "Willie and I are friends. The three of us are friends. But you don't treat me the same as him. You treat me different."

"That's 'cause you are different," I said. "I paid attention when we was studying the human body."

"See, when you say 'different' and when I say 'different,' we're meaning two different things," she said. "Because, yeah, we're different. Obviously. I'm a girl. We have different anatomy. I look at the world a little differently than you do. I have different issues you don't have."

"Exactly," I said.

"But when I say you treat me different, I'm not talking about that. I'm talking about the fact that you take all those differences we have and you decide that I'm weaker, dumber, more emotional, more manipulative, or less in touch with reality than you are. Like I'm some stupid china doll or a frail flower that you need to be delicate with and protect from the world."

It's funny, I'd actually written down once that she was like a china doll and I was her superhero. I didn't see how that was insulting.

"What's so bad about wanting to protect you and impress you? Thinking you need a little bit of special attention?"

"It's not your job," she said. "I never asked you to protect me. And to act like you and Willie aren't just as fragile and frail and in need of special care as I am is what makes you a pig," she said. Then she turned and stormed off.

I couldn't believe she just said that. I had to blink back a few tears, and worried somebody'd call me a sissy or something. Once I got myself in order, I ran on over to Mr. Thomassen's.

The door was locked when I got there, which wasn't no surprise, 'cause Mr. Thomassen had been pretty fickle about working ever since he got his money back from Cuba. He still opened up shop most days, but there wasn't no consistent time or nothing. I asked him once why he even bothered since he was rolling in cash, and he told me it was 'cause it was important to have a good work ethic so folks knew you wasn't lazy. Then I asked him why he was making so many sideburns uneven, and he told me to go on home. So I stopped asking him.

I looked in through the window and Mr. Thomassen was leaning on his counter next to his cash register, talking to Short-Guy and the other Caballeros. And also a couple other fellas I wasn't expecting to see with them. Bob Gorman and Bull Connor.

I knocked on the window and Carlos came to let me in.

"*¿Por qué están aquí?*" I asked him, which means "Why are they here?"

"*Esperan información de Short-Guy que podría ayudarles,*" he said. Which means, uh, well, I ain't exactly sure what it means. Something about Short-Guy getting information that might help them, I reckon.

I walked over to stand next to Short-Guy. He had all the keys taken off a key ring and had them lined up between the shaving cream and the jar of razors. He was looking in his notebook and reading what it said.

"So, we traced this safety deposit key to a bank in Mobile," he said. "And this is a house key. The etching here on the corner shows that it was made in a factory in Florida, and that factory only ships in-state, so it's probably to some place there."

"What about this one that says 'Do Not Duplicate'?" Bull Connor said, pointing to a square one. "Looks like a government key to me."

Short-Guy cleared his throat.

"That one's a little unsettling," he said. "It's a key to a federal building in Texas."

"Where in Texas?" Mr. Thomassen said. Short-Guy glanced at Bull and Bob.

"I'm not at liberty to say," he said.

"I don't care about that," Bob said. "Will any of these keys help me find my boy? Every minute we ain't looking is a minute he could get strung up by the Tiggers that's out in the woods, or worse."

Mr. Thomassen cleared his throat.

"I've told you not to use that language in here," he said.

"My boy is gone," Bob said. "And you read that letter the

which might finally make my life resemble normal. I had to come up with a way to stop him.

"You're going to go see your people with that face?" I asked.

He stopped and turned around. "What's that supposed to mean?" he asked.

"Well, you got five-o'clock shadow so bad I think Peter Pan's going to come and try to glue it to his face."

He blinked at me like he didn't get it.

"You know, 'cause he's hunting his shadow and all?" I asked.

He looked over at Mr. Thomassen. "Does it look bad?" he asked, and he rubbed his cheek.

Mr. Thomassen shrugged. "It could be closer," he said. Then he went over and sat down at his piano and started playing a jazzy tune. "But you'll probably be fine."

Short-Guy nodded and turned back to the door, still rubbing his cheek to feel his stubble.

"Unless you're trying to impress some lady," I said. Tommy once told me that, when in doubt, bank on the fact that fellas are always trying to impress girls. It worked, too, 'cause he stopped in his tracks and looked at me.

"How'd you know about that?" he asked.

"It's pretty obvious," I said.

He looked sheepishly at them other fellas.

"Marge is our secretary," he said. "She's so dainty and pretty.

Like a china doll." He went over and sat down in the barber's chair. "I better get cleaned up."

"Do you ever tell her she's a china doll?" I asked.

"Oh no, you can't tell them those things. Girls don't like to hear the truth about themselves," he said. Then he snapped his fingers at Mr. Thomassen. "Let's get to it."

Mr. Thomassen kept playing his piano.

"I'm sorry," Mr. Thomassen said, "but George Gershwin's work deserves to be finished once it's started."

"Fine," Short-Guy said, and he got back up. "I'll hit a barbershop on the way." He started back toward the door.

"I'll do it," I said. Couldn't believe it myself when them words came out of my mouth. Mr. Thomassen hit a sour note. Short-Guy started laughing. Even my own pa giggled a little at that.

"What?" I asked. "I've watched Mr. Thomassen do it a thousand times. And y'all know he's the best there is. Plus I'll do it for free."

"There's a difference between watching and doing," Carlos said. "I've watched the birds every day of my life, but I still haven't learned how to fly."

"That's 'cause you ain't got wings," I said. "I'm a man—"

"A boy."

"A man. And shaving comes naturally."

"You got whiskers I don't know about?" Pa said.

"Not yet, but still."

Short-Guy went back to the chair.

"Free shave is nothing to sneeze at," he said. "Besides, what's the worst you could do to me?"

I hurried over to grab the equipment before he changed his mind. I got the shaving soap and the brush and the leather strap and the razor blade. The supersharp razor blade. So sharp it could probably slice through skin and maybe even bone.

I reckon you ain't supposed to think like that when you're fixing to shave a fella.

I took it all over on a tray and got started.

"You gonna take off your jacket?" I asked.

"Nope," he said. "So don't make a mess."

I gulped so loud I figured they'd probably all heard it, and then I picked up the dish that had the shaving soap in it and used the brush to work up a pretty good lather.

"Ain't you going to do the hot towels first?" Pa said. I looked over at him, he was hiding a smile behind the newspaper. And here I thought parents was supposed to support their kids.

"Uh, yeah, let me get them."

Short-Guy grabbed my arm.

"No time for that, just shave my face," he said. "But be mindful of this mole here under my cheek." He pointed to a ripe bump under the jawline on the right side of his face. "Make it fast but not too fast."

I nodded and started slapping shaving cream on his face. I got some in his eye.

"Ow!" he hollered. He reached up to rub his eye and his sleeve got into the lather.

"Oh, here, you got some on your coat. Go ahead and take it off and we'll get it cleaned up," I said.

"No," he said. "It's fine. Just shave me."

There wasn't going to be no getting him out of that jacket, not without drastic measures. But I wasn't real sure yet of what those drastic measures was going to be.

After I got the lather all over his cheeks and such, I picked up the straight razor to start scraping his stubble off. I touched my fingertip to the edge. It was danged sharp.

I started working around his face just like I always saw Mr. Thomassen doing, scraping the lather off along with the whiskers. I got all the way done with the left side and started working on the right, and then I figured out exactly what my drastic measures was going to be.

I closed my eyes and asked the Good Lord to have mercy on me for what I was fixing to do, and then I moved the razor down right next to that mole on his jaw.

"Yeah, that's where that mole is, so—" he started.

I flicked my hand and the razor sliced right through it. It went flying over his shoulder and then it was followed by a squirting stream of his blood.

He started screaming like I didn't reckon CIA agents was supposed to and he grabbed at his face.

"Oh, dadgum," I said. "Here, let me help you." I squeezed on his cheek and directed the stream of blood so it got all over his jacket. He kept on screaming.

Mr. Thomassen jumped up from the piano and ran over, and so did Pa and Carlos.

"Here, I've got a first aid kit in the back, let's go fix you," Mr. Thomassen said.

"Better get this off of you," Pa said, and took the jacket off. He threw it over onto the counter and they all went to the back.

I jumped over and grabbed the envelope out of the pocket. I emptied them keys into my hand and put them in my pocket. I looked around for something to put back in it so he might not notice that the keys was missing, and I landed on a stack of spare blades for the razor. I shoved about four into the envelope and put it back in his pocket.

"What were you doing?" Carlos said. He'd just walked back into the room right when I was doing that.

"I was looking for health insurance," I said. "Just in case he needs surgery or something."

Carlos didn't say nothing else, but he grabbed the jacket and took it to the back with him.

My heart was racing as I left the building. Knowing that I'd just stolen from anybody would make me panic, but that I'd just robbed a CIA agent after I lopped off his favorite mole made me think I might die right there on the sidewalk. I looked over at the soda shop across the street to see if maybe Short-Guy had a band of other agents that was watching or something. The only person over there was Martha. She was sitting outside, sipping a root beer float through a straw. I reckoned she was the opposite of interested in whatever I was doing, so I hurried off toward Snake Pond. Of course, I had to find a way out there, but I reckoned I could borrow Molly Turner's bike again. After all, if you're going to be a thief, you might as well be a good one.

I went over to their house and grabbed the bike, and I'd already started riding it when I realized that Molly's brother had left his bike out there too. Oh well, it was too late to be concerned about looking manly. Them tassels was sort of fun to look at while I went, anyway.

I rode out of town and started along the road to get to Snake Pond, and every once in a while, I felt like somebody was following me. But I didn't hear no cars behind me and there weren't very many people who could keep up with me on a bicycle, so I reckoned I was just being paranoid.

It took me a good twenty minutes of riding, but I finally got over to Snake Pond and Rudy and Eddie's campground. I parked the bike and hurried through the woods.

"I got them," I said. "I got them keys for you."

Rudy was smoking a cigar and as soon as he heard that, he tossed it into the fire and ran over to me.

"All of them?" he asked. "Did you get them all?" He held out his hand and I dropped them all in there.

"One's missing," he said. "A square one."

I dug in my pocket and found the one Short-Guy had said went to a federal building. I put that one in his hand too.

"What's that to?" I asked.

"Don't worry about it." He went straight over and started packing his stuff into a backpack and was folding the tent up. He did it real fast, like it was a habit or something.

"Wow, you're good at that," I said.

"Not my first time packing on the run," he said with a smile. "Now we just need to go get the car and then we're home free. Let's get a move on, Edward."

"Edward?" I asked.

Eddie shrugged.

"New start, new name."

"You should come too, Jonathan," Rudy said. I shook my head.

"It's Johnny," I said. "There ain't no amount of trouble that'd make me go by Jonathan. Besides, I ain't got no reason to leave. And who'd watch out for Sora?"

Rudy acted a little funny when I said that, but he kept right on packing. Meanwhile, Eddie grabbed me for a great big hug.

"I ain't never had no friends like you, Johnny," he said. "You really got my back."

"I reckon so," I said, and tried to wiggle out of his grip. He smelled like wintergreen, just like Rudy, and I was beginning to think I was allergic.

They didn't say no more, but they hurried and took their things and left. I sat down by what remained of their fire and took a breather. They was about to be out of my hair, and it felt good to see them go.

A twig snapped behind me. Did they forget something? I got up to see what they needed.

But it wasn't them.

It was Martha.

And she was as mad as the devil himself. Or herself, I reckon.

My day was just getting better and better.

CHAPTER TEN
SNAKE POND

Y ou've—you've got his *back*?" Martha said. She looked like her red hair was about to ignite into flames. "You know that some people have started thinking he's been kidnapped or killed or something, right? And you know that people are taking it out on the Parkinses, right? But you're watching out for Eddie?"

"Look, it ain't exactly—"

"Don't start," she said. "How long have you known he wasn't in danger?"

"The whole time, I guess, but you got to understand, I took an oath."

She rolled her eyes.

"What you mean is that you did some bullheaded boy promise that you'd take care of him, and now your pride won't let you do the right thing because you're worried it'll make you look like less of a man."

"No," I said, though it was hard not to see how she might have been right. "I'm just doing this 'cause it's the right thing to do."

"This is the right thing to do?" she said. "Helping a juvenile delinquent is the right thing, but helping your best friend when he's in real trouble, that's totally optional?"

I groaned.

"You're painting it all wrong."

"I'm not painting anything, I'm taking a photograph," she said. "And you just don't like looking at your picture."

"You're only seeing one side of this whole thing."

She shook her head and backed away from me.

"I was wrong when I called you a pig," she said. "You're a snake."

Dang, that hurt. I started to follow after her.

"What are you doing?" she asked. "I don't want to be with you right now."

"But it ain't safe down here at Snake Pond. Let me walk you out."

"What did I tell you? I don't need you to protect me. I don't want you to protect me. I don't even want to look at you again, ever."

She kept walking toward the woods that was around Snake Pond. Away from the road.

"But you ain't going the right way."

"And if we were still friends, I would be listening to you right now." She kept on walking.

"But you're probably gonna get bit by a snake!"

"I already did." She disappeared around the trees.

Tommy once told me that there ain't no worser place to be than on the receiving end of a girl's anger, 'cause they'll say things they don't mean. Then when you don't listen and do what they really need, they'll get real mad at you for it. But if you do listen, they'll get mad at you for not doing what they really wanted in the first place. It was like the opposite of having your cake and eating it too. It was getting punched in the face and kicked in the gunnysack at the same time.

But, you know what, maybe the reason girls kept on doing stupid stuff like that was 'cause boys was always swooping in to help them. Like, maybe Lois Lane would be a little more careful up on them building ledges if Superman made her sew her own parachute first. Though I ain't so sure she knows how to sew, but still. It's the principle.

Besides, Martha'd find her way around eventually. And snakes only bit you if you was getting in on their dens. And, anyway, you'd have to be pretty dadgum stupid to get bit by a snake.

I headed to the road. If she wanted me to let her alone, then I'd let her the heck alone. That'd teach her.

I got out to where I'd put the bike and saw that the boy bike was parked next to the one with tassels. Martha must have ridden it out there. Explained a lot. One thing everyone in Cullman could agree on was that stuff always went wrong when girls tried to act like boys.

I hopped on the boy bike and left the girl one behind for her. It was my way of bringing balance back to the world. Then I headed on over to the Parkinses' house, 'cause I wanted to see if what Martha'd said was true.

When I got there, Willie and his ma and his sister was scrubbing a whole mess of busted eggs off their front porch. Yeah, I reckoned it was true.

I didn't say nothing, just grabbed a rag and started wiping up.

"Where's your pa?" I asked.

"Went into town to find Bob," Willie said. "Wants to make sure he knows he didn't mean what it seemed like he meant with that letter."

"I'll bet that's going to go real well," I said.

Mrs. Parkins threw her rag into the bucket of soapy water and went inside. Willie sighed.

"Anyway, I talked to Short-Guy about the cipher," he said.

Dang, he was still working on my mess. I wondered if that was 'cause he was a better friend than me or if focusing on my stuff helped him take his mind off his own. Either way, I reckoned I'd let him.

"What'd you figure out?" I asked.

"He told me it seems like the code needs a key to solve it. Like a code word."

"What you mean, like 'abracadabra' or something?"

"No, that wouldn't work, there's too many repeated letters."

I blinked a few times, hoping my brain's vision would clear up and I wouldn't seem so stupid. Didn't work. He could tell.

"It's like this," he said. "Whoever is writing the message and whoever is getting the message will both agree on a code word."

"Me and Tommy never agreed on no code words."

"That's beside the point. The code word has to be a word or a phrase or something that don't repeat no letters. Like 'Quick as brown' or something. So you put that down on paper, then you put the rest of the letters of the alphabet that don't fit after it. You do all that on one line, then on the next line you put the alphabet down like normal. And that's how you figure out how to substitute the letters."

I nodded like I understood, but he knew me well enough to know I didn't. He set down his rag and pulled a paper out of his pocket.

"Here, look. I did it using 'bread' as the code word." He pointed to the line on the paper.

B R E A D C F G H I J K L M N O P Q S T U V W X Y Z
A B C D E F G H I J K L M N O P Q R S T U V W X Y Z

"So, to tell somebody to run for their lives, I'd make a message that instead had these letters." He scrunched up his forehead and started figuring it out. "Um, let's see, *Q. U*, oh, that's funny, 'cause it's the same. Then *O. C—*"

He kept on going, but it was just getting more and more confusing for me.

"So you reckon 'bread' is the code word?"

"No, that ain't what I'm saying," he said. "But maybe he gave clues to the code word to you, or maybe to Sora or something."

Mrs. Parkins came back out with a fresh bucket of water.

"Why don't we go ask her?" I asked. He nodded and tossed his rag into the new bucket. It splashed up onto Mrs. Parkins.

"What do you think you're doing?" she asked.

"Got to go check on something at Johnny's," he said. "I'll be back in a bit."

Before she could start hollering at him, we hurried off as fast as we could what with him and his bum leg. Which wasn't too terribly fast, but still. She wasn't too quick on the hollering that day.

We got up there and busted into the living room 'cause we was both so eager to talk to Sora, but it turned out somebody else had gotten to her first. Mrs. Macker. They was drinking together, but not tea like you see women doing in the movies. They was both drinking bottles of beer. And Mrs. Macker didn't look too good.

"So how old is she?" Sora said.

"She's a nineteen-year-old sweater-buster, a sophomore at Auburn," Mrs. Macker said. "And he says she makes him happy." She wiped at her eyes.

Me and Willie both looked at each other. This was not the kind of talking that we was meant to hear.

"So that's why he hasn't come home," Sora said. Mrs. Macker nodded.

"He's been living in her apartment." She sobbed a little. "I don't know what I'm going to tell Martha."

I cleared my throat.

"Where is Martha, anyhow?" I asked.

Mrs. Macker wiped her eyes again and looked at me. Her face was a little puffy.

"She's supposed to be with you and Willie," she said.

"I ain't seen her at all," Willie said. "We've been working on cleaning our house."

My stomach started to feel sick. "She ran off from me a little bit ago," I said. "I was hoping she'd found her way to you."

"She's not a dog, Johnny," Mrs. Macker said, then she winced. "I'm sorry, you didn't deserve that. Where did you leave her?"

I swallowed real hard. "Snake Pond," I said.

She jumped up. "You left her there?"

"She asked me to."

She grabbed her purse and started toward the door. "I have to go get her."

Willie elbowed me in the stomach.

"We'll come with you," he said. "It'll be easier to find her if we all go."

We ran out and got in her car and she drove us on down the hill. I told her where to park, which just so happened to be where that girlie bike was still laying in the tall grass. We ran through the woods to where Rudy's campsite had been and we fanned out, me and Willie going around Snake Pond one way and Mrs. Macker going the other. Every three steps or so, we'd holler out for Martha.

"Why was she down here?" Willie said, and he kicked a beer can into the water. "Martha! Martha! What got in her head to go off on her own like this?"

"She got mad at me and stormed off," I said. "Martha! Martha!"

"Got mad at you? Martha! Martha! What was she mad about?"

"On account that she found out I was sort of helping Eddie hide out from his pa," I said. I stepped over an old car tire. "Martha!"

Willie stopped right were he was at. I thought for a second he'd seen a snake wiggle through a gas can or something.

"Wait, Eddie wasn't kidnapped or nothing? And you're *helping* him?" he asked. "I don't—"

"Now ain't exactly the time," I said.

He stared at me for a bit, then he shook his head and went on ahead of me.

We worked our way all around Snake Pond and met Mrs. Macker on the other side, but none of us had no luck.

"Maybe she found her own way home," Willie said.

"The bike is still by the road," I said. We all three got quiet. Too quiet.

"Dadgummit!" I yelled. "Why'd she have to take off like that?"

"Can't say I blame her."

Mrs. Macker was fit t

"She might have come

"We should drive down a bit an

I nodded, but I was still so frus

leave the pond just yet. I picked up a

water's edge a bit.

It didn't splash.

I walked over to where I'd thrown it, into

grass, just for the heck of it.

Just barely peeking out of the grass was a foot wea

leather oxford that was getting real waterlogged 'cause

about four inches of water around it.

My heart started pounding in my chest as I ran over and pull

the grass apart to see what it was hiding.

Dadgummit. I found Martha.

"She's here!" I yelled to Willie and Mrs. Macker. They ran to

me as fast as they could. Meanwhile, I tried to pull Martha out of

the grass. She was facedown, her hair floating in the water around

her head.

I got her to dry ground just as soon as they got to me. I rolled

her over, and then I froze. Her face was as pale as a ghost and she

wasn't moving none at all. Her eyes had started to get dark circles

around them. Her mouth was open, but she wasn't breathing for

nothing.

As soon a

"Move!"

She po

side, the

fished

breatl

time

Mrs. Macker got to me, she shoved me away.

she said.

unced down onto Martha and turned her head to the

n brought it back normal. She opened up the mouth,

ut some mud and such, pinched Martha's nose, and started

ing into Martha's mouth. She breathed real hard about four

s, then she checked Martha's neck for a pulse.

Then she cussed.

"No pulse," she said. "And her throat is swollen up." She put her hands on Martha's chest and started shoving down on it, real hard. I was afraid she was going to break her bones or something.

Then I noticed something on Martha's arms. Two little holes. Bite marks.

Snake Pond.

"I think—" I started to say, but Willie beat me to it.

"She got bit!" he said.

Mrs. Macker looked at the bite and cussed again. She tried to breathe into Martha's nose. She checked her pulse again.

"We need to get her to a hospital," I said.

She started pumping her chest again. "Of course we do, but she'll die on the way if we don't get her breathing."

All the blood and all the smarts and everything else I had inside of me felt like it died on its own, right then. I didn't know what to do, or what to say, or nothing.

"There's got to be something we can do," I said.

She tried breathing in Martha's nose again. Four big breaths, then back to pumping her chest.

"Try to find a tube, or a hose, or something, and something to pump with," she said. "Now, go!"

I didn't bother asking her what she was going to do. Instead, I took off running.

'Cause I finally had an idea.

I found it, sure enough, hanging out over in the mud, an old bicycle pump. I brought it back to her.

"Dadgummit, Johnny," Willie said. "That ain't what she—"

"That's perfect," she said. "Willie, start doing what I'm doing."

He nodded and got down and started pressing on Martha's chest. She grabbed the bicycle pump from me.

"Do you have a knife?"

Of course I did. I gave her my pocketknife. She cut off the end of the tube.

"Okay, Johnny, I need you to hold her head steady and her neck straight, got it?"

She tilted Martha's head back, opened up her mouth, and then she got set to put the tube of the bicycle pump in her mouth.

"Can you get the mud off?" I asked.

She wiped the tube off on her shirt. She put the tube in Martha's mouth while I held her head just like she'd told me.

"You might want to turn your head," she said. I didn't want to.

She closed her eyes, took a deep breath, and then she pushed that bicycle pump tube down Martha's throat. It took her a couple of tries, but she finally got it down a couple of inches, and then she began pushing on the pump handle, not a whole lot, but about halfway up and down. And then, I'll be darned, Martha's chest started moving.

"Has she got a pulse yet?" she asked.

Willie felt for it, then he shook his head.

"Not yet."

"Let's go," she said. She nodded for me to pick up Martha and we moved as fast as possible back around the pond to the truck. She kept on pumping air into Martha's lungs the whole way.

I put Martha into the backseat of her car. Mrs. Macker got in there with her, still pumping the bicycle pump.

"Willie, get back to the chest compressions," she said. He got in there with her and Martha and went back to saving her life. "Johnny, you drive."

I broke probably a billion speeding laws as I got us down the hill and into Cullman. Just in case, I opened the window and made the sound of an ambulance siren. I figured the sheriff would know what I meant.

I pulled us up right outside the hospital and the nurses came out to meet us. I reckon they could tell that it was an emergency.

"She got snake-bit," I said as I got out. They was already getting her onto one of them rolling beds. "And she fell into the water and she ain't breathing."

One of the nurses took over breaking her chest from Willie. Another tried to push Mrs. Macker out of the way. But she wasn't moving.

"Get your defibrillator ready. Now!" Mrs. Macker said. The nurse ran inside.

A doctor ran up to us and grabbed hold of the bed.

"We need to get this thing out of her so we can intubate," he said, and tried to move Mrs. Macker again. Me and Willie followed them inside. Mrs. Macker wasn't about to leave Martha's side.

"Do you have your intubation kit ready?" she asked. "Show it to me and I'll move."

"Please trust me," he said. "We know what we're doing."

"Show me."

They stared each other down for a bit, and finally he ran off and grabbed a kit that had a tube and a balloon and a couple of other things in it. Once she saw it, she let go and let him take over. He pushed Martha over to a room, and a nurse was standing with some fancy handles that had wires connected to them. They went to rip open Martha's blouse, so I turned my head.

"Clear!" one of them said. Then there was a popping sound.

"Again!" they said. Then another popping sound. "We got a pulse. Get the tube in."

I could finally breathe better. I went over to Mrs. Macker. She stood in the center of the floor, folks buzzing around her, and she had her fists clenched, her eyes glued on her daughter getting worked on in the room. As I looked at her, I got the feeling that this might have been the closest I'd ever gotten to a real live super-hero.

"You saved her," I said. "You're a real hero."

"No," she said. "I'm a mother."

As I kept on watching her, I started to realize that there wasn't much of a difference.

CHAPTER ELEVEN
WHERE THERE'S SMOKE

Willie wouldn't look at me. We was sitting outside the hospital room Martha was in. There was three wooden chairs which was being occupied by me, him, and Pa, and Willie stared straight ahead at the wall. He had been for the last twenty minutes, ever since Martha'd woke up and asked Mrs. Macker where her pa was. That's when Mrs. Macker sent us out into the hallway.

"The devil is attacking this town," Pa said. "First he got you to get drunk, then Eddie went missing, and now this."

Willie shot me a look, but I wasn't ready to start giving out the truth about all that. Pa hadn't believed me when I tried that before, why would he start now?

"Yessir," I said. "It's the devil all right. After all, that's what I was drinking, the devil's brew. It was probably a mess of goat-footed demons that took Eddie off too. And the snake, everybody knows that's the devil's favorite costume. But, don't you worry, I ain't going to let my lips be touched with his poison again."

He looked me square in the face for a good two seconds and then he cussed. That made both my and Willie's jaws drop, 'cause neither of us had ever heard Pa cuss before.

"You was telling the truth before, wasn't you?" Pa said. "'Cause you're lying now. 'Cause you think that's what I want to hear."

I glanced at Willie and he looked away again. I held my tongue. Pa cussed again.

"Then this whole thing is my fault," he said. He let out a big sigh. "I'm going to go to the prayer room. Come fetch me when they're ready to let us back in."

He walked off and left me and Willie alone.

I tried to think of something I could say that might maybe get me and him talking again. I decided to try a history fact.

"I know it ain't the sixth yet, but I'll give you a preview of tomorrow. September sixth is the day that the Pilgrims left Plymouth to head to America, and also the day that the Puritans first settled around Salem. So, really, September sixth is all about new—"

"Shut up," he said. Then, after a bit, he looked me square in the eyes. "Are you really going to let your pa think you're as innocent as a baby?"

"Well, I sort of am. I didn't do nothing to nobody."

"See, that's your problem. You don't understand that you can be just as guilty for not doing something as you can for doing something."

Right then Mrs. Macker came out of the room.

"Come on back in," she said.

We both got up and I didn't go fetch Pa yet, 'cause I knew how long he liked to pray and I'd hate to interrupt when he was having a little talk with Jesus. I wasn't so much scared of Pa smacking me for it, but if the Good Lord felt so inclined, he'd probably knock me into the next week.

Mrs. Macker went and sat next to Martha's bed and Willie went over and joined her. I couldn't make myself walk all the way into the room. I just stood there and watched as Willie grabbed hold of Martha's hand. She turned her head and looked at him and a tear sort of formed in her eye.

"So, where is Mr. Macker, anyway?" I asked. Willie and Mrs. Macker both gave me the stink eye, so I reckoned that meant the answer wasn't a good one.

The doctor knocked on the door behind us. Mrs. Macker told him to come on in.

"We got some of the lab work back already, and it seems as though she's out of the woods."

"I want to go home," Martha wheezed out.

The doctor clicked his tongue and got the sort of smile you get when a kid asks you a really stupid question.

"Oh, sweetheart, I don't think so. You have a lot of recovering to do."

"I can do that at home," she said.

Mrs. Macker looked over at the doctor. He cleared his throat so he could talk a little more stern-like.

"I'm sorry, but on this I must be emphatic," he said. "Your heart stopped beating. You had no oxygen flow to your brain. We have no idea how bad the damage really was. You need to have at least forty-eight hours of observation."

"So, she just needs observation?" Mrs. Macker said.

He winced.

"Yes, but observation by medical professionals. People who know what they're looking for."

Mrs. Macker nodded.

"You mean like someone who went to the University of Pennsylvania and specialized in cardiothoracic surgery? Would that person be medically trained enough for you?"

"Well, certainly, but where are you going to find someone like that?"

"I just need to look in the mirror."

He glanced over at the mirror like he was trying to figure out what the heck she was talking about. Even I got it before he did.

"Wait, you mean you?" he asked. She nodded. "You're a surgeon?"

"Was. But then I had my baby and my husband—" She

coughed and rubbed Martha's forehead. "Well, he asked me to give up a lot of things."

"Nevertheless, I must insist—" he said.

"Nevertheless nothing. You can't keep her here against my wishes," she said.

"I should call your husband," he said. "Get a clearer head on this."

"Go ahead and call him," she said. "And while you're at it, will you let him know I told his daughter about his girlfriend? Oh, and that I'm selling his golf clubs."

The doctor looked like she'd punched him in the nose. He threw his hands up in the air. He started to storm out, then he turned and gave Mrs. Macker the meanest look I'd ever seen a doctor give.

"I might add," he said, "it's no surprise your husband looked for a little understanding in the arms of another woman. Nobody likes a shrew."

"You might want to go check your blood pressure, Doctor," Mrs. Macker said, her fists clenched. "You're looking a little flush. And you're sounding somewhat stupid. But that could be normal for you."

He left in a huff.

There was another knock on the door. Pa came walking in, and he was joined by Carlos and Mr. Thomassen. Carlos was carrying a big vase of flowers, a gift from the Three Caballeros.

"Some flowers to brighten the room," Mr. Thomassen said.

"I'm going home," Martha said.

All them fellas looked at each other real awkwardly.

"Uh, did the doctor say it was okay?"

"Yes, I did," Mrs. Macker said.

Another couple of awkward seconds. Carlos cleared his throat.

"So, do you want these flowers in here or should we take them downstairs?"

I didn't much care what they decided on that, and I was tired of looking at everything and everyone in that room, so I went over to look out the window. Out there, on the streets of Cullman, there wasn't none of the mess that was inside that room. I sure did wish I was out there.

Then out from the shadows of one of the alleys, two people snuck across the street and ducked behind another building. Then they snuck a little farther down the street and hid again. They was doing a pretty good job of keeping out of sight from the pedestrians.

"Is that Eddie?" Willie said. I hadn't even realized he'd come over to the window with me.

The Three Caballeros hurried over to look for themselves.

"Well, I'll be, it *is* Eddie," Pa said. "But who's that with him?"

Mr. Thomassen peered real close.

"Oh my God," he said. "That's Rudy."

That was weird. How'd he know that?

ISAIAH CAMPBELL

"Rudy?" Carlos said. "You don't mean—"

"Yes. Eddie Gorman is tangled up with Rudy Trafficante."

I felt my brain exploding in my head.

"Wait, Trafficante?" I asked. "Like Santo Trafficante?"

"Yes, Rudy is his son."

Willie leaned in to whisper to me.

"So does that mean Rudy is from Florida, like ol' Trafficante?"

"I reckon," I said. Didn't see why that was important, but who knows what goes on in Willie's brain?

Eddie and Rudy got over to Bob's auto shop and they slipped inside.

"What do you think they're doing?" I asked.

"I don't know," Pa said. "But I reckon I ought to call the sheriff." He headed over to the phone. We kept on watching the empty street.

After a little bit, the street wasn't empty anymore. Instead, that brand-new Corvette peeled out of the garage, fishtailed and nearly took out Mrs. Buttke, who had just come out of the beauty parlor, and then the car zoomed away from us. Mrs. Buttke fell down on the sidewalk.

"Oh, dang, they almost killed Mrs. Buttke!" I said. And then I forgot all about it.

'Cause right then, Cullman finally got its fireworks show.

The front of Bob's shop flashed red and yellow and we heard a real loud bang, then a whole mess of smaller bangs. And whistles.

And crackles. Plus there was rockets shooting, and green and red sparks flying. It was like the *Reader's Digest* version of the Fourth of July. The explosions just kept going and going.

And then I remembered them cars that was in the shop.

"Oh, dadgum, I hope the sparks don't—"

I didn't get to finish. There was an even bigger explosion than the one before. Then another, and another. If I had to guess, I'd say each one of them cars in the shop blew up, one right after the other, like a set of dominoes. The roof of the shop flew up into the air, and then the whole thing started falling in on itself. And the buildings around the shop started falling apart and crashing down on top of it all.

And then the explosions stopped and it got quiet, which was almost more creepy and scary than the explosions. There was smoke and fire blowing in every direction, running across the sidewalk and down the street. Folks that had been walking nearby was on the ground, some of them it looked like they was knocked over, others looked like they was taking cover.

Carlos dropped the vase of flowers and it broke all over the tile floor. Mrs. Macker came running over, but she didn't seem to care one bit about them flowers.

"What happened?" she asked, then she saw the scene down on the street. "Oh my God."

The flaming smoke was gone and it was just regular black and gray soot and dust that was blowing around down there, along

ISAIAH CAMPBELL

with torn-up papers and stuff from inside the auto shop. Some of the folks that had ducked for cover got up and you could tell they was trying to get their bearings back.

Some of the other folks stayed down on the ground. It looked like they couldn't get up at all. Mrs. Buttke was one of them.

Mrs. Macker took off running out of the room. Us menfolk looked at each other and realized we probably should have done that too, so we all headed out. Willie stopped at Martha's bed, grabbed her hand, and told her we'd be back real soon. She seemed thankful for that and so I went to grab her other hand. She flinched away from me.

"Come on, let's go," Willie said. I ran out with him.

We got into the elevator and headed down to the first floor.

"Why was you holding her hand?" I asked.

He glared at me.

"After everything that's gone on, that's the only thing you can think to say?"

"You don't want to hear none of the other things I got to say."

He stared straight ahead.

"I was holding her hand 'cause she was scared and 'cause that's what a friend does. Not making her go running off at Snake Pond, or getting her bit by a water moccasin, or anything else you did."

"Hey, I didn't make her go running off from me."

He shot me a death look.

"Sure you did. When you teamed up with Eddie Gorman, you made her run away from you. You didn't leave her no other options."

I was tired of arguing about that, so I let it go.

"What about you?" I asked. "Did I make you run away too?"

He sighed.

"We're blood brothers, Johnny. That means I'm stuck with you."

I started to smile.

"That ain't meant to be a happy thing," he said. "I'm stuck with this bum leg, too. So keep in mind what sort of company you're keeping."

The elevator doors opened and we went as fast as we could out onto the street. All the doctors and nurses had already run out and was trying to help folks. Mrs. Macker, too, with her hair pulled back into a ponytail, was running around and checking on folks. She got over by Mrs. Buttke and stopped. Mrs. Buttke was clutching at her chest. Me and Willie hurried over.

"Eleanor," Mrs. Macker said. "Tell me what's wrong."

Mrs. Buttke was breathing real quick and short.

"My heart, I think—"

"Are you having a heart attack?" Mrs. Macker said.

"No, it's my pacemaker," Mrs. Buttke said. "Something's wrong."

"Johnny," Mrs. Macker said. "Go get a gurney and tell the

doctor that Mrs. Buttke needs to get into an operating room immediately."

I nodded and ran. I ran past folks that had giant pieces of glass sticking out of their shoulders and folks that was bleeding 'cause the bricks hit them. I found the doctor that had been up in Martha's room. He was over barking at the nurses to hurry up so he could stitch up a couple of fellas.

"Mrs. Buttke's over there and she's in a bad way," I said. "She said something about her pacemaker."

He didn't need nothing else to be said. He had a gurney he was sitting on, so he jumped off and pushed it through the street to where Mrs. Buttke was at.

"She says her pacemaker is malfunctioning," Mrs. Macker said. The doctor ignored her.

"What seems to be the problem, Mrs. Buttke?"

Mrs. Buttke just glared at him.

"Pacemaker," Mrs. Macker said. "She needs to go into surgery."

The doctor clicked his tongue.

"Well, let's get her into an ambulance so she can get down to Birmingham."

"Birmingham?" I hollered. Probably shouldn't have, but it was Mrs. Buttke we was talking about. "What if she don't make it to Birmingham?"

"She'll be fine," he said, and patted Mrs. Buttke on the

shoulder as they put her on a gurney. I think she almost bit his hand off. "We don't have a cardiothoracic surgeon here, so we don't have a choice."

"I told you that I am—" Mrs. Macker started.

"Were," he said. "You *were* a cardiothoracic surgeon. Now you're a mother. Maybe you should tend to your job and let me tend to mine."

Mrs. Buttke yanked on my sleeve.

"Johnny," she whispered, "hand me my cane, please."

I grabbed it up off the ground and gave it to her. She poked him right in the gut with it.

"If she's a cardiothoracic surgeon, then let her do the surgery," she said, still wheezing and gasping for breath.

"Mrs. Buttke, please, you have to trust me. You'd be much better off to go to Birmingham."

"I buttered your bottom when you had diaper rash, Percival. Don't you dare let me die because you're too stubborn to let a woman do a man's job."

They stared at each other for a spell, and then he huffed.

"Fine, if you would rather die in Cullman, be my guest." He turned and yelled at one of the nurses. "Go with them and get an OR ready!"

Mrs. Macker gave him a hug.

"Thank you, Percival," she said, trying real hard not to laugh at his name. She pushed the gurney along with some of them nurses and they went to go get Mrs. Buttke all fixed up.

Me and Willie moved on to try and help wherever else we could. Thankfully, nobody'd been close enough to the blast to get killed or nothing, so there wasn't any real messy cleanup to do. After a few minutes of helping folks walk to a gurney or get their car pushed out of another one's fender, I noticed that the Three Caballeros wasn't around.

"Where do you reckon they are?" Willie said. "You don't think they went after Eddie and that other fella or something, do you?"

"I don't rightly know," I said. "There really ain't no telling what they do. Heck, I'm about done trying to figure out what's going on with anybody anymore."

He nodded and we both kept right on helping out. After a bit, the sheriff's car pulled up and Sheriff Tatum, Pa, Carlos, and Mr. Thomassen all got out. But they wasn't in handcuffs, so I reckoned they hadn't gotten in trouble. Me and Willie went over to see what was going on.

Sheriff Tatum walked around, looking at the damage with his hands in his pockets, every once in a while patting his big belly or twisting the ends of his mustache. He'd occasionally mutter to himself about how terrible a thing it was and such. Finally he came back over to all of us.

"All right, I think I've seen enough for now. I'm going to do everything I can to find whoever did this and get them locked up."

"Ain't going to be too hard," Willie said. "We all saw Eddie and his buddy do it."

"Hmm," Sheriff Tatum said. "Blowing up his own daddy's shop. That's dirty." Then he lowered his voice. "Though, I can't say I blame him."

"Where is Bob, anyway?" Pa said. "I'd have thought he'd be burning rubber to get over and check this all out."

I looked over at the pile of burning rubble that used to be Gorman's Auto Shop and I started feeling sick over it again. Bob had lost his airfield earlier that year in the tornado, and now this. Plus his son had done run off. It might have been the worst year anyone ever had. Except for those folks that lived in Europe in 1348, when the bubonic plague broke out. Then again, it got rid of half the folks that lived back then, so if you was sort of a loner, you might have appreciated it.

"It is weird," Willie said. "My pa was trying to meet with him too. He came into town to look for him at his shop earlier."

"What's your pa drive?" Sheriff Tatum said.

"Our station wagon," Willie said. "A brown Ambassador."

"Thought I saw one while I was driving over. Parked around the corner."

I was still looking at the wreckage. Thought I saw something moving, but I wasn't too sure.

"Funny." Sheriff Tatum kept talking. "It was parked behind Bob's tow truck. Bob must not have had room in his shop to park."

"Wait, so they're around here somewhere?" Willie said.

Yeah, I definitely saw something moving. I took off running toward the rubble.

"Johnny, come back here. That ain't safe!" Pa said. I didn't listen.

I got over to the mess of metal and bricks, and it was as hot as the fires of hell over there. The flames was still burning, probably thanks to the oil and gasoline. But I was sure of what I saw.

Under a great big slab of concrete I'd seen something moving.

I got there and looked in the little opening there was, and I was met by a set of eyeballs. And a voice.

"Johnny, please get help." It was Reverend Parkins.

"Get over here!" I hollered to them other fellas. They all came running and as soon as they saw what I saw, they started pulling on the slab to move it.

"Daddy," Willie said as he got up next to me. "Try and push it off."

"Can't," Reverend Parkins said. "I can't move my hands."

The Three Caballeros was heaving as hard as they could. Carlos grabbed a piece of rebar, but then dropped it 'cause it was flaming hot. He pulled off his shirt and grabbed it again and stuck it under the slab to start prying it off.

"Are you paralyzed?" Willie said.

"No," Reverend Parkins said. "I just can't do it right now."

"Where's Bob? Was he in there too?" I asked.

"Yes, we were together," he said. "Please, get this off of me."

I started pushing on the slab myself. After a few seconds of nearly popping all our back muscles, we got it moved. Reverend Parkins's foot had been under it and it was pretty bad mangled up, plus he had pretty bad burns all over his legs and back. But not a one of us focused on those things, 'cause all of a sudden, we knew why he hadn't been able to use his hands.

He was laying on top of Bob Gorman, like he'd jumped on him to protect him from the falling slab. And he had his hand in a deep gash on Bob's throat, pushing real hard like he was trying to keep him from bleeding to death. There was a bloody piece of glass on Bob's smoldering chest, which must have been inside his neck before Reverend Parkins moved to save him.

Meanwhile, Bob, who probably would have been better off to be knocked out, was wide awake, his eyes bulging, staring at Reverend Parkins's face, his mouth gurgling but not saying nothing.

"It's going to be okay," Reverend Parkins kept whispering to him. "The Lord is our shepherd. It's going to be okay."

Mr. Thomassen jumped up.

"Get a doctor over here! Now!"

It only took a couple of seconds for Dr. Percival to get a gurney and two nurses over with him. When they saw the scene, they all froze. Reverend Parkins kept whispering a prayer to Bob.

"Move!" Mr. Thomassen said.

Dr. Percival sent a nurse to get more help and another gurney. All the while, Reverend Parkins kept on whispering the same thing over and over to Bob.

I glanced over at Willie. I could tell he was freaking out something fierce. Even though it was probably weird and wasn't what you was supposed to do with another fella, I reached over and grabbed his hand. He didn't pull it away.

When they got another gurney over, we all scrambled and started working on moving Bob onto the first of them. After we got him on, Dr. Percival moved around and worked to replace Reverend Parkins's hand with his own. Right after Reverend Parkins's blood-covered hand came out, they went to move him onto his own gurney, but Bob's hand snapped up and grabbed Reverend Parkins's wrist. He wouldn't let them move Reverend Parkins away from him.

"Somebody break his grip so we can move them," Dr. Percival said. The nurses tried, but Bob was holding on for dear life.

"We can't," one nurse said. Dr. Percival growled.

"Fine, then bring the other gurney closer so we can move them together."

They did that and got Reverend Parkins onto the other one, and Bob didn't let go of his wrist, not once. Reverend Parkins called to Willie to come closer.

"I'll stay right by you," Willie said to him.

"No, go on home and tell your ma that I'm okay," Reverend

Parkins said. "She's probably worried enough as it is, and I don't—" He coughed a whole mess of stuff up. "I don't want you seeing me like this. So go on. For me."

Willie didn't seem happy about that, but he nodded. They started to move them along and Willie was left standing there. He hollered after them to stop and he went real quick to Bob.

"You need to stay alive," he said. "It wouldn't be right for you to die after my dad acted like a SuperNegro for you."

Bob nodded a little and they hurried to get into the ER so they could save his life.

Willie went and asked Pa if he could take him home so he could do what his pa had said, and so we went and got into our truck and left all that trouble behind so Willie could be a good son. I probably needed to be taking notes, but I didn't have no notebooks with me, so I hoped I'd just remember it later.

On our way up the hill, Willie stared out the window and I figured he was real worried about his pa, so I patted him on the back, which was somehow more awkward than when we'd been holding hands. He looked at me.

"Hey, Johnny?"

"Yeah?"

"I was thinking," he said. "Mercury needs a hideout."

It took me a second to respond.

"Mercury? You mean your made-up superhero?"

"SuperNegro, and yeah," he said. "If Mercury had a hideout,

like the Batcave or something, he could have a whole mess of computers and such and probably be able to do things like figure out the cipher in that letter and all that lickety-split."

"Boy, I can't believe you're thinking of that letter at a time like this," I said.

He shrugged.

"It's easier than the alternative."

I nodded.

"On top of that, I can't believe you'd default to the Batcave for the hideout. What about the Fortress of Solitude? Superman's got Kryptonian computers in there that can do what them Batcomputers couldn't never do."

"But Mercury ain't Kryptonian," he said. "And, anyway, the Batcomputers are more realistic."

Now, normally that would have set off an hour-long argument over which was better, Superman or Batman, and we'd both get real mad at each other and dig out comics to prove our points and all that. And normally, I'd have won, but he'd claim he did, which would have started another argument. And it'd be a grand old time of fun arguing.

But a lightbulb had just went off in my head that made me not feel up to arguing. Instead, it made me feel up to mystery solving.

"'A solitary fort,'" I said. "Ain't that what the hidden message said?"

He blinked a couple of times. "Yeah," he said. "'If a solitary fort is a Scottish lake.'"

"The Fortress of Solitude," I said. "That's the solitary fort."

His eyes got wide. "Whoa, that makes sense. But what's a Scottish lake?"

Pa must have been listening. "It's a loch," he said. "Like Loch Ness."

Me and Willie both had more lightbulbs busting. "The Fortress of Solitude is the lock!" we said at almost the same time.

"What's the next part?" I asked.

"'Then what is its resident?'"

"Superman," I said. "Obviously."

"But it didn't say 'who,'" Willie said. "It said 'what.'"

"Well," Pa said, "I don't rightly know what y'all are talking about, but it would seem that if the first line is about the lock, then the second line is about the key. That's how riddles usually work out."

"Superman is the key," I said. Then I realized what that meant. "It's 'Superman'!"

"Dadgummit," Willie said. "Of course it's Superman. How come we didn't think of that before?"

"You didn't have me around," Pa said with a chuckle. "I'm real keen at riddles."

Willie leaned into my ear and whispered to me.

"Go get the letter and bring it to my house. We'll figure it out now, that's for darn sure." He looked out the window and got that glimmer in his eye. "Meanwhile, I need to get a hold of Short-Guy."

We dropped Willie off at his house and his ma was standing on the porch, watching the road real worried-like. I reckoned that wasn't going to be the best of conversations he was about to have, telling her what happened with Reverend Parkins and all. Which meant he'd be primed and ready to scat as soon as I got back. Which was fine by me.

We went up to our house and I hurried inside to grab the letter. Sora was sitting on the couch with a wet rag covering her eyes, and she was holding on to a pillow like it was a parachute.

"You all right?" I asked.

"I don't feel well at all," she said. "I think this baby's trying to kill me."

"Well, don't let it. There's already been enough folks getting rushed to the hospital today for my taste." I ran up to my room and grabbed the letter. I peeked at it for a minute to see if I could figure it out on my own, which of course I couldn't, but I still owed it to myself to try. I could hear Pa checking on Sora the same as I had, and him saying just about the same thing I did. Then he went out to his radio shack and I reckoned I was clear to run back over to Willie's.

I started out the door, but Sora stopped me.

"Did something happen with Rudy today?" she asked.

"More like Rudy happened to something," I said.

"He called me," she said. "He seemed in a panic. Insisting

that I come and meet him. Like it was life or death."

"I don't reckon you ought to," I said. Then I told her the whole story about Rudy blowing up Bob's shop, and about him being a Trafficante, and the whole shooting match. She clutched the pillow harder to her chest while I told it all. She shook her head and I almost thought she had tears in her eyes.

"I knew he hadn't changed," she said. "Once a Trafficante, always a Trafficante."

"Wait, you knew he was a Trafficante?"

She nodded. "But he swore he'd left that lifestyle behind. Trying to be a better man. Making his own name in the world. A name worth taking." She breathed out a long sigh.

I didn't really much care for that sigh. "I thought you was Tommy's girl," I said. She looked startled at that.

"I am," she said. "Rudy is just—he's like a brother to me. He's always taken care of me. And I know he's so in love with me, because he always tells me." She looked me in the eyes. "Tommy never said that to me."

He should have. But that was Tommy.

"Well, I don't reckon Rudy's as different as he claimed."

"I know," she said. "And I don't feel the same for him as he feels for me. I've just never really told him. But I need to, for both our sakes. I'll go meet him and tell him to leave without me."

She started to get up, but then she groaned a little and sat back down.

"Just leave him be," I said. "He'll get the hint. And maybe get picked up by the sheriff. That'd be a happy ending, for sure."

"I can't do that to him. Regardless of what he's done, he's always been good to me."

She tried getting up again, but groaned even louder.

"You're going to kill yourself if you try heading out there right now."

"If he gets arrested or killed before I get the chance to talk to him, I won't be able to live with myself. He's staying around for my sake. It'd be my fault."

Now I was the one that groaned. Why'd I have to be so danged addicted to doing things for other folks that wasn't helping me live my life one bit?

"I'll do it," I said. "I'll go talk to him."

She didn't seem like she believed me and started to try and get up again.

"No, really," I said. "I'll do it."

"Because you think it's safer for you to go than for me? Trust me, Rudy is a shoot-first-ask-questions-later kind of guy. If he thinks you're trying to get him in trouble—"

"He won't," I said. "He don't know I know he's a Trafficante, or that he blowed up half of Main Street. I'll just tell him I'm bringing a message from you. Besides, I'm a shoot-first kind of guy too. So I'll be fine."

She probably would have kept fighting me on it if it wasn't for the fact that she felt like a dead squirrel that had been left out for two days and then reheated in a pie pan for dinner. She told me where he was planning on meeting her, which was down by a stream just about thirty yards out our back door. Which wasn't very far at all, when you're walking it to skip rocks or something.

But, when you're headed to talk to somebody that likes to shoot before he says hello, it's the longest walk you'll ever take in your life.

And there I was without my gun.

CHAPTER TWELVE
BLOOD AND GUTS

I found them two crazy fellas right about where Sora said they'd be, but I didn't barge right in between them off the bat. Instead, I hid behind a couple of trees so I could listen in on their conversation. 'Cause, brother, was they having a conversation.

"No!" Rudy said, waving his arms around like a chicken trying to learn how to fly. "No, we can't go back into town, you idiot! They're looking for us."

"But . . . but what about them fellas we left in there?" Eddie said. "What if they didn't get out? What if we—what if they're dead?" His voice quivered a bit when he said that.

"Did I know it was going to blow?" Rudy said. "No, no I didn't. I lit my cigar for effect. It's what you do, you leave an impression so they're afraid of you. Oldest trick in the book."

"But you threw your match on them fireworks."

"Who leaves boxes of fireworks in an auto shop? If the idiot owner died, he deserved it."

Eddie got real quiet after that.

"Anyway," Rudy went on, "that Tigger was strong enough to drag him out of there. And getting hit with a tire iron won't kill you. Trust me, if I had a nickel—"

Didn't really want to hear the end of that sentence, mainly 'cause I could tell Eddie was real close to blurting out some truth that he wouldn't want Rudy to hear. So I stepped out of the trees.

"Hey there, fellas," I said.

Rudy whipped his gun out of his shoulder holster and spun around. I raised my hands in the air.

"Sora sent me," I said.

Rudy stared at me and his eye twitched a bit. Must have been a trait he got from his pa. One of many, I was beginning to believe.

"Why didn't she come?" he asked. "We have to get out of here."

"She ain't feeling up to it," I said. "She's sick as a dog."

He put his gun back in the holster.

"She's not going into labor or something, is she?"

"No, it ain't nothing like that," I said. "She just ain't feeling up to it."

He didn't seem too convinced.

"You'd tell me if she was going into labor, right?"

"Can't see any reason why I wouldn't," I said. Course I didn't tell him I couldn't see any reason why I would, either. Didn't want him pulling that gun out again.

He glanced at Eddie again, who was sitting on a log with his head in his hands.

"Okay, okay, okay," Rudy said, nodding and thinking while he talked, which never was a good idea 'cause that's how you blurt out what you got your brother for Christmas. "This is okay, she'll feel better soon. And then she'll join us."

"She said something about you going on your own. Leaving her behind."

"No!" he said. "No, I'm not going to do that. She's got to go with me. I can't—" I'll be darned if that fella didn't start crying out of his eyeballs. He wiped them tears off with his wrist. "She's all I've got anymore. She has to go with me. With us."

"I don't know what to say," I said, 'cause I really didn't.

He fumbled around in his pocket and pulled out a notebook, then he used a tiny little pencil to write something down. He ripped the paper out, folded it up, and handed it to me.

"Give this to her. Please," he said. "As soon as possible. There's not any time to lose."

I turned to run off, just glad that I didn't have no bullet holes in me. I heard Eddie sob a little and realized how ate up he must have been over his pa. I looked over at him.

"Bob's gonna be okay," I said, almost without thinking.

He shot me a look, then he glanced at Rudy, but Rudy seemed too messed up over Sora to have heard nothing I said. Eddie nodded at me and pulled himself together. And I ran off, 'cause I'd done more than I needed to as it was.

I got up to the house with that little note in hand, intending to give it to Sora and then run over to Willie's with my letter so we could finally solve the mystery. Pa stopped me before I headed inside, though.

"Sora is laying down," he said. "So don't you go bothering her none. She said she feels worse than she's ever felt before. I tried to call the doctor, but they're all busy with the folks from the explosion."

I reckoned Rudy's note would have to wait.

"Where you off to?" I asked, 'cause I saw that Mr. Thomassen was in his Cadillac, waiting in the front.

"Short-Guy contacted me," he said. "He's heading back to town. Said he lost something and asked me to meet him at Mr. Thomassen's so we could try to find it. You want to come?"

Not even if he paid me. If I knew Short-Guy, he knew exactly why he'd lost them keys and he was ready to use his fancy CIA interrogation methods to get me to squawk.

"Nah, I ain't good at finding nothing, you know that."

He chuckled and headed off, and I walked on over to the Parkinses' house.

Mrs. Parkins was on the phone, talking to somebody that was

apparently giving her the runaround at the hospital. She was asking to get connected to Reverend Parkins's doctor, and they kept setting the phone down or something. As soon as I got inside, Willie grabbed me and we went to his room. He took the letter out of my hands and started blabbering.

"Okay," he said. "Since the word 'Superman' has a lot of letters from the second half of the alphabet, we'll line up the letters in reverse order after the *N*, starting with *Z*."

I still didn't understand a bit of that, but he showed me by writing it down.

S U P E R M A N Z Y X W V T Q O L K J I H G F D C B
A B C D E F G H I J K L M N O P Q R S T U V W X Y Z

Then he wrote down the coded words under it.

JVSJN IND KQUZT

"Okay, so here we go," he said. "*J* equals *S*. *V* equals *M*. *S* equals *A*. Then there's *J* again, which is *S*."

"The first word is 'smash,'" I said, "and the second one is 'the.'"

He grinned at me.

"Good job, see, I knew you'd get it eventually," he said. "Okay, so the last word is *KQUZT*. *K* is *R*, *Q* is *O*, *U* is *B*, *Z* is *I*—"

"'Smash the Robin,'" I said. "What in the heck is that supposed to mean?"

He shrugged.

"Maybe another code, or—"

I jumped up and hollered.

"That dadgum Robin statue!" I smacked myself on the forehead. "Tommy knew I'd want to smash it anyway. He probably did this code as a last resort, just in case I didn't."

He hurried and put on his shoes.

"Let's go smash the Boy Wonder, then," he said. "And then I can tell you about something else Short-Guy and I figured out."

We went and told his ma where we was going, though I don't think she really paid no attention on account that she was still yelling at whoever she was on the phone with. Then we went and hurried as fast as we could over the hill and back to my house.

We got to my porch and we was both all set to bust in through the door, but then I remembered that Sora was bad off, so I told him we had to be as quiet as church mice. Then he reminded me about them rats we caught at his church back in July that was squealing and carousing like a couple of drunk sailors home on leave. In Texas, which is where the loudest drunks live. But I told him they was rats, and I said mice, so we was having a wasteful conversation.

I gently pushed the door open and tried my absolute hardest to keep it from creaking, which was a stupid thing to try and do, 'cause that door had creaked ever since my great-grandpa had been running booze up into Chattanooga during Prohibition. But still, we tiptoed in and we was pretty sure we was in the clear. Sora wasn't on the couch no more, so I reckoned she'd done gone up to bed.

Willie spied the Robin on the mantel and grabbed it. He turned it over and under, and then he shook it.

"Yeah, there's something in there, definitely," he said. "Dang, it's a real shame to have to break it. I mean, look at this craftsmanship, and the way they got his eyes just right."

I'd heard enough. I grabbed the statue and slammed it down on the ground in between us. Robin's head exploded like the Joker had stuffed a grenade in his ear, and I felt real good about myself. Even if there wasn't anything inside that darn statue, it was still plenty worth it.

But there was something in there.

It was a reel of tape, like what Willie used in his recorder. He bent over and picked it up.

"Will you look at that!" he said. "Look at this label, it says 'For Johnny's Ears Only.'"

"Well, my ears is itching to hear what's on it, that's for darn—"

There was a bloodcurdling scream that shot out from behind us. We both spun to see what it was. It was Sora. She hadn't gone up to her room after all, she'd only been in the kitchen.

And I reckoned she was real mad that we'd just broke the one thing she and Tommy ever bought together.

"Oh, gee, I'm sorry, Sora. But it ain't what it looks like," I said.

She screamed again. She grabbed the doorjamb around her and bent over a little bit, probably to get her breath in order for another scream to come popping out.

"Listen, if you'd just stop screaming," I said, and I went to get closer to her, thinking it might get her to quiet down a bit.

It didn't. She screamed even louder.

"Hey, look, you gave it to me, and I can do with it what I want," I said. Had more to say too, but I slipped a little when I got close to her and it made me forget what I was going to say. I looked down to see what was so slippery.

There was a puddle on the ground right underneath her.

She screamed again.

"Oh, dadgum, did you just pee yourself?" I asked. "Hey, it ain't nothing to get this worked up over, we all do it sometimes."

"No, you birdbrain!" she hollered, and her face was contorting up like a spasmodic banshee. "I'm having my baby!"

Willie dropped the tape. I just about dropped some poop into my pants. There's a lot of things they teach you in school, but what to do when a girl has just peed herself *and* she's having a baby? They must save that for senior year.

"Here," I said. "Let's get you onto the couch." Actually, I screamed it. Not so much 'cause she was still screaming herself, but 'cause that was the only volume that felt about right. "Willie, call the doctor."

Willie was already on it. He grabbed the phone and called up the doctor, but there wasn't no answer.

"They must still be messing around with folks from earlier."

She was still screaming, her whole body was tensing up, her legs was kicking at me. I tried to get away from her, but she grabbed me by the wrist and her nails started trying to draw blood.

"Call your ma, then," I yelled.

He nodded and dialed his home number.

"Dang, it's busy."

"Oh my God!" Sora hollered. "Do something!" Then she screamed again.

"Hey, do you still have that book of medical facts I gave you?" Willie said.

"Yeah, it's up in my room, keeping my desk level."

He ran up the stairs and, after a second, came back down with the book that was three times the size of the Bible, which I always thought was wrong but didn't never say it.

"Okay," he said while Sora kept on screaming, "let's see, let's see. How are babies born? Uh, page two hundred seventy-five."

"Hurry!" Sora and I screamed at the same time.

He flipped through them pages real fast and found the section.

"Okay, here goes." He cleared his throat. "When a man and a woman love each other, and they're ready to spend the rest of their lives together—"

"Dadgummit, Willie, skip to the end!"

He nodded and flipped another couple of pages.

"Um, it says to get to the doctor right away," he said.

I was just about ready to start using some cusswords I'd sworn off of, both 'cause I was afraid Sora was going to cut my wrist with her nails so bad I'd die in my own living room and also 'cause I was afraid she might join me if we didn't do something for her.

Right then, the phone rang.

Willie answered it.

"Hello, Cannon residence," he said. "Oh, hey, Ma! I was just trying to call you."

Sora screamed again and then I heard Mrs. Parkins holler into the phone.

"Yeah, she's having her baby," Willie said.

There was more hollering from Mrs. Parkins.

"Oh good, you're gonna come on up?" Willie put the phone to his chest. "It's going to be all right, my ma's going to come up. She's birthed about a hundred babies, including her own kids. We'll be fine."

Sora screamed again, but this time it was so panicked, and so loud, and so right on the edge of heaven and hell that it made all the other screaming she'd been doing seem like she was singing Christmas carols or something.

"It's happening!" she said. "It's happening, the baby is coming now!"

ISAIAH CAMPBELL

"Any chance you could hold it in for just a little longer?" Willie said. "Ma's on her way."

Another scream that made him turn just about white, which was a real feat.

Willie went back to the phone.

"Ma, she says the baby is coming right now. And she ain't going to wait, no matter how nice I ask." He listened for a bit. "Okay, I'll put him on."

He put the phone to my ear and I held it with my shoulder, 'cause my hands was occupied with getting ripped off my arms at that exact moment.

"Johnny, you're going to have to listen to me and do exactly as I say," Mrs. Parkins's voice said.

"Okay, how soon you going to get here?" I asked.

"I'm not. I'm going to talk you through this. You're going to have to deliver this baby."

I was about to protest that I didn't know nothing about birthing no babies, but I reckoned that'd get me slaughtered like a pig, so I agreed.

Now, I got to tell you. There's some things that you do in life and you talk about it forever after. You brag about the part you played and how neat it was. You always make sure you remember every single detail so you can tell your story for the rest of your life.

This wasn't one of those things.

Mrs. Parkins was in my ear, telling me what to do. To get my hands down there and grab the head, which was apparently already turning Sora inside out or something, from the looks of it, 'cause there was blood and all sorts of nasty stuff happening under her skirt. And then I had to hold on to it while she kept pushing, and that was real hard, 'cause the baby was the slipperiest thing I'd ever held in my entire life, including bullfrogs.

Sora kept screaming, and I wanted more than anything else to just pull that baby on out of her, but Mrs. Parkins kept telling me not to. So I held on to its head and waited while Sora looked at me like she hated me for not pulling on it. But Mrs. Parkins was older, so I listened to her.

The baby started turning on me, and I at first tried to hold it steady, but Mrs. Parkins told me to let it turn if it wanted to, so I did. Then Sora screamed another good one, and she kicked me right in the belly button, and the next thing I knew, I had a whole baby in my hands, from head to toe.

"Get something and start rubbing it. Get it warm and make sure it's breathing."

I pointed for Willie to hand me my work jacket off the back of the door. He handed me my church jacket instead, but I didn't reckon it was time to start splitting hairs. I used my nice coat to get the goo and disgusting jelly off that little baby, and that's when I realized what exactly it was.

"It's a girl," I said. And then, I'll be a monkey's uncle if I didn't start to cry.

Mrs. Parkins was crying on the phone, too.

"*Good job,*" she said. "*Good job, Johnny. Make sure her mouth is clear, wrap her up, and let Sora hold her baby. I'll be up there in a few minutes.*"

The little girl still had her extension cord on her tummy, but I didn't reckon I wanted to try cutting it, so I handed her over to Sora as she was. And then Sora started crying herself.

I looked over at Willie. He was blubbering like an idiot. Or like me. Either way, he was crying.

Sora kissed the little baby girl on her chest.

"What you going to name her?" Willie said.

"I don't know," she said. Then she looked at me. "What's her name?"

It took me a second to realize she was asking me to give her baby a name, and I tried hard to not freak out. Then I realized what her name was. What it ought to be.

"Tammy," I said. "If that's all right with you."

She nodded.

"Tammy Jane," she said.

Mrs. Parkins and her daughter got there right about then and started hustling and bustling, got the cord tied off and cut, and got Sora to start letting the baby feed off her and such, even after I pointed out that wasn't what Mrs. Macker would have said to do. But Mrs. Parkins told me even doctors don't know everything. And then she told me how proud she was of me. It felt real good.

"I'll tell you, you sure are lucky Johnny was here, aren't you, Sora?" she said while she wrapped the baby up in a better blanket than my suit jacket. Sora didn't say nothing. "Sora?" Mrs. Parkins said.

Sora's head dropped to the side. Mrs. Parkins handed me Tammy Jane and checked Sora's pulse.

"She's passed out," she said. She looked at the bloody mess that was Sora's skirt and my couch. "She's lost way too much blood. We need to get her to the hospital."

I jumped up.

"Okay, let's get going."

She shook her head.

"I don't have our car. Is your pa's truck here?"

I ran and got the keys.

We hurried and got Sora loaded up in the back and Mrs. Parkins made Willie and the baby get in the front. She told Willie to hold her steady for the ride.

"You want me to ride in the back with Sora?" I asked. "Keep her steady?"

"You're exhausted. You've already done a good job. Now stay here and rest. There's nothing more you can do."

I didn't like that too much, but you just don't argue with Mrs. Parkins, so I went and sat on my porch.

"You know where my tape player is, don't you?" Willie yelled out the window as she backed our truck up to take off. "Go ahead and listen to the tape. I won't mind."

They went off in a cloud of dust and left me all by myself. I reckoned he'd done forgot what he was going to tell me that he and Short-Guy figured out, but it didn't seem near as important now. It dawned on me that everybody I knew was at the hospital right then, except for the Three Caballeros, who was looking for them keys. And there I was, just watching the world go by on my porch. It was the biggest letdown I'd ever had.

After a little bit of staring down the road, I headed back inside. There was still blood and birthing mess and junk everywhere. Somebody was going to have to clean all that up. Maybe I could leave it for Sora when she got back, considering she made most of it. I went over and got the tape we'd found in the Robin, and then I headed back over to the Parkinses' house.

I popped the window open in Willie's bedroom and climbed inside. I got his tape player ready to go, loaded up that tape, and then I strapped on the headphones so I could listen.

There was some noise at first while he must have been working on figuring out how to work the recorder. And then, for the first time in six months, I heard Tommy's voice.

"Hey there, little brother. If you're listening to this—"

I clicked it off for a minute. I was probably really tired and worn out, and that's why I was crying like a girl again.

Which I didn't honestly mind. I was finally starting to realize that doing things like a girl wasn't the worst thing you could do. In fact, sometimes it was the best thing.

Finally, after a bit, I got myself put back together and got ready to hear the rest of the tape. I backed it up, flipped a switch, and started it over again. While I was listening to it, I started imagining what it must have looked like when he was recording it. Tried to imagine the room, the air he was breathing, everything. It wasn't as hard as it sounded, since I could hear some things happening in the background and such. Best as I could figure, it went something like this.

CHAPTER THIRTEEN
THE TAPE

Tommy sat in his room on the base down in Mobile. It was late, the clock in the room chimed midnight. He cussed at it, 'cause he'd always hated clocks that chimed. Especially when it was late. And especially when he was drunk. Which he was. That's why he accidentally hit the microphone with his glass that was half full of whiskey. He cussed again.

He put his feet up on the table, grabbed hold of the microphone, and held it while he took another sip of his drink. The ice clicked around in his glass, which must have worked to make him feel a little less frustrated and a little more focused. He cleared his throat and then he began.

"Well, little brother, if you're listening to this, then I reckon I'm as dead as Grandma. I also reckon this fool's mission we're sending these poor folks on failed, just like most of us think it will."

He sighed and looked around the room. He spied the Superman

action figure I'd given him just a couple weeks before. He got up and grabbed it, then he sat back down.

"I'm holding on to that Superman you gave me. Since you don't remember nothing from before Ma died, I don't reckon you remember when I gave it to you. It was the day I left you all in Guantánamo, down in Cuba. You was begging me not to go, begging me to tell why I was leaving, and I couldn't do it. I'd promised Ma I'd keep my trap shut. So instead I gave you this. Thought, somehow, it'd make it easier on you."

He coughed as the memory started making his heart hurt something fierce. He wiped at his eyes.

"When they told me about the accident, I was sitting in my room in Grandma's house, where we live now, and the first thing I asked about was this dadgum toy. I don't know why, but I wanted to know if he was with you. They told me he was, and somehow I felt better. Like you wasn't as alone as—like I hadn't abandoned you when you needed me the most."

He sighed and tossed the toy onto his bed. Superman bounced a couple of times, which made him let out a chuckle.

"Anyway, turns out, I'm doing that exact thing right now. Abandoning you when you probably need me more than ever before. And I'm sorry about that." He coughed again. "So, so sorry."

He poured himself another glass of whiskey. He took a sip and let it settle in, then he went on.

"Anyway, as I hope you've figured out by now, you aren't Pa's son. You're the son of that coward, Captain Morris. I've known that since before you were born, 'cause Ma was dating Morris in secret while Pa was in the hospital. And she let slip to me that she was pregnant when there wasn't no chance it was Pa's baby. But she promised me she'd break it off with Morris if I'd keep it secret. Which is why I ain't never told you. Out of respect for her.

"Of course, then after we was all a nice little family in Guantánamo, I found out she was still seeing that scoundrel. So I left you behind, and I'll always be sorry for it. Left you to stay with her, to look up to him, and to not have a single person around that would tell you the truth about nothing. Nobody to keep you out of trouble.

"But now, whether you know it or not, you've got trouble. 'Cause it turns out Captain Morris wasn't just a coward and a scoundrel. He was also working for the Trafficante family, one of the biggest Mafia groups in Havana. And he screwed up. He messed up on a dosage for Nell Bianca, Santo Trafficante's mistress, and she died. And Santo loved Nell more than he even loved his own wife, and he was heartbroken. Couldn't accept that it was an accident, he was convinced Morris killed her on purpose. So he swore a blood oath that he'd have revenge on Captain Morris, and even on his children.

"All that happened about a week before the accident. Though, it's probably not right to call it an accident. What happened that night, what killed Ma and nearly you, wasn't no accident. It was a hit on Captain Morris's life. But he got away. And then word got back to Trafficante that Morris had lived, and so had his son. And that's when you got tied up into this whole mess.

"You might be wondering how I know all this. Well, Nell bore one child to Santo back in '38. A son named Rudy, and he's here in Mobile working to make sure we get into Cuba so Santo can get his power back. He's also here hunting for Captain Morris, 'cause Santo heard Morris was getting involved somehow. Anyway, Rudy is bad at keeping secrets when he's sauced, so he spilled the whole story to me."

Tommy started to pour himself another drink, then he thought better of it and dropped his glass on the floor.

"Which brings us to Sora. And the biggest lie I've probably ever made you believe. See, she's been telling you and everybody else that she's pregnant with my baby. But it ain't true."

He took a deep breath and leaned into the microphone.

"She's pregnant with Captain Morris's baby."

He sat back in his chair, letting those words sink in. Then he went on.

"Turns out, he got himself a girlfriend that's twenty years younger than him. And he promised her he'd take care of her. And she promised she'd take care of his other child. You. Though, he didn't tell her your name. I reckon he wasn't ready for that yet or something. But what he did tell her was to stay close to Mobile and he'd come get her once he'd gotten you, and y'all would all move off to another country and be happy together. Him and Sora and you and your other sibling. Like a nice little family on the run.

"Same kind of promises he made Ma back in the day."

He stopped and got his glass up off the ground and poured himself another shot. He downed it and went on.

"Which is why I'm so fired up to help her. 'Cause I wish to goodness I wouldn't have run the last time he had somebody tied up over him. I wish I would have stuck around and maybe I'd have saved Ma's life. And you, too.

"Anyway, I met Sora at church a couple of Sundays ago, and she told me her whole story like she hadn't never even thought about keeping it a secret. She was already starting to second-guess Captain Morris and whether she really was in love with him. Then I told her about that price tag, 'cause I'd just heard about it from Rudy. We agreed that she had to keep quiet about it or she might not have a baby to raise.

"Now, I ain't going to lie to you. I've sort of gotten real fond of her. And I think she's real fond of me, too. More than any other girl I've ever met. Heck, maybe it's love or something. Whatever it is, I reckon that's why we came up with this plan.

"When she's just about due to have the baby, she'll head up to Cullman, and either I'll be there or I won't, but she'll be protected by you and Pa. And she'll tell folks it's my baby. And no matter what, she'll be taken care of. 'Cause nobody takes care of folks better than you do, Johnny.

"But I also know you good enough to know you'll figure things out eventually. Which is why I'm making this tape. 'Cause you'll listen to it when the time is right, and then you'll know the truth. You're the sort that always does better with the truth than with a lie.

"And, hopefully, Morris will either be in prison or dead by then. And hopefully you won't have gotten caught in his web, either. It's dadgum the most important thing in the world that nobody know you're his son, or that this baby is his either. 'Cause Santo's going to kill you if he finds out. I know that for a fact."

He breathed a little into the mike, probably trying to get his brain to move past all the alcohol it was swimming in so he could finish what he was saying.

"One thing, and I ain't even sure if it's worth mentioning, but Rudy met Sora last night at the bar. And I ain't ever seen anybody as smitten as he was over her. And they hit it off pretty good, too. She seemed to really enjoy his company. But she told him flat out, she couldn't ever be courted by someone that was a Trafficante. Then to make sure he was off her tracks, she said she was being courted by me. Which I didn't mind so much, and it seemed to ease his interest a bit. So it probably won't be nothing, but just in case."

He sighed again.

"All right, little brother, I got to ship out in the morning. I'll have Superman with me, though, so who knows. Maybe I'll live through this. Take care of yourself, okay?"

He leaned forward to flip off the tape recorder, then he grabbed the microphone again.

"I love you, Johnny."

Then he clicked it off.

"I love you too," I said as the tape went stone quiet.

I sat on Willie's bed, not sure what to do with myself. I wanted to listen to it again, hear his voice again, be with him one more time.

But I also needed to wrap my brain around what he'd said.

Sora's baby, Tammy Jane, wasn't his. Willie and Short-Guy had been right to be suspicious all along. Tommy was still just as dead as ever, and there wasn't even a piece of him I could hold on to.

Tammy Jane was Captain Morris's. Which meant somehow, Captain Morris had managed to take my brother away from me all over again. Even from the grave. That dadgum polecat.

Tammy Jane was my little sister.

Dadgum.

I reached into my pocket for a stick of gum or maybe a piece of bark or anything that was worth chewing. My fingers brushed against that note from Rudy that I hadn't given Sora, since she was too busy pushing a baby out and all that.

I opened it to read it.

Sora—

I messed up. I'm so sorry. It's in my blood, I guess. I know we said we'd take care of Morris's child and keep him from my father, but I don't think that's going to work anymore. The only chance we have of protection is to ally with my father. Which means we need to take this boy to him. I swear to you, I will live the rest of my life to make penance for this. But we need my father's hand on us now more than ever before. Or else, I may go to prison forever.

All my love,

Rudy

Well, that wasn't no good.

I'd have to think all about what Tommy'd said to me some other time, 'cause right now, I had to get back to Rudy and Eddie. 'Cause Eddie was on a fast train to the devil himself. And by that, I mean Santo Trafficante. But maybe also the devil. I hadn't never paid attention to if Eddie prayed at church or not.

I ran as fast as I could back over to where I'd left them two yahoos behind. I sure hoped they'd still be sitting there, waiting for Sora like a couple of chumps.

They was still there, but they wasn't sitting.

Rudy was on top of Eddie and he was beating the living tar out of him. Actually, it was worse than that. It looked like he was trying to kill him.

He was hitting Eddie in the face, and blood was coming from just about every place it was possible to bleed from. But Rudy didn't care. He just kept on going.

"Hey, stop!" I said.

Rudy jumped up and yelled back at me. "He's not Morris's son!"

Oh good, maybe the problem was solved on its own. I looked over at Eddie. He was crying and trying to cover his face, but it looked like his arm was pulled out of its socket or something. So, maybe only part of the problems was solved.

"Okay? So what?" I asked.

"So what? Do you have any idea what that does to my plan?"

I tried to tell Eddie telepathically to crawl off and get away, but he seemed too busy having a panic attack to do any of that. I tried to think of a way to distract Rudy.

"It don't matter right now," I said. "Sora had her baby. A girl."

Rudy's whole face changed. He looked both happy and surprised and sad and scared all at once.

"Is she okay?" he asked.

"Yeah, she was borned all right and she's breathing and all."

"No, not the stupid baby," he said. I got a little mad at that, but I let it go. "Sora, is she okay?"

"No, she ain't. She had to get taken to the hospital."

"Oh my God," he said. "Oh my God, oh my God."

"Will you shut up, you idiot?" I said. Something about hearing Tommy's voice had reminded me what it meant to have a few pounds of courage strapped onto your hip. "This ain't about you, and fact is, it don't concern you. She wanted you to get out of town and leave her be. So maybe that's what you ought to do."

"No, no, she needs me."

"Like a heart attack," I said. "She's fine and dandy without you or anybody else. She barely even needs me and Pa. Heck, the only reason I had to deliver her baby in my living room was probably 'cause she couldn't reach to catch it coming out herself."

"No, you don't understand—"

"What? The price tag?" I asked. He looked shocked. "Yeah, I know that baby I delivered was Captain Morris's, and so she inherited a price tag that your pa says will only be paid in blood. I know all about that, and I ain't scared one bit. Let him come try and take Tammy Jane away. I'm a crack shot and he's got a big head. This is Alabama, so there ain't no way I'd get in trouble over it."

He stammered a bit.

"The baby is Captain Morris's?" he asked.

I cussed inside my head.

"You didn't know that?" I asked. "Then what was you so all-fired concerned about protecting Sora for?"

"She's like a china doll," he said. "And I'm her hero."

Oh, for crying out loud.

"Look, just get in your dadgum car and get out of Cullman. Leave poor Eddie be, and we'll pretend you never existed. All of our lives will be better for it."

His face was pale as a sheet, but he nodded.

"Okay, okay, I'll go," he said. "But you don't understand what this will do to her. She loves me."

"No she don't. Not like how you want her to. She told me herself. But I'll tell you who she does love. She loves her baby. She loves that little Tammy Jane enough to die a thousand times for her. And there ain't no way she'd ever do that for you."

He looked real hurt by that, and he mumbled something I couldn't understand, then he took off into the woods. A few seconds later I heard that Corvette engine start up and he went roaring down the road. And I breathed a sigh of relief.

We was finally out of the bull's-eye.

I hurried and helped Eddie sit up. Then I real fast cracked his shoulder back into its socket before he knew I was going to, 'cause that's the best way to do something like that. He screamed something fierce.

"You okay?" I asked.

He nodded.

"So that baby is the Morris kid he's looking for?" he asked.

"No, she ain't. She's just a Morris kid, but there ain't nobody looking for her."

He groaned as he got up. "Well, wherever that Morris kid is, I sure hope he's never found."

"Yeah," I said. "Me too."

He started working on wiping all the blood off his face with his hankie and I was worried he was going to start talking about Morris again, so I decided to change the subject.

"Hey, you reckon we ought to head into the hospital?"

"No, I'm fine," he said. "I been beat worse than that for looking at *Playboy*s."

"No, not for you. We got a whole mess of folks there that it'd probably be good for us to go check on. Martha. Mrs. Buttke. Your pa. Sora. And of course my new baby sister, Tammy Jane."

He grinned at that.

"You mean you want me to meet your family?" he asked. "Does that make us friends still?"

"Something like that, I reckon," I said. "Come on, let's go."

We started walking down the road, making some jokes about life and such and the mess we'd been getting into. After a bit, a farm truck came along and offered to give us a ride. We was real grateful for it, even though we did have to ride in the back with his dogs. They wasn't bad company, and we made it all the way to the hospital without no problems.

When we got to the hospital, though, the problems started right back up again.

To say the place was chaotic would be like saying a tornado was a strong breeze. There wasn't a single person that didn't look like they was a chicken trying to find its head on the other side of the chopping block. The Three Caballeros was all there, but they was so busy yelling and shouting and asking questions and speaking all at once, there wasn't no telling what had happened. The sheriff was there too, but he looked as shocked and scared as everybody else. Short-Guy was there, and he at least seemed like he knew what he was doing. He was writing in his notebook. I thought about asking if he'd found them keys, but it was pretty obvious he wasn't up for no questions.

Me and Eddie hurried inside and I finally found somebody that looked like she might be open to talking. Her mouth was open, anyway, and she was staring outside.

"What's going on?" I asked her.

"A man. With a gun. A man with a gun came in and—oh God."

I wasn't liking where this was going at all.

"What you mean? Everybody in Cullman's got a gun. What happened?"

"He came in, the man with the gun, and he pointed it at all of us, and he demanded to know where—" She started sobbing. "Where the babies are."

Oh no.

"What'd he do?"

"He went up there and—and he took her. The baby. He took little Tammy Jane Cannon, the newest newborn, and he drove away with his gun pointed at her little head."

And all of a sudden, I done forgot how to breathe.

CHAPTER FOURTEEN
TUNNEL VISION

Me and Willie was sitting in the backseat of Short-Guy's car, zooming down the country roads on the way from Cullman to Birmingham. The Three Caballeros were off on a different route, and Short-Guy had already contacted the state troopers to set up roadblocks on the highways. The sun was starting to set, and I sure didn't want it to be dark while we was hunting Rudy. Besides, I'd come clean about taking them keys, and I had a feeling Short-Guy was aiming to pistol-whip me later. He was just too busy at the moment.

We was heading to Birmingham 'cause he'd heard from Marge in his office, and she'd told him that they'd tracked down the warehouse in Birmingham the key went to. Turns out it had been bought by Santo Trafficante himself in June, or rather, it was bought by his representative, Rudy. It had been Rudy's job to go buy these warehouses at different spots around the country, but they was all left abandoned. Some loose-lipped fellas that Short-Guy knew pretty well told him that them warehouses was meant for one purpose. Finally having revenge on those pesky Morrises, whenever they'd finally turn up.

Which meant that's probably where Rudy was taking Tammy Jane. Or, at least, that's where he was headed. We was going to catch him before he got there. I hoped.

"You know, Bob hasn't let go of my pa's hand one time, the whole time he's been in the hospital," Willie said. "Even when Eddie went in there, I heard one of them nurses say he kept on holding on. Ain't that something?"

Dadgum Willie. Always trying to find something to take our minds off of things.

"Yeah, it's swell," I said.

He looked out the window, like he was trying to think.

"Hey, did you see that slick stranger that was waiting in the lobby? That was Mrs. Buttke's son. Flew down from Detroit," he said. "Must be nice to have that kind of money. Of course, he's apparently the chief of surgery at Henry Ford Hospital, so I reckon he's got money to spare."

"That's great," I said.

He looked down for a second. "Hey, I talked to Martha for a bit. She's warming up to you again, I think."

"Look, Willie—"

"So, I'm thinking we can get Operation Happy Ending going again."

"Willie—"

"In fact, I'm already coming up with a humdinger for you."

"Willie!" I said. "Shut up."

He looked like I slapped him, but he kept quiet. For about five seconds. Then he spied something in the floorboard. A manila envelope.

"Is that it?" he asked. Short-Guy nodded.

"Marge is a miracle worker," he said. "Even I can't believe how fast she got it."

I was wondering what they was talking about, but I wasn't all that interested in asking about it, so I went back to watching the road in front of us. We was coming up onto a fork.

"Which way you going to go?" I asked.

Short-Guy looked at the seat next to him. "Let me find this on my map."

"You don't got to, I can tell you where both ways head," I said. "To the left you'll go back toward the highway, which is the smart way to go if you're aiming for Birmingham. To the right will take you down to Flood Creek, which ain't the way anybody'd want to go, 'cause it's prone to doing what it's named for, especially this time of year."

"It floods?" he asked.

"Yup, the whole road goes underwater about five miles from here."
He headed to the right.

"Wait, what you doing that for?" I asked.

"If he goes to the highway from here, the troopers will get him. But that Corvette trying to drive through water? If he went that way, he's ours for the taking."

The road was gravel and dirt, and he was driving so fast the rocks was pelting the bottom of his car and making it real loud inside. Which was fine by me, 'cause I reckoned that meant Willie wouldn't try to say nothing else. Of course I was wrong. It just meant he was going to yell.

"It's going to be okay, you know," he said, real loud. "It's like you was saying before about the Pilgrims and September sixth. Tomorrow's a day of new beginnings. When the sun comes back up, it'll be a new start, and you'll have your baby sister back home, and it's all going to be okay."

"I ain't so sure about that," I said. "You know what happened on September sixth, 1901? Leon Czolgosz shot President William McKinley in Buffalo. Assassinated him. So, sometimes September sixth is a day for terrible endings."

"Well, it's also John Dalton's birthday," he said. "The father of atomic theory. And you know what he did?"

"Willie," Short-Guy said. "Shut up."

He put on the brakes right before we went around a turn in the road, and he pointed on the other side of the trees.

Just through the leaves we could see a cherry-red Corvette. And a dadgum kidnapper that was trying to push it through two feet of water.

Short-Guy turned off the car, dug under the seat next to him, and pulled out a walkie-talkie. He handed it to Willie.

"Radio the others and tell them where we are."

Short-Guy pulled out his gun, checked to see that it was fully loaded, and quietly opened up his door.

I didn't figure I'd be staying behind, so I opened mine, too.

He shot me a look, but since he was trying to be quiet, he didn't say nothing. He pointed for me to get back in the car.

I shook my head. And he knew I wouldn't budge without a tongue lashing, which he couldn't give right then. So he pointed for me to get right behind him.

Willie started whispering into the walkie-talkie, telling whoever was listening that we was at Flood Creek and that they needed to get their behinds over there as fast as possible, speed limits be darned.

I got in behind Short-Guy and we started sneaking along toward them trees, which would be a real good place to stake out if we was hunting deer. We crept along, crouched down like we was ducking under a low hanging branch or something. As we got closer, I could hear Rudy cussing up a storm while Tammy Jane did her own baby-cussing, squalling in the seat of that car.

Short-Guy didn't notice it, saw some turkey feathers peekin headed for.

But I didn't notice it in time.

Short-Guy bumped right into tha went nuts and started gobbling and tu us. Short-Guy grabbed me and pulled r on the ground. The turkey went runnin place to have a nap.

Rudy stopped cussing. Tammy Jane didn't

After a few seconds, Short-Guy peeked over breathed a sigh, held his finger up to his lips, an up again. So I got up right behind him.

Rudy was standing with his back to us, still faci he wasn't pushing it no more. He was just standing t

Then I noticed his shoulder holster was empty.

Short-Guy took another step.

Rudy spun and fired.

Short-Guy dropped back to the ground, so I dropped rig to him.

Rudy shot another couple of times, hitting the trees nex us and sending chips of bark flying all over us. Then he stoppe I rolled over behind a tree and peeked to see what he was doing.

He'd gone and picked up Tammy Jane, and he'd started running on down the road.

back over to Short-Guy.

to get going. He's on foot, we can catch him easy."

groaning something fierce. I looked down at his gut.

lutching his side, but blood was already dripping from

rtips.

ve a kit in the car," he said. "Go get it."

didn't have to tell me twice. I jumped up and ran back to

. Willie was sitting with his back to the front seat, which

ctually a pretty smart thing to do since there'd been bullets

g and such.

I already told them we was in a shooting match over here. They

they're on their way."

I nodded and reached under the seat. There was a second radio

d a first aid kit.

"Short-Guy was hit," I said. "Bad. C'mon."

I didn't have to tell him twice, either. He got up and hurried with me. We got over to Short-Guy and he started telling us what to do, which bandages to get out, and all that stuff.

"Hey, remember when I shot you?" Willie said.

"Shut up, for the love of God," Short-Guy said.

Willie got in there with all that mess and started trying to stop the bleeding. I probably should have helped, but I only had one thing on my mind.

I picked up Short-Guy's gun, put it in the back of my pants, and grabbed the second radio.

"What are you doing?" Short-Guy said.

"Going after him."

"No!" he said. "You will not do that, do you understand me?"

"He's going to get away," I said. "And then Tammy Jane'll—" I couldn't finish that sentence.

"We already have men at the warehouse. At all the warehouses. We'll catch him."

"But what if he throws her down? What if she slips out of his arm? It's going to be dark soon, and then we'd never find her." I shook my head. "Nope, sorry, I'm going after him."

"He's had too good of a head start, and there's no way he'll stick to the road."

"I'm fast. And there ain't nobody that knows these woods like me. It's just like tracking a bobcat. Easy as pie. Plus I'll have this radio, so I can let y'all know where we're at and such."

He was probably about to say something else, but Willie stuck him with one of the suture needles and distracted him. I thought it was an accident at first, but then Willie shot me our blood brother look, and I knew he'd just opened the door for me.

I took off running.

Short-Guy started shouting, but I ain't never been too good at listening, especially when the folks I love are bad off.

I went down the road, the same way I'd seen Rudy go, and once I'd gone a little ways, I stopped. 'Cause that's what you do when you're tracking something, you have to stop and look around.

Rudy wasn't going to stick to the road, that was pretty clear. But he was in a hurry, which meant he wasn't going to be aiming to trail-blaze either. I spied a path off to the right, which was where I'd go if I was running from the law. So that's where I went.

There was some freshly broke sticks and dirt scuffs over there, about the size as might be made by a man, and I reckoned I was going the right way. Of course, if he was an animal, there'd be some poop nuggets to confirm, but that didn't seem likely in this case. Not impossible, but not likely.

I followed that path, checking for broken branches and other signs that I was still hot on him. I kept going along, and the path turned deeper into the woods. The branches was getting broken more often, which meant he was starting to panic. Which wasn't good, 'cause panicked people holding babies was a pretty bad combination.

I came to a clearing that you could just as easily head off to the left or to the right. The real bad news was, there wasn't no clear signs to show where he went.

But that's where the woods was able to help me.

See, the funny thing about nature is that it likes to keep a good balance in the way things are happening. Especially noise. If you're as quiet as can be, the forest can be as loud as a hi-fi, blasting nature noises all around you. But if you're busting through trees, carrying a squealing baby? Well, then nature decides to shut itself up.

I closed my eyes and listened. To my right, the birds was chirping good night to each other, the bugs was humming as they got ready for the moths to wake up, and there was even some squirrels scurrying around to find them some last-minute nuts. To my left, it was stone-cold silent.

I went left.

After a little bit that way, I caught up to a footpath that had been set up, and from the looks of the mud prints, Rudy'd decided to follow it off to the south. As I kept going, I started hearing the faint sound of Tammy Jane's cry.

I started running along the path.

The path led along to a footbridge, which I could see coming up ahead. The footbridge went over a railroad track.

And, standing right in the middle of that footbridge was Rudy, still holding Tammy Jane. And also still holding his gun.

I dropped and hid behind a rock. I figured I'd give him a few seconds to cross the bridge, then I'd radio Short-Guy with where I was. Wherever it was that I was.

I peeked out again. Rudy hadn't moved.

What in tarnation was he waiting on?

Then I heard it. The train was coming.

But there was no way he was that crazy, was there?

He climbed up onto the railing, still holding the baby.

Yup, he was that crazy.

I jumped up.

"Hey! Get down from there!"

He real quick turned that pistol and fired a shot. I ducked back behind the rock. The bullet knocked some pieces off the top and they showered down on me.

The train was getting closer. About to come around the bend and go under the bridge. I reached behind me and grabbed that gun. Then I pushed the button on the walkie-talkie.

"He's fixing to jump on the train," I said. "I ain't exactly sure where it's going, though it's headed south. Maybe to Birmingham, or something. Anyway." I took a deep breath. "I'm going to try and stop him."

I turned the walkie-talkie off so they couldn't try to tell me nothing, tossed it to the side, and jumped back up. I aimed that gun right for his head. Wasn't really sure what I was fixing to do, but I knew I had to do something.

The train arrived and the engine went under the bridge.

Rudy looked at me, but he didn't fire at me.

I started running, gun still aimed at him.

"I'm a darn good shot, Rudy," I hollered.

There was several cars on that train. The first ones passed underneath.

I got to the bridge.

"Give her to me. Then I'll let you run off as far as you want," I said. "Just give me the baby."

He closed his eyes, the way you do when you're preparing yourself for something reckless.

"Don't you do it!" I yelled. "Don't you dare!"

He dropped off the bridge, clutching Tammy Jane to his chest.

I tried to catch him, tried to run over and grab him by his hair or something, but I wasn't fast enough.

My heart wasn't beating at all as I got to where he'd been and looked over the edge. He had rolled over in the air and landed on top of the train, on his back. He'd slid a bit, but he'd caught his foot on a railing that kept him on top of the train car. Still holding Tammy Jane. And still holding his gun.

He was getting away. He even had the smuggest smile I'd ever seen on a fella that probably had broken a rib or two on landing. I imagined he figured he was another one of them great mobsters that never got caught by the police.

But I wasn't the police. I was a pissed-off big brother from Alabama. We don't give up nearly that easily.

I took three steps back from the edge, said a prayer that I reckoned might be my last, and dove over the side of that bridge.

Now, I don't know nothing about science or physics or anything like that, so I can't exactly tell you what happens when a body that's going one speed in one direction comes in contact with a train that's going about fifty times that speed in a different direction. All I can tell you is, when that happens, the little fella gets hurt. Oh, and it's dadgum hard to stay on top of the train.

I slid and rolled along, which spread all that pain on impact to every single muscle and bone in my body, and I almost went sailing off the back end of the train. But my hand, right before I went off, found a chain that was spread tight across the top, and I grabbed hold of it. Nearly jerked my arm out of its socket as I got myself adjusted from hitting a train to riding one.

After a bit, I stood up. I reckoned it was the hands of angels that helped me keep holding on to Short-Guy's gun, so I held it out in front of me and aimed it at Rudy. He was standing too, with his gun aimed at me. He was on the car in front of me, and he was walking my way. Still holding Tammy Jane in his arm.

If it was good for the goose it was good for the gander, so I started walking toward him.

He fired and his bullet bounced off the metal of the train. Either he was the worst shot ever, or he wasn't actually trying to kill me.

Of course, right in that moment, the feeling wasn't mutual. But I wasn't going to shoot him as long as he had my sister.

He came to the edge that separated the car he was on from the one I was on.

"It doesn't have to be like this, Johnny."

I spit at him, but the wind caught it and it hit me in the eye. Took me a second to recover.

"Give me my sister."

"I'm not a monster," he said. "I'm just—wait. Did you say your *sister*?"

I wasn't in the mood for playing no games, so I went ahead and spilled it.

"Yeah, you stupid idiot. I'm Captain Morris's son. Which makes her my sister." I sort of leaned forward a bit, to try and look more menacing. "So, give her to me."

He took a step away from me, which wasn't the right direction one bit, and I was about to get up the courage to jump over to the next car, but then we hit a bump. And if you think it's hard to hold steady when a train is moving, you ought to try doing it when it's got the shakes.

I tried to stay upright, but the shaking from the bump knocked me off to the side and I was just about ready to fall off the edge. I crouched down to get my balance back and grabbed hold of the bar that was at the edge of the car. When I did, Short-Guy's gun went flying. There went my upper hand.

I tried to stand back up, but we hit another bump and I had to fall down on my belly. Which wasn't the best idea I ever had, 'cause now I was slipping all over the place. And my hands was starting to slip off the bar that was holding me on.

I looked up at Rudy. He was crouched down, holding steady onto the bar on his side. Tammy Jane was still in his arm, but his gun was gone. He must have dropped it.

My pinky came off the bar. Then the next finger.

Rudy watched me for a bit, then he stood up and jumped into the air. He landed right next to me and he grabbed my hand. With his help, I got back to my feet.

"Why didn't you tell me?" he asked.

I looked at Tammy Jane's face. She wasn't crying no more. She was staring at me. In spite of everything, I smiled at her. It's against the law to frown at a baby. Or at least it should be.

"'Cause I didn't want to get taken to your pa," I said. "Didn't want to get killed. But I sure ain't going to let you give him that baby. He can kill me instead."

We hit another bump, but he grabbed me and steadied me. He had his foot wedged under the bar so he wouldn't slip. That was pretty smart.

"I'm not going to let him kill her," he said. "Like I said, I'm not a monster."

"Well, I ain't so sure if you've heard or not, but your pa is aiming to hold the Morris heart in his hand and all that. And, I ain't good at biology or nothing, but I'm pretty sure you can't live through that."

"My father will listen to me."

"Really? 'Cause you been sort of acting like he won't."

"I was angry. But he's a reasonable man, and he wouldn't do something like that to a baby. I'll explain things to him, and he'll understand."

The wind was rushing past us, nearly knocking me off my feet, but what had me so uneasy wasn't that. It was the fact that I was sure he was wrong.

"He wouldn't do something like that to a baby?" I said. "Then can you explain why he did that to me back when I was just barely past being one? He ordered the accident to happen, the one that killed my ma and made me lose half my brain. So I ain't so sure he's as reasonable as you think."

He looked up ahead of us on the track.

"We'll find out soon enough," he said. "See that tunnel?"

I did. It was a real tight tunnel into the side of the hill, just barely big enough for the train to fit through. Even with the sun barely peeking out over the top of it, I recognized it. It was the one I'd seen from Nicole's Diner.

"When we get to the other side of that tunnel, the train will slow down because it's entering the city, and we'll jump off. We'll meet my father, and if you want, I'll keep your secret. And I'll convince him to let me and Sora take care of this baby. You'll see."

I wasn't feeling like arguing with him. Mainly 'cause I was staring at where we was headed.

"That tunnel? It's going to be a tight fit with us up here," I said.

He pointed to a ladder that went down into the gap between the cars.

"We'll climb down there. I've already planned this whole thing out."

The engine of the train was starting to go into the tunnel, which meant we really needed to get down. He motioned for me to go ahead and start down the ladder, so I moved as fast as I felt comfortable and got my feet onto the top rung. It started getting a lot easier once my bottom half was out of the wind. I made my way down to safety.

We hit another bump. Which wasn't so bad for me this time, since I was on the ladder. But it was real bad for Rudy.

He dropped Tammy Jane.

It was like I was watching it all happen at half speed. She slipped out of his arms and fell right over the ladder. As she came past me, I put both my arms out and grabbed her right out of the air. Which was great, except that it meant I wasn't holding on.

Next thing I knew, I'd done fallen off the ladder and was headed straight for the ground below and the sharp edges of them train wheels.

Rudy's hand grabbed my arm. He was straining to hold on to me without slipping off himself. Probably had his whole foot under that bar up there.

"Get back on the ladder!" he said.

I looked up ahead. The first couple of cars were through the tunnel and we was coming up lickety-split.

I tried to grab the ladder, but kept missing. Plus I was trying real hard to hold on to Tammy Jane, which I wasn't nearly as skilled at as he'd been.

The tunnel was only four cars ahead.

I finally kicked my feet out and got my legs over the rung of the ladder, then I was able to loop my arm through. It wasn't pretty, but I was secure.

"Get down!" I yelled.

He nodded and started to move. But he couldn't.

"My foot is stuck under the bar," he said.

I looked ahead. The tunnel was only two cars away.

"Pull it out!" I said.

He tried a couple of times, then he stopped. He looked ahead of us. The tunnel was just at the end of the car in front of us.

"So, this is how I pay for the sins of my father," he said, then he closed his eyes. "Tell Sora I—"

We went through the tunnel.

Me and Tammy Jane and the train went through the tunnel.

But not Rudy.

Rudy went to heaven.

I had my eyes closed, so I didn't see what happened, but that didn't make it any less horrible. Didn't make me cry any less.

It might have been the worst thing I'd ever gone through in my entire life.

When the train got through the tunnel, it got a signal or something to stop in the tracks, and we screeched to nothing.

Once we stopped, I climbed on down from the ladder and got back onto solid ground. I looked at my baby sister again.

She smiled at me. Either that or she had gas, but right then I needed a smile. So that's what it was.

I started walking toward the engine, and that's when I saw that there was a dozen state troopers all coming down from the road. And so was the Three Caballeros.

Pa got to me first, and he hugged me so hard I thought I

might pop. Which was exactly what I needed right then.

After a bit, I realized we might have been making Tammy Jane uncomfortable, mainly 'cause she was crying, so I pulled away and handed her to him.

"Rudy's back there," I said. "He's—" I couldn't say it. It made me gag. I didn't throw up, though, but I came real close.

Mr. Thomassen put his arm around me.

"It's okay," he said. "It's going to be okay."

Once they was sure I wasn't aiming to die or nothing, he and Carlos went to go see if they could find the remains of Rudy and maybe get them keys Short-Guy needed, 'cause they was real focused like that. Pa stayed with me as the state troopers asked a billion questions. An ambulance came along eventually, carrying Short-Guy and Willie. Apparently Short-Guy had threatened to arrest them all if they took him to a hospital instead of to where we was, which I was grateful for, 'cause that meant Willie was there for me to talk to. And to do what he did best, take my mind off of things.

When we finally could, he and I went off on our own away from all the commotion, just up the hill a little ways. We stood there in the dark, with the stars over our heads, and we didn't say nothing. Just let nature remind us that we was still alive.

"Hey, look at that," he said. "The diner is still open. Bit late, ain't it?"

I looked at where he was pointing, and sure enough, Nicole's Diner still had their lights on. But there was only one car in the

"Oh, I do thank the Good Lord for that," Willie said. "But I ain't lying. Maybe I wish I was, but I ain't." Willie opened the envelope he was carrying and pulled out a great big piece of paper.

It was a birth certificate.

He slid it over in front of Mr. Trafficante. On the top it said "Panama City Hospital." Under that it had the baby's name, Rudy Trafficante. And then it had the parents' names and, sure enough, right there where it asked for the father, it said what Willie'd claimed.

It said "Richard Morris."

Mr. Trafficante stared at that for a bit, then he shot his eyes back up at Willie.

"How did you get this?"

"Getting things is sort of what I do," Willie said. "Me and Johnny was given the address of that there hospital, so I called them up and they was happy to oblige."

"The city in the letter?" I asked him. "So it *was* another code. Dadgum." That sort of put the brakes on what I was going to say. I reckoned telling Santo that I was Morris's son would probably be anticlimactic now.

Santo slammed the table with his fists. Yeah, I should just keep my mouth shut.

"You smug little punk," he said. "Did you come here to hurt me? Do you have any idea who I am?"

Willie shifted in his seat real awkward-like and reached into his pocket for a second. Couldn't be sure, but I thought I heard a click or something.

"I got some kind of an idea," Willie said. "You own buildings, right?"

Santo actually started laughing at that, but not in a happy kind of way.

"Sure, kid. Sure."

Willie picked up the envelope again.

"That's what these say, at least," he said. He pulled out three more big papers. At the top of each one was a photo of a key. Specifically, it was them keys that Rudy'd had. Under each one was another photo showing an address. And under that was a list of dates.

"See, here's some buildings you own. And those dates at the bottom, those are times them buildings have been the target of FBI raids. You know, for all them drugs and prostitutes your fellas keep pushing."

Santo picked up one of the pictures, glanced at it, then put it back down.

"I don't own any of these."

"I guess technically that's true," Willie said. "But you do own a company in Texas, don't you? East Texas Financial, or something like that?"

Willie pulled out another paper. This one had a fella's picture on it.

"This fella here is on the payroll, right? He also works in a federal building at night. Which is where he makes sure the records of all them building purchases gets swept under the rug."

Now Santo started looking worried. He picked up that photo of the fella.

Willie wasn't done talking.

"Too bad that fella loaned Rudy his keys a little while ago, huh? And too bad each key's got an ID code on it so they know whose it is."

Santo crumpled the photo up and threw it across the room. He stood up and towered over Willie.

Now Willie started looking a little worried.

"Who are you working for?" Santo said. "Who's trying to do me in?"

The fella with the sandwich came running out of the kitchen again, followed by another fella about the same size and probably about as intelligent.

"Everything all right, boss?" the one fella said.

Santo grabbed Willie and pulled him up from his seat. "This kid's pegged me. He knows too much."

"He knows about the hit you called on Ken—"

"Shut up!" Santo hollered. "He knows about ETF and the racket we're running."

Santo shoved Willie into them thugs' arms. They grabbed him and held him up off the ground.

"But my question is," Santo went on, "how do you know? You working for the Feds?"

Willie started wiggling his feet. I wasn't entirely sure what to do for him, but I reckoned I could maybe fight one of them fellas off with a fork or something. Might not win, but it's the thought that counts.

"What if I am working for the Feds?" Willie said. "You wouldn't kill a Fed, would you?"

Santo got the creepiest, sickest smile I've ever seen.

"Tigger, you've got no idea who I'm willing to kill."

I jumped up. "He ain't working for the Feds. He's working with me."

Santo narrowed his eyes at me. "That doesn't tell me anything."

"It does so," I said. "'Cause I'm working for the Three Caballeros."

Santo huffed. "I knew Thomassen was a Caballero."

"No he ain't. You don't know who they are," I said. "In fact, you don't really know who we are."

"Oh, I know you," he said. I reckoned he was aiming to scare me. Didn't work.

"You really don't know me," I said. "But I know you. We know you and all the underhanded things you been doing. And that's why we came to give you a message."

He didn't say nothing back, so I figured that meant I should tell it to him.

"Don't get in our way," I said. "And we won't get in yours. For now."

"Or else what? You take me to the Feds?" he asked.

"Maybe," I said. Then I tried to think of what Mr. Thomassen would say right about then. "Or maybe we'll deal with you ourselves."

"Kid, you got some mighty strong *cojones* to be threatening me."

"Say," Willie said, still dangling his feet in the air, "speaking of the Feds, unless I'm mistaken, that's them coming up over the hill."

They all looked out the window and, sure enough, Short-Guy was heading our way with his posse of fellas. They was state troopers, but I reckon when you're feeling real guilty, you can't much tell the difference between them and federal agents.

Santo stared for about two seconds, then he grabbed all them photos and everything else and ran out to his car. Them two other fellas dropped Willie, followed him, and they ripped out of that parking lot like a bat out of hell.

Willie picked himself up off the floor. He reached in his pocket and I heard another click.

"What's that?"

He pulled a little box thing out of his pocket. There was a wire coming off of it and going up his shirt.

"This here is a CIA-commissioned mini–tape recorder. And we got him admitting to all that mess right here on the tape."

Well, dadgum.

"So you was putting all this together? Getting all this ready just in case something like this happened?"

Willie grinned. "I've learned to expect the worst when I'm helping you out."

That made sense.

"Still, it's a real stroke of luck that you figured out what Tommy meant about that address, ain't it?"

Willie grabbed the envelope and folded it up.

"Huh?" he said. "Oh, the birth certificate thing? Yeah, no, Tommy was drunk when he wrote that address. It didn't go to nothing."

"But the certificate—"

"Was fake. Short-Guy had Marge make it for him real fast after I told him my idea." He laughed at the look on my face. "Ain't it something what the CIA can do when they're put on the spot?"

"Yeah," I said as Short-Guy and them other fellas started to come in. "Especially when they get a little help from a junior agent."

"Except I wasn't being a junior agent when I came up with this," he said. "Lying, cheating, jumping headfirst into danger without a second thought? I was being like Johnny Cannon."

I was sure glad at least one of us was.

CHAPTER FIFTEEN
THE END

And that's why Short-Guy moved in with us, 'cause he ain't so sure Trafficante's going to keep his distance," I said to Ma's gravestone. "Which has been real weird, 'cause I don't reckon we've had a house this full since forever."

It was September 23, a little over two weeks after Rudy died and Tammy Jane was born. It also just so happened to be Ma's birthday. And this time I'd brought her some really good flowers. Sora'd helped me pick them out. And she promised to keep on doing it every year, for as long as she was living with us. Which Pa said was maybe going to be forever. And I was fine with that.

"By the way, did you know that on this day back in 1806, Lewis and Clark arrived back in St. Louis after they had their big adventure? Funny thing is, that's where Mr. Thomassen is at too. Apparently he tracked down the fella that sold Rudy the federal key and he's going to see what them Trafficantes was planning."

I heard a car pull up to the front gate. I looked over and saw it was the Mackers'. Martha got out and walked over to where I was at.

"Hey," she said. It was the first real word she'd said to me since Snake Pond.

"Hey," I said. "You finally came to meet Ma?"

She looked at the gravestone, then she smiled. She knelt down.

"Hello, Mrs. Cannon. My name's Martha. Your son and I—" She looked up at me. "We're friends."

She let that settle in for what it was worth, and it worked just fine to me. At least it was a step forward. Then she stood back up. I reckoned maybe we could start Operation Happy Ending again.

"Hey, you want to come fishing?" I asked. "Me and Pa are taking Tammy Jane and Sora down to the lake to catch a few, or at least to waste some time together. Short-Guy's going too. And, if you want to come along, it could be a lot of fun."

She sighed and stared at Ma's gravestone another couple of seconds, then she looked back at me. Her cheeks was wet.

"I can't. I'm moving away. That's why I came out here to see you," she said, and I forgot what I was saying.

"You're what?"

"Moving. My mom and I. We're leaving Cullman. Leaving Alabama."

It felt like I got punched in the gut.

"What do you mean? Where you going?"

"Mrs. Buttke's son offered my mom a job at his hospital

in Detroit. And, since my dad sent up the divorce papers, she's decided to take the position."

All of a sudden, everything around us got darker and uglier. All of a sudden, I felt like I was in a cemetery.

"But, I come here and tell my ma stories, all these stories. And you're—" I swallowed real hard. "You're the girl in my stories. I *need* you to be the girl in my stories."

Her eyes started watering up real bad.

"No, Johnny, I need to be the girl in my own stories." She grabbed me and gave me a hug. "I'm sorry. We're leaving now. Please tell Willie I said good-bye."

"You ain't going to tell him?"

"No, I can't. It's too—I can't. Please, just tell him, okay?"

I nodded, she hugged me again, and then she walked away.

She got ten steps off before she stopped. She came running back to me.

"I almost forgot," she said.

Then she kissed me.

Right on the lips.

All the blood in my entire body went straight to my feet and I felt like I might pass out. She let go of me and I couldn't wipe the goofiest grin of my life off my mouth.

"There," she said. "Operation Happy Ending is accomplished."

My brain started sounding the fire alarms.

"Wait, you knew?"

"I'm a girl," she said. "We always know."

She turned and ran back to the car. Mrs. Macker honked and waved to me, and then they drove on down the road. Just like that.

After a bit, I told Ma I'd see her later. I went and got into the truck and drove on up to the Parkinses' house, where Pa and Sora was waiting for me with Tammy Jane.

Everybody was real happy when I walked into the living room. Short-Guy was down there too. He was in the kitchen with Mrs. Parkins and she was teaching him how to make cornbread. Apparently that girl of his, Marge, really loved cornbread, so he wanted to surprise her when he saw her again. Plus it'd be good to take with us fishing.

As soon as I walked in, Willie started talking ninety miles an hour.

"Hey, guess what just happened? Bob Gorman called, and you know how he's been in my dad's fan club ever since the explosion? Well, Bob decided that it was about time Cullman had some diversity, and he'd rather it be 'a colored man he can trust,' so he's going to run a joint campaign with him running for sheriff and my dad running for county commissioner."

Dang, it was a whole day of shocking news. It had already been weird seeing Bob acting like a new man, swearing he'd never lay another finger on Eddie again and that he reckoned Reverend Parkins was the finest man that ever walked the earth, a real exception to the "colored epidemic" or whatever. But this? This was mind-boggling.

"Wow," I said. "So does that mean—"

"We ain't going to move!" he said. "Which means you and me and Martha can keep on being friends forever."

I didn't know what to say to that, since it made me real happy and real sad at the same time.

"Of course, Bull Connor pulled his endorsement of Bob when he heard about it, but still," Willie said. Then he saw my face. "Wait, what's wrong?"

I told him about Martha moving, and he went from happy to sad maybe even harder than I had.

"That messes up everything," he said. I thought he might be about to cry.

"Not quite everything," I said, trying to find a happy side. "She did kiss me at the graveyard, so Operation Happy Ending worked out."

"She—she kissed you?" he asked. He looked even worse off at that.

"Yeah, and it was real nice, even though I reckon it didn't mean much to her," I said. Then my brain started working and I had one of them eureka moments like what Archimedes had in the bathtub back in the third century before Jesus was born.

"Wait, are you ate up over Martha?" I asked.

"Well, yeah, I'm sad she's leaving," he said. His lip looked like it wanted to tremble but he was holding it back.

"No, that ain't what I mean. Did Cupid get you in the butt with one of his arrows for her?"

"Look, that don't matter," he said. "She's your girl, and—"

"No she ain't. She told me that herself."

He blinked a couple of times when I said that and I thought he might have almost smiled, but then he remembered that she was moving.

"Well, anyway, I'm your guy, so I ain't ate up over her."

He refused to talk any more about it. We sat down to wait for the cornbread so we could get going. But, after a little bit, the Mackers' car pulled into the driveway and Mrs. Macker walked up to the door. Mrs. Parkins came out of the kitchen and answered it.

After some quick greetings between them, Mrs. Macker told the news to Mrs. Parkins and to everybody else, which led to a whole mess of hugging and some tears and such. Then Mrs. Macker asked if she could write down the Parkinses' address and phone number, in case she needed any mail or something, since she wasn't yet sure of where they'd be living up in Detroit.

The whole time they was talking, Willie was looking out the window. He was staring at Martha, who was sitting in the car. I went over next to him.

"Go out there and talk to her," I said.

He shook his head. "Ain't nothing much to say. We're just friends."

I socked him in the shoulder for being stupid, 'cause that's what blood brothers is supposed to do.

"You're ate up over her. And I have a feeling that she feels close to the same about you. So go talk to her."

"No, it ain't right," he said. "I'm your guy."

I remembered what Martha had said in the cemetery.

"Maybe it's about time you be your *own* guy for once," I said. "And get out there. Or I swear I will kick your butt, crippled or not."

It took him a second, but he finally agreed. I watched through the window as he made his way over to her door. She got out of the car and he started talking. Then he started crying. Then she started crying.

And then she grabbed him by the face and they kissed.

And it sure looked like she enjoyed it a heck of a lot more than the kiss she'd given to me.

Part of me was real happy for them. Like, maybe about a quarter of me was. The other parts of me was hurt real bad. Watching the girl you're hung up on get tangled up with somebody else is bad. Watching her get in with your blood brother is torture. But I wasn't about to cry. No sir, not going to let that happen.

Dadgummit, my eyes started leaking.

Thank goodness Short-Guy didn't know how to cook to save his life, 'cause he started burning the cornbread and tried to pull it out, but he forgot the oven mitts, and so he screamed something fierce. Mrs. Parkins ran in to help him out, but he didn't stop his screaming. He screamed more than he had when he'd gotten shot in the gut.

Woke up Tammy Jane, too. She started crying, which made me stop.

Sora went and grabbed her and pulled out the bottle. Then she saw my eyes and handed my sister to me. I put the bottle in that little girl's mouth and watched her as she started eating. The sparkle in her eyes and the little grunts she was making started to do what Willie always tried to do, it made me forget about my problems.

I glanced back out at Willie and Martha, they was hugging on each other now. Then I looked back at Tammy Jane.

"I reckon you're the girl in my stories now, ain't you?" I asked.

Pa came over to me. "So, Martha's leaving. You going to be okay?"

I kept on looking at Tammy Jane's face. "Yeah. I'm going to be fine."

"You sure?"

I shrugged. Then Tammy Jane pooped. Seemed about right.

After a little while, Carlos's truck pulled around Willie and Martha and he hopped out and ran in. He scanned the room real fast and landed on me.

"*Chico*, are you busy?" he asked. Then he looked out and saw Willie and Martha a-hugging away, and Tammy Jane still pooping away, and me trying my best to look away from it all 'cause I wasn't about to let myself end my day with a bout of crying. "Ah, you are busy, but you'd prefer to be distracted, yes?"

I nodded and snorted up them tears that was working their way down my nose pipes.

"Then you should come with me."

I didn't put up no arguing, especially 'cause folks was finally noticing Tammy Jane's odor and they probably was about to expect me to change her, which really ain't exactly up my alley at all. I handed her off to Pa, ran out and hopped in the passenger door of his truck, and we took off down the road.

We was quiet for a bit, which I was glad for, 'cause I sure didn't feel like talking.

"Is all okay?" Carlos said.

"Yeah," I said. "I guess I'm just really learning some hard lessons for my life."

"Such as?"

I sighed. "Like that there ain't no happy endings. Not a darn one of them."

He waited for me to go on, but like I said, I wasn't down for talking. So he turned on the radio to the only Spanish station there was in the entire South, and we listened as it faded in and out with trumpets blowing and fellas squalling and the occasional guitar playing a tune. It was all punctuated with static and noise, sort of like how my life was, and so I didn't complain none.

We drove for a good while, outside of Cullman County and on down to Birmingham, straight to the Greyhound bus station.

We got out and we went over and sat on a bench. Still not saying much at all. Finally even I got tired of the quiet.

"So, what are we doing here?" I asked.

"Do you remember me telling you about Operation Pedro Pan?"

I did. It was back when we was finding our way out of Havana and we'd seen an airplane getting ready to head back to America. He'd told me that there was a priest in America that was arranging for kids from Cuba to get sent on up to the States for safekeeping. Operation Pedro Pan was the name of it all, and it was doing pretty good at flying under everybody's radar.

The bus came around the bend and pulled into the station.

"Well," he said, "I think you're about to learn something about happy endings."

I didn't get no chance to answer him before the bus pulled up and the doors opened and folks all started pouring out. Carlos stood up, so I did too.

We was watching the folk as they came off the bus, all of them looking tired and wore out and not a single one of them looking like the ending of the trip they'd just had was a happy one. I reckoned maybe that was the lesson.

I was wrong.

'Cause after all them folks came off the bus, there was a lull in the traffic, and then another person came off.

She was brown skinned, just like Carlos, and her eyes had the color that firewood gets right before it catches. Her hair was pulled back into a ponytail, but it still made sure you noticed it and said "wow."

She looked around until she spied Carlos. When she did, she smiled.

And that's when I learned the lesson.

See, her smile wasn't like no other smile I'd ever seen before in my entire life. You could search a million art museums, dig through a thousand magazines, or watch every movie that's ever been made, and there ain't no chance you'd find a smile like hers. I halfway wished Mrs. Macker was around with one of them defibrillators, 'cause I swear my heart plumb stopped. Then it started again, all its own, but beating a different tune for the first time in forever.

'Cause that's the deal about happy endings. They don't exist. But there is something that does.

Happy beginnings. Those are the best thing in the world.

While I was standing there with my jaw dangling down around my ankles, she came over to us and gave Carlos a hug.

"Primo!" she said, which is Spanish for cousin.

He picked her up and swung her around. Then he set her down and pointed her toward me.

"Here's someone I want you to meet," he said to her. "This is Johnny Cannon. Johnny, this is my little cousin, Caridad."

She held out her hand to me.

"You can call me Cari."

I shook it and I'm pretty sure she could feel my pulse pounding through my fingers.

"Johnny?" Carlos said. He nudged me with his elbow. "Do you have anything to say?"

I stammered for a bit, but then I got my footing. This wasn't like how it'd been with Martha. Not even for a second.

"Yeah," I said. "How do you feel about fishing?"

Her smile got even wider. Which was all the evidence I've ever needed that there really is a Good Lord up in the heavens.

"That's not the question to ask," she said with a Cuban accent that probably made even her cusswords sound good. "The real question is, how do you feel about a girl that can fish better than you?"

Now I was the one grinning.

"Cari, I ain't going to lie. I reckon this is the start of something real good."

And let me tell you, I was more right than I could have dreamed.

Johnny Cannon

November 13, 1961

Biography Project

Well, Mr. Braswell, this here's my biography
project, as you can tell 'cause I put it right
up there in the title of it so you'd know what it
is for sure. And I reckon you're going to give me
an A on it, for reasons I'll tell you down there
at the end. Just you wait, it's a humdinger.

I decided to pick somebody for this biography
project that you don't get to hear about nearly
as much as you should, and who deserves a lot
more credit than they get for all the things
they've done.

I'm writing this here biography on the
American Woman.

She was born, I reckon, back in 1620, when
Mary Winslow, who was only about the same age
I am, stepped off the Mayflower and became the
first woman settler to the New World. She didn't
have an easy time of it, though, which you're
going to see is sort of a theme of this whole

biography. Mary Winslow's pa died on the boat before they got off and her ma died in the horrible winter they had to endure. But I reckon that's sort of fitting for the beginning of this story, 'cause if there's one thing that's a fact about the American Woman, it's that she has a tendency to shine through the worst challenges a body can face.

Of course, Mary Winslow wasn't the only woman on the Mayflower, and she sure wasn't the only woman that came to settle the New World. But all them women had it real hard, especially the ones that would come over later. Since a lot of folks reckoned the new frontier was more of a man's place, a lot of the women that came had to be servants and slaves just to get passage from England. But they did it, no matter the cost. That's another theme you'll see in this biography.

Of course, there was already some women that lived on this spot of land we call America, the natives. And from Pocahontas with the settlers to Sacagawea with Lewis and Clark, they worked to adapt and interact with the folks that wasn't like themselves, all 'cause they realized that, for the most part, them white folk wouldn't survive without their help. Heck, Pocahontas married John Rolfe and made even the most racist fella get all romantic about a mixed marriage. And that's something. That's the American Woman.

Of course, there's women we've all heard about, especially from the Revolutionary War, like Martha Washington or Betsy Ross. But what I've started realizing is that we hear more about them 'cause us menfolk like how they sort of fit into the mold of what we think a woman ought to be, sewing by the fire or making Martha Washington candy.

But you never hear about Deborah Sampson, who cut her hair and called herself Robert Shurtleff, or about Ann Bailey, who did the same and went by Sam Gay. They both enlisted into the Continental Army and fought alongside them musket men we always hear about. In fact, Ann Bailey got promoted all the way up to being a corporal before they figured out she was a woman. Then they threw her in jail. For being a woman.

See, that's the amazing thing about the American Woman. Even though the whole society made it seem like they wasn't wanted or wasn't needed-'cause they wasn't allowed to vote, wasn't allowed very often to choose who they'd marry, or whether or not they wanted to have babies, or any of that stuff-those women still fought for freedom. Fought for the right to be an American Woman.

The best examples of that are the women who was slaves, like Harriet Tubman. Did you know that, after she escaped from the South to the North for her freedom, she turned right back around and snuck back down to start helping other slaves find their freedom too? Not only that, but during the Civil War, she was a spy for the Yankees and helped Colonel Montgomery capture Jacksonville, down in Florida. All the while there was folks that didn't believe she ought to be doing that stuff. And not just 'cause she was black, though that was part of it. 'Cause she was a woman.

But she didn't care. 'Cause she was an American Woman.

The American Woman really started flexing her muscles after that, 'cause she started seeing that the only way to change society was to make her voice be heard. And it wasn't enough to whisper her thoughts to her husband for him to speak it from the pulpit or whatever. She deserved to be heard on her own.

Take Susan B. Anthony, for example. She was one of them that was fighting to get rid of slavery before the Civil War, and then after that, she started fighting for the chains of society to be taken off of women. She got arrested for voting, which sounds crazy these days, but back then men was real scared of women with power. I reckon they still are. Anyway, she helped start the suffrage movement in hopes to give women more rights, especially the right to vote. She wouldn't get to see that right come before she died, though. But that's the thing about the American Woman. She never stops fighting, even if she knows she won't get to see the victory.

When the twentieth century rolled around, all that investment in all them women finally started paying off. In 1917, Jeannette Rankin became the first woman to get elected to Congress, then in 1920, women got that right to vote they'd been after. And just in time, too, 'cause when the Great Depression hit and then World War II came around, women had the sense to help vote in FDR, and his powerful wife, Eleanor, into four terms as president.

The American Woman also proved, just like she had before, that she could take care of herself too. When menfolk was heading off to go fight the Nazis, the women of America stepped up and started filling in their spots on the assembly lines and in the factories. They built planes and weapons. Heck, the WASPs down in Texas flew them planes for the Air Force and some was even killed in action. They helped remind folks that being an American Woman was just as much about being an American as it was about being a woman. Maybe even more so.

See, the more and more you look at history, the more you realize that America probably wouldn't be America if it wasn't for the American Woman. In the fifties, when Senator McCarthy was going crazy and hunting all them Communists, it was Senator Margaret Smith that denounced him for being a nutjob. When it was getting more and more obvious that President Eisenhower wasn't going to end segregation anytime soon, it was

Ethel Payne, a black reporter from Chicago, who called him on it and asked when he was going to speak up. And when all that segregation on them buses was oppressing the black community here in the South, it was Rosa Parks who dared to sit at the front of the bus.

Now, it ain't no lie that there's still a ways to go. Women here in America can't get jobs like fellas can, they can't get into all the places men can, and Lord knows they don't get treated like they match up on the same yardstick as the average man on the street. But it'll be okay. They've come this far, and the American Woman will keep on going.

So, that's the end. And I know that your first inclination is going to be that I don't deserve a good grade on this paper, if I even deserve one at all. But you're going to give me an A, and I'll tell you why.

First off, you're going to give it to me 'cause I did exactly what I was supposed to do. I wrote a biography on somebody that I could talk to, 'cause the American Woman is everywhere, and I get the privilege to talk to her anytime I speak to Mrs. Buttke, or Mrs. Parkins, or Mrs. Macker, back when she still lived here.

And I wrote a biography on someone that's alive. 'Cause, even though she's pushing three hundred years old, the American Woman is alive and kicking. And she looks to stay around for a really long time.

But here's the honest-to-goodness biggest reason you're going to give me an A: Ethan Pinckney has promised me that, if I say so, he'll tell the whole town that you really did make me drink Jack Daniels down at the cemetery. I reminded him that liars go to hell, and so he said he'd like a clean conscience. He might even spill that you stuck your pasty white booty out the window at me, which won't just get you fired, but might make it hard to get hired at any other school.

And if you're wondering how I learned to blackmail so good, let's just say I haven't changed the last seventy-two of Tammy Jane's diapers 'cause I wanted to. I've only got twenty-eight more to go before I can stop worrying about Sora spilling to Cari that I cried watching <u>West Side Story</u>.

American Women. They're a dadgum force to be reckoned with.

ISAIAH CAMPBELL